Hans Werner Kettenbach was born near Cologne. He is the author of several highly acclaimed novels, including *David's Revenge* and *Black Ice*, also published by Bitter Lemon Press. He came to writing late in life, publishing his first book at the age of fifty. Previous jobs he has held include construction worker, court stenographer, football journalist, foreign correspondent in New York and, most recently, newspaper editor. His thrillers have won the Jerry-Cotton Prize and the Deutscher-Krimi Prize; five of them have been made into successful films.

Also available from Bitter Lemon Press
by Hans Werner Kettenbach:

Black Ice

DAVID'S REVENGE

Hans Werner Kettenbach

Translated from the German
by Anthea Bell

BITTER LEMON PRESS
LONDON

BITTER LEMON PRESS
First published in the United Kingdom in 2009 by
Bitter Lemon Press, 37 Arundel Gardens, London W11 2LW

www.bitterlemonpress.com
First published in German as *Davids Rache* by
Diogenes Verlag AG Zurich, 1994

Bitter Lemon Press gratefully acknowledges the financial
assistance of the Arts Council of England

A CIP record for this book is available from the British Library
ISBN 978-1-904738-39-8
Typeset by Alma Books Limited
Printed and bound by CPI Cox & Wyman, Reading, Berkshire

David's Revenge

1

Ninoshvili's letter has made me curiously uneasy. It's ridiculous, but I felt something like a presentiment of disaster at the mere sight of the dingy grey envelope when I came home today after teaching five tedious lessons and found it lying on the hall table. I stared at the stamp, with its colourful picture of King David the Builder swinging his sword against the Mussulmen. I deciphered the postmark as Tbilisi, removed an imaginary speck of dust from my coat sleeve, and began to feel afraid.

Ninoshvili writes to say he is very happy to tell me that, after persistent efforts, he can travel to my country at last. The Cultural Ministry of the Republic of Georgia has officially commissioned him to visit the Federal Republic of Germany, where he is to get in touch with publishing houses interested in bringing out Georgian literature in German translation. Unfortunately, he adds, Matassi can't come with him, but he looks forward to picking up our friendship again, seven years after we first met.

The letter has taken a good four weeks to get here from Tbilisi, and since Ninoshvili says that "all being well" he will be "making my final preparations in about a month's time", he could turn up on my doorstep at any moment.

I actually rose immediately from the desk where, with a stifled groan, I had just sat down, lifted the net curtain and looked out. The street lay deserted in the midday sun. No taxi in sight.

Or perhaps he's coming from the bus stop on foot to save money, bringing only a small, well-worn case with him? Perhaps he's already walked past the house, sizing it up. Perhaps he's on his way now, stepping quietly, coming through the garden, looking around with those inscrutable dark eyes.

Oh, that's enough of such absurdities! I have no real reason to be afraid of this visitor. He'll mean a certain amount of inconvenience for me, of course, I can see that in advance. The postscript to his letter, in which he hopes that I can help him "to find inexpensive accommodation", is clear enough. He probably thinks it will be only natural for me to ask him to stay here. Every other toast we drank in Tbilisi was to the hospitality of the Georgian people, and now, seven years later, I have to suffer the consequences of that admirable quality.

But what's our spare room for, after all? It can't be permanently reserved for Julia's old school friend, Erika, who likes her pleasures and uses it as a base for her excursions to the West every six months, leaving it impregnated with her aggressive perfume. Or for Ralf's friends, a couple of whom have already slept off their hangovers in the bed under the sloping roof, after having too many beers to ride their mopeds home. They probably didn't even remove their trainers. David Ninoshvili will appreciate being asked to stay in our spare room. Let him have it.

2

I'm only trying to fool myself. It remains to be seen whether this visitor from Georgia is really as harmless as he seems.

Matassi. That evening in the bar of the Hotel Iveria. The next afternoon, when Ninoshvili invited me to his apartment.

And last but not least, the middle of the following day, when Matassi knocked at the door of my hotel room, bringing me the article she'd photocopied for me in the library.

Matassi wore pale blouses and skirts in plain colours, and once I saw her in a bright summer dress with a white collar. No tall circular cap, no laced bodice, no strings of beads dangling from her temples. No long, plaited braids lying on her breast; she wore her black hair cut short. Yet she had the same exotic charm as the women in Georgian national costume smiling at visitors from the posters at the Tbilisi branch of the state-run Inturist travel agency. Round cheeks, dark thick eyebrows and lashes, shadows around her eyes. Full lips.

On the evening when Ninoshvili brought her to the hotel bar with him and introduced her as his wife, Dautzenbacher and the bearded Slavonic lecturer from Heidelberg – I forget his name – immediately sat up and took notice. Dr Bender, the only woman in our party, went to her room in a fit of pique on finding herself increasingly left out of the conversation. She pleaded a headache, but didn't bother to make it sound plausible. I had stayed in the background, and found myself rewarded by the intriguing impression that Matassi was casting me glances of much greater interest than those she gave the other two, who went on tirelessly posturing. I even received a dazzling smile now and then.

Next day, Ninoshvili didn't tell me that she'd be expecting both of us at his apartment. Instead he asked casually, after our group had all lunched together, whether I would like to visit a Georgian home, and I instantly decided to skip the afternoon's study programme. I followed our interpreter through the winding streets of the Old Town, immersing myself in a flood of strange smells and sounds. I thought, with growing alarm, that if I were to lose sight of my guide I'd never find my way back through this teeming labyrinth.

When Ninoshvili, with an inviting gesture, opened a small gate in a high wall, I found myself in a quiet courtyard surrounded on three sides by balconies. I saw wooden balustrades, elaborately carved and painted sky blue. Washing lines crossed the courtyard up to the second floor. On the wall of the house there was a large stone tank with a tap above it. Two children, sitting in the shade on the trodden mud of the courtyard floor, inspected me with dark eyes.

The round table in Ninoshvili's living room was laid with three cups and three plates, and the aroma of fresh coffee hung in the air. As I looked around me, Matassi appeared in the doorway leading to the kitchen. She was wearing the summer dress with the white collar. She smiled at me and said, in English, "Good afternoon, Mr Kestner. How are you?"

Ninoshvili said he would just go out to the confectioner's for something to nibble with our coffee, and when I protested that I couldn't possibly eat anything else after our lavish lunch, he waved the objection away with both hands, smiling, and went off. Matassi brought the coffee. I asked her if she didn't have to go to work. No, she said, not today. And how, I asked, had she known that I'd be coming? She hadn't known, she replied, but she had hoped I would. Hoped I would? Why? A silent glance and a smile were her only response to that.

Perhaps it was the wine and vodka freely dispensed by our hosts at lunch, when toast after toast was drunk, and anyone who didn't empty his glass every time was offending the sacrosanct table manners of the Georgians. But be that as it may, as soon as Ninoshvili had set off for the confectioner's I embarked on a determined flirtation with his wife, threw my ideas of a guest's proper conduct overboard, and began to feel I was hovering under the blue sky, in the summer wind wafting in through the balcony door.

When Matassi showed me a little book written by Ninoshvili, and leaned over my shoulder to translate the Georgian print of its title for me, moving her pale brown forefinger along the line, I turned my face to her. The tip of my nose touched her cheek, and I breathed in a perfume that I had never smelled before. The Orient and myrrh sprang to mind and remained lodged in my memory, although to this day I don't know what myrrh really smells like. I kissed Matassi's cheek. She did not draw back. I took her in my arms and kissed her on the mouth. She returned the kiss before, smiling, she freed herself.

I felt no scruples about deceiving my host. If I did feel a little sorry for anything afterwards, it was only that when Matassi showed me first the kitchen and then the small, shady bedroom, I didn't pull her straight down on the bed, which was covered with a woven spread and provided with plump pillows. I was afraid that Ninoshvili, swinging a bag of pastries, might surprise us in a situation that couldn't be satisfactorily explained in a hurry, my trousers around my feet, her summer dress pushed up to her armpits. At that point I imagined him dropping the bag and reaching for a knife, washing away the shame with blood, Matassi's blood, but also, and fatally, mine.

As I thought later, with annoyance, I need not have feared the Georgian's revenge, or at least not that he would catch us in the act. Ninoshvili didn't come back for a full hour. He said he had been held up.

3

Only later, when we had left Georgia and were travelling on through the Armenian Soviet Socialist Republic, did I begin to wonder about the division of labour between Ninoshvili and Matassi when they entertained a guest. We were sitting in a bus on our way from Yerevan to Ejmiadzin, where we were to have the honour of an audience with the Catholicos, when Dautzenbacher, for whom no joke was too tasteless, grabbed the woman interpreter's microphone and bellowed into it, in his beery bass voice, "Attention, everyone, please, here is an important announcement!"

He cleared his throat, making the diaphragm of the microphone crackle, and went on. "Don't forget the bugs! We may be on our way to a monastery, but don't you go thinking the head of the Armenian Apostolic Church despises those dear little creatures, not him. So no hostile questions, please, and most important of all no negative criticism of Soviet power! It'll all be recorded, and then you'll be sorry. Thank you for your kind attention." And with that he handed the microphone back to the interpreter, some Irina or Natasha from Inturist, who took it with a rather forced smile. Dautzenbacher dropped back into his seat, very pleased with his performance – his broad shoulders were shaking.

I suddenly thought of the memo that had been handed out at home along with the programme for the trip. I'd just shaken my head and thrown it into the waste-paper basket. Our study group, this memo told us, could expect a friendly reception, but nonetheless we must not forget that the Soviet Union had a highly developed intelligence system which took a particular interest in foreign visitors.

I don't remember the details, but this document warned participants in the study tour against bugging devices in not only our own rooms but also those of the people we'd be meeting, all of them "top professionals from the educational institutions", although that did not, unfortunately, mean that some of them might not also work "for the intelligence services". There followed several categorical imperatives for unsuspecting participants in study trips, which as far as I remember ran: *Do not go out alone! Beware of incriminating situations!* And the crowning injunction, with three exclamation marks, was: *Do not give your hosts the chance to put you under pressure in any way whatsoever!!!*

I had thought this list of banalities was mere pomposity on the part of the Federal German authorities financing our study tour, who were obviously not too happy with its stated aim, i.e. to foster cultural exchange between Germany and the Soviet Union. But at the same moment as I remembered these infantile rules of conduct, I thought I saw the writing on the wall in them, an awful warning of something I'd only just escaped. I felt hot, I began to shift restlessly in my seat as my memories of Tbilisi inexorably turned into an embarrassing and alarming nightmare. Why hadn't I put two and two together?

Matassi, who worked at the university library, and Ninoshvili, the writer, translator and interpreter, now appeared to me in a new and ominous light. Two pleasant people, forthcoming, frank and open? What a wicked deception! Behind that hospitable façade, the couple were really a pair of agents in the Soviet secret service. And now I had a plausible explanation for Ninoshvili's hour-long absence at the confectioner's.

The trap had been set when he invited me to his apartment. A bug in the bedroom, not a permanent installation, of course, but specially fitted by Ninoshvili for my visit, perhaps with help from some kind of KGB technician. Ninoshvili leaves the house after handing me over to Matassi, tells the children in the courtyard to go and buy him some pastries in the shop next door, immediately takes himself off to a windowless room near his apartment and switches on the listening apparatus. He waits there for Matassi to call for help, removing his headphones only once, when the children knock on the door and deliver the bag of pastries.

After an hour, when nothing useful for his purposes has happened, he calls the whole thing off, comes back to have coffee, carrying his purchases, and explains that he was held up. But they are already planning the next attempt. Matassi, her white teeth biting into a crisp croissant, brings the conversation round to a French ethnologist's account of his visit to Tbilisi at the turn of the century, and when I show interest says she'll photocopy his article from the journals archive in the library and leave it at my hotel tomorrow.

And shouldn't I have smelled a rat, at the very latest, when the next day came?

Matassi wasn't content just to leave the photocopy at the hotel reception desk. Instead, she appeared on the twelfth floor, unannounced, and knocked at the door of my room when I'd gone up there after yet another tiring lunch, meaning to take a nap before the next excursion on the study programme.

When she explained this delightful surprise – unfortunately, she said, the hotel service wasn't very reliable, even letters from abroad were lost now and then – I didn't stop to think of anything that might have aroused my suspicions. I went to the bathroom, brushed my hair, rinsed out my mouth, did up my shirt buttons. When I came out she was sitting on the bed, leafing through my bedtime reading, a Simenon crime story.

I offered her some of the duty-free bourbon I'd bought at the airport, stocking up for the journey, and she didn't hesitate for a second. "Oh, wonderful, thank you! Just a little bit, please," she said, again in English. I sat down beside her with both glasses, drank to her, and as her dark brown eyes gazed at me over the rim of the glass I jettisoned the prelude I'd been contemplating, some idle chatter about Georges

14

Simenon and the erotic component of his work. Waste of time. Throw it out, unnecessary.

I took her glass from her, drew closer, putting one arm on the bed on the other side of her thighs, said I really had to breathe in the scent of her skin again, just once more. She laughed. I ran my nose gently over her cheek, her eyebrows, then down over her nose, her mouth, her throat. I kissed her throat and then her lips. She responded to the kiss, so I never got around to asking her whether she used myrrh as a perfume. We sank on the bed; I put a hand between her thighs. The skin there was smooth and cool. Matassi didn't object. She closed her eyes.

There were three sharp knocks at the door, a short pause, and then they were repeated. David Ninoshvili with the knife in his hand! Matassi opened her eyes, but she lay where she was. I fear my reaction made her doubt my virility. I snatched my hand out from under her skirt as if a vicious insect had stung me, jumped up and stared at the door.

It wasn't David the Avenger, it was Karl-Heinz Dautzenbacher. "Open up in there, Kestner!" he called. "Or are you going to sleep the whole afternoon away?"

Matassi rose, put the Simenon that had fallen to the floor back on the bedside table, picked up her glass and sat down in an armchair. When I didn't move from the spot, she smiled and asked, "Why don't you open it?" I opened the door. Dautzenbacher raised his eyebrows when he saw Matassi, grinned, said, "Why, hello, Mrs Ninoshvili!" and apologized for disturbing me, still grinning. He'd only come, he said, to tell me that the bus for the sightseeing trip to Narikala Fortress was leaving half an hour earlier than originally planned.

I could have murdered that smirking troublemaker, I could have rammed King David the Builder's hunting spear through

15

his thick skin – to think of that great elephant trampling all over my little oriental garden! On the way to Ejmiadzin later, when I thought I saw the facts of the matter, I reluctantly began to do him justice: Karl-Heinz Dautzenbacher, an uncouth fool of a guardian angel who, unwittingly but reliably following the dictates of Fate, had saved me from the honeytrap.

Once again I picture David Ninoshvili sitting next door, in a hotel room booked by the KGB, headphones on his ears. Waiting beside him stands a militiaman: calf-length boots, round peaked cap with a red band and a gold star. Ninoshvili is listening in, raises his head as he hears me mention the scent of Matassi's skin. Then, unexpectedly, he hears the knock on the door, recognizes Dautzenbacher's voice. Cursing, he takes off his headphones and slams them down on the desk.

If Dautzenbacher hadn't barged his way in, the scene as staged could have come to quite a different end. A nasty end. Ninoshvili, listening intently, raises one finger. The militiaman parts his hands, which he's been holding clasped together behind his back, and juts his chin. A shrill scream comes from the room next door, *my* room. It is Matassi's cry for help. Ninoshvili kicks back his chair, races out of the room, hammers at the door of my room. It opens; Matassi appears in the doorway.

Her blouse and bra are torn, she clutches the rags together, pressing them to her bare breasts as she sinks back against the wall. Her other half asks her a question in Russian or Georgian, she replies in a faint voice. I don't understand a word of it.

Ninoshvili slowly approaches, stops in front of me. Balancing on one leg, I struggle with my trousers: one foot is tangled up in them. The Georgian looks at me, asks tonelessly, as if he can't believe something so outrageous, "Is this true,

16

my friend? You tried to rape her?" I cry, "No! If she says that, she's lying!"

The burly figure of the militiaman appears in the doorway; the door is still open. After a glance at Matassi he scrutinizes me, adjusts his belt and says something in a sharp tone, more of an accusation than a question. Ninoshvili turns back, speaks to the militiaman, pushes him out into the corridor and closes the door. Then, his footsteps dragging, he goes over to the armchair, drops heavily into it, looks at me almost without interest as I do up my trousers. "This is a bad business, my friend. Very bad. You can think yourself lucky I arrived in time." He shakes his head. "But I don't know what will come of it now."

He looks at Matassi, who is still leaning against the wall, her eyes cast down. Before I can work out what to say without digging myself even deeper into the hole I'm in, Ninoshvili stands up. He wraps his jacket round Matassi and leads her out.

He comes back in the evening, on his own. He accepts a glass of my bourbon, walks up and down the room with it, stops by the window now and then and peers down at the street, while I sit on the bed, feeling numb.

He's been out and about all afternoon, says my Georgian friend, he's done his level best to avert a scandal. But the militiaman – who by some unfortunate chance happened to be coming along the hotel corridor – has reported the incident, there'll be police inquiries, and they could take a long time. The authorities won't let me leave the country. They have made it very clear to him that they are, after all, ready to let me go only on one condition.

He sips his bourbon, turns away from me, and continues with some hesitation, peering out through the net curtain. It would be a two-way deal, he says, a deal of a kind that,

17

very sad to say, is not unusual in the Soviet Union. And this shameful practice is also now the standard in Georgia, once a free republic fit for human beings to live in. To tell me the bitter truth plainly: the authorities will waive prosecution and allow me to leave if – and here he takes a deep breath – if I declare myself ready to supply them with information now and then, once I am back in the Federal Republic of Germany. Nothing world-shaking, nothing that could really be called espionage. But the authorities, he says, are pathologically obsessed with gathering information of every kind.

When I try to protest, my voice shakes pitifully. I manage to say that I didn't offer Matassi any violence. I was caressing her, yes, I can't and won't deny that, and I'm extremely sorry to have forgotten myself so thoughtlessly. But there was no question of rape, not even an attempt at such a crime. I can explain the state of Matassi's clothing only by supposing that she herself – perhaps overreacting in panic – had torn her own blouse and bra before she opened the door.

Ninoshvili shakes his head, as if in sorrowful regret. "I believe you, my friend. And Matassi wouldn't want to get you into trouble either. But the militiaman has given a different account. And the authorities won't believe either me or you, they'll believe that overzealous police officer."

He has brought with him a written statement, prepared by the authorities, of my willingness to work for the promotion of world peace. He takes it out of his breast pocket and hands it to me with a regretful expression. I have only to sign this paper, he says, and then I'm at liberty to travel on.

4

Julia and Ralf take it even worse than I'd feared when I tell them, at supper, about Ninoshvili's forthcoming visit. My lout of a son throws his fork down on his plate, frowns and leans forwards. "*Where* did you say this guy comes from? Georgia? Hey, look, they're cutting each other's throats there at this very moment, right? Is he going to apply for political asylum here or something?"

I ask him, raising my voice, kindly to spare me his *idées fixes*. When, I say, is he finally going to get it into his head that foreigners usually have far better things to do than to exploit our German fatherland? David Ninoshvili is an educated man, highly regarded in his own country, and he's coming on behalf of the Georgian Ministry of Culture.

While my wife eats in silence and looks at her plate, that oaf Ralf stuffs his mouth with food, chews and grins. He breathes heavily out through his nose. "Ministry of Culture, ho ho, what a hoot! What sort of culture do those Georgians have? All of them running around with knives between their teeth. Or anyway with Kalashnikovs." He clenches his right fist, aims his outstretched forefinger at me. "Bang, bang, bang!"

I lose my temper. I throw my napkin down on the table. "Are you actually proud of your ignorance? Your total lack of historical knowledge? People were living in towns in the Caucasus when your ancient Germanic ancestors were still squatting behind bushes gnawing bear bones!"

"Yes, teacher, sir!" He puts his fork down, wipes his mouth, pushes his chair back and gets up. "Just could be I know more about the Caucasus than you, though." He leans over the table. "So can *you* tell me what happened on Mount Elbrus fifty-one years ago?"

19

I stare at him. He grins. "Twenty-one mountaineering infantrymen planted the German flag there, that's what. And it would still be flying on the mountain peak if Army Group A hadn't run out of petrol."

"Oh, get out of here!" I shout.

"Okay, I was going anyway." He slouches casually towards the door on his air-cushioned rubber soles. "I'm off to get some fresh air before that Georgian wop turns up."

I've put up with the way Ralf carries on for too long. The hopeful idea that he might turn out better than the recalcitrant little bastards who do their best to pollute my lessons every day was an illusion. I expected to see him develop into an enlightened human being of his own accord, but I was wrong. I ought to have revised my educational principles ahead of time. Corporal punishment for good reasons, a few sound slaps now and then – that might have worked wonders. But it's too late for that now, never mind the fact that by this time he's probably physically stronger than me, and wouldn't hesitate to dislocate his own father's arm if I raised it to chastise him.

And I ought to have turned my attention to young Herr Schumann earlier: Gero Schumann, in whose summer house my son and his friends hang out, leading their own lives and pouring beer down their throats. Unfortunately I was depending on Julia. Herr Schumann did his probationary period as a qualified trainee in the legal practice where she works, and ended up with glowing reports: an affable, highly intelligent man who'd make his way in the world as a lawyer. Nice manners, well-to-do family – the summer house belongs to his grandmother, who owns a number of properties.

Herr Schumann has now successfully stood as a candidate for the city council, on which he sits representing a party of the far right. And my son and his friends put up his election posters and distributed unspeakably idiotic leaflets. *Against xenophobia – but against foreign domination too! Foreigners yes, freeloaders no! For a confident, independent Germany!*

I have always assumed that my wife finds this inflated babble as abhorrent as I do, despite her constant attempts to calm my anger: now don't get worked up, it will all work out, he's at the awkward age, just suppose he'd taken to drugs, to be honest I'd rather have him spouting this silly stuff, he'll get tired of it some time… and so on and so forth. Ah, the maternal instinct: come what may, the mother will love her black sheep.

After this evening, however, I doubt this explanation of her attempts to mediate. Once our son has stormed out uttering deplorable invective of some kind, I look at her, breathing heavily. Julia does not return my glance. In silence, she finishes eating her supper. I ask her, "Did you have no contribution to make to that conversation?"

She shrugs her shoulders, shakes her head. "Oh, you know how he reacts to these subjects. Arguments make him even angrier. He'll calm down."

I don't believe I'm hearing this. *Who* will calm down? I suppose we're talking about that lout's state of mind, not by any chance mine? My tone becomes a little sharp. "The subject was not the question of political asylum, but a visit from a man who's a friend of mine." (A friend of mine – oh, God.)

"You're right, his behaviour really is impossible." She folds her napkin. A few seconds pass, then she comes out with the question her son would already have asked if he hadn't preferred to make a dramatic and ill-mannered exit. "How long is this man going to stay?"

I don't know, damn it. There's no indication in his letter. And I can understand that. He's not to know how long it will take him to get people over here interested in publishing Georgian literature. (I hope at least he knows where to go to find such people.)

She looks up from her napkin. "You haven't forgotten that Erika wanted to visit us at the end of this month, have you?"

Erika?

"That's right, Erika. I told you some time ago." She didn't, but never mind; I could have guessed that her school friend from Halle was feeling tired of her dreary home town yet again. When did she last visit us? In spring, that's not even six months ago. Sometimes I still feel bothered by the way that heavy perfume of hers hangs around, but of course that's not Erika's problem. No doubt she's already shifting about restlessly on her curvaceous behind, longing for all the distractions the West can offer.

I try to control my tone of voice. Well, I say, it's perfectly possible that Herr Ninoshvili will be on his way home before the end of the month. If he does want to stay any longer, or if he *has* to stay any longer, which I don't anticipate, then just for once maybe it wouldn't be too much to expect Erika to go to a hotel.

The answer comes promptly and baldly, nothing to soften it. "That's not how I see it. Why can't Herr Ninoshvili be expected to get a hotel room?"

"Because he's sure to be short of cash."

"So is Erika."

"You're overlooking one considerable difference." I pause for a moment while she looks at me, her eyes flashing. "Erika is travelling for her own pleasure. Herr Ninoshvili, on the other hand, is making this journey on behalf of a cultural project of some considerable importance. And also, not least, to earn his living."

She nods, smiles wryly as if my comparison had shown me up in some way and was also an insult to her old school friend. "I'm afraid *you* have overlooked another considerable difference."

"Which is?"

She hesitates, but not for long. "Ralf did have a point. This man comes from a country engaged in bloodthirsty civil war. Do you know which party he belongs to, and what he may have done in this war? You can't be sure he's not getting out of the country to escape retribution. And you say yourself that he doesn't have any money. So how do you know he won't want to take refuge with us? And then, once we've taken him in, he might hang around for months and months."

I say, "You're describing the situation of a political refugee. The classic case of a human being with a right to claim asylum."

She shrugs. "Call it what you like. As you know, I've often enough supported the principle that such people should have their rights. But does it really have to be at your own family's expense?" She leaves the dining table and goes to her study.

I clear away the dishes and take them to the kitchen. A cup slips out of my hand and breaks on the stone floor. I tread on the broken pieces, and they fly all over the place.

I'll show those two what a guest means and how civilized people treat their guests! Yes, yes, perhaps Ninoshvili is in fact coming because he can't stay in his own country and hopes to begin another life here, build up a new future. Then let him stay in our house, damn it, until he's found his footing. If necessary I'll celebrate Christmas and see the New Year in with him.

I don't suppose he'll be planning to stay until Easter.

5

I should add here that seven years ago Julia's legal practice was defending a qualified engineer from the Federal Office of Defence Technology and Procurement who was an alcoholic, and had let himself be recruited by the KGB. The case for the defence was rejected, and the provincial Supreme Court sentenced the man to three years behind bars, as far as I remember, for giving away a few ridiculous state secrets for an equally ridiculous sum that didn't even cover the delinquent's bills for spirits.

I hadn't known anything about this client of my wife's when I set out on my trip to the Soviet Union. It was only after my return that Julia happened to mention casually what a lot of work the case was making for her. It was a mild autumn evening, and we were sitting on the terrace watching twilight fall slowly over the garden. Julia had said she must go back to her desk, but she obviously didn't want to, and was trying to postpone the moment by telling me about all the trouble she was having with the unfortunate procurement technician.

When she had finally gone in I mopped the sweat from my brow. Luckily she didn't seem to have noticed my uneasiness. I'd almost forgotten my nightmares about Ninoshvili and Matassi – with some difficulty, but successfully in the end – by calling on sound human reason. After all, if the couple were really working to entrap people, why would they want to lure an ordinary secondary-school teacher of German and history into their clutches? Any information I could have given the KGB about Germany would have centred on my experiences with pupils who liked to waste time behaving like pigs, and teachers who suffered from having to be their swineherds, and that would hardly have been of any material interest.

But now my fantasies began running wild again, preying on my mind: suppose the Komitet Gosudarstvennoy Besopasnosti, the Soviet secret service, had been trying to gain access to the Federal Office of Defence Technology and Procurement through schoolteacher Christian Kestner and his lawyer wife Dr Julia Kestner? Maybe they hoped, by those means, to get an insight into top-secret documents from which they could discover how many screws held the Leopard tank together, or which of the civil servants employed by the Defence Office was as notorious a drunk as the qualified engineer Julia was defending, or how many bucketfuls of jam a division of the Federal Armed Forces consumed on average per month.

Enough of this foolishness. I will also add that over the last few years Julia and her firm have defended several clients working in those fields that are absurdly described as "sensitive", (as if making your living by dealing with armaments and their accessories calls for profound sensitivity). But this participation by my wife in the affairs of state of the Federal German Republic doesn't really constitute reasonable grounds for me to feel as if I ought to anticipate Ninoshvili's visit with misgivings.

Even if the Georgian and his wife were trying to get me into the clutches of the Soviet secret service, the Soviet Union as such no longer exists. And the Republic of Georgia certainly has weightier matters on its mind than blackmailing Christian Kestner, senior schoolteacher, by holding over him a crime that he would have liked to commit but, thanks to Karl-Heinz Dautzenbacher, never did.

6

In the morning twilight they looked to the east, and halfway between the sea and the sky they saw snow-crowned peaks rising above the clouds, bright and glittering. And they knew that they had reached the Caucasus, at the ends of the inhabited earth. The Caucasus, the highest of all mountain ranges, father of the rivers of the east. Prometheus was once chained to its summit, for the eagle to gnaw his liver day after day, and at the foot of its slopes whispered the dark forests around the magical land of Colchis.

That is vividly written, although sad to say by an Englishman, not a Georgian. I'm acquainting myself with Georgian literature a little in order to do my guest justice, but I'm not getting on very well with it. Hardly any modern texts exist in German translation, and the older works I've found in libraries have a musty odour of the past about them that sometimes puts me off. Or makes me yawn, to confess the truth (and I do want to stick to the truth here).

The Georgians must be strange people if it's true that every other man and woman among them can quote from Shota Rustaveli's *The Man in the Panther's Skin*, and quote from it with feeling. Yet this "book of books of an entire nation", of which I knew nothing before, is almost eight hundred years old, and its venerable metaphors would never trip off anyone's tongue in this country today. What does a Georgian feel when he declaims lines claiming that Queen Tamar had "the countenance of a rose", "crimson lips" and "teeth like polished crystal" set between rubies?

I also have to ask myself why I feel considerably greater interest in Rustaveli's account of the lovelorn Patman, who falls for the wrong man and afterwards complains, "Unlucky that I am, I was no more than the female goat to his buck."

And the book's antiquated illustrations, where knights sit with their ladies behind portières and on cushions, remind me, I am ashamed to say, of the pornographic interiors depicted by Chinese and Japanese artists, although Rustaveli's ladies wear high-necked gowns and the knights' private parts are not on display.

Do I lack moral seriousness because I can't understand this cult of courtly love? Have I been, unknowingly, a guest in a country where women are still put on a pedestal just as they were eight hundred years ago, to be defended against all attacks – defended, perhaps, with the murderous tools so famously manufactured by the Georgians over the ages?

I found a macabre tale illustrating the efficacy of this renowned Georgian craft in Pushkin's travel journal. He writes that weapons from Tbilisi "are highly prized all over the Orient", and continues, "Count Samoilov and W., who were known here for their physical strength, generally tried out their new swords by chopping a ram in half or beheading an ox with a single stroke." Heaven help us. Disgusting!

Why am I doing this? Well, my study of Georgian literature does offer more than just sensations of tedium and horror. In a novel published in 1937, I have come upon an idea which helps to explain the uneasiness that Ninoshvili's letter aroused in me without the need for any outlandish fantasies.

Grigol Robakidze, the author of this novel, describes a banquet to which writers, actors and painters from Tbilisi are invited. It is held in a castle not far from the city. The guests sit down at a long table on the veranda, and the leaves of an old walnut tree with many branches allow dappled sunlight to fall on the table. As they are drinking their first glasses of Maglari, a wine made from a grape variety that grows wild on date palms, they choose the Tamada, the master of ceremonies, who will now be in charge of the banquet and whose orders are to be obeyed to the letter, whether he tells the guests to drain their glasses or commands one of his companions at table to sing a song or perform a folk dance.

Robakidze was well advised to let his readers know first that a banquet was essentially a religious celebration in ancient times, and remains so in Georgia to this day. Without supernatural assistance, the guests at that 1937 banquet could hardly have consumed the full menu served to them under the walnut tree.

First they eat young green beans mixed with ground paprika leaves and walnuts, accompanied by two kinds of cheese and hot maize cakes. After the Tamada has struck up a hymn in praise of the Upper Imerians, an ancient Georgian tribe, this first course is followed by boiled chicken and baked trout. When the fish bones and chicken bones have been taken away, the Tamada calls for the recitation of a poem. One of the literary men composes, extempore, a sonnet in honour of a beautiful woman. His companions applaud him and the lady, and they all rise to dance.

After they have given their digestions a little help in this way, they are served roast mutton on twelve long spits, sprinkled with barberries and with a pomegranate-juice sauce poured over it. They get to work on the mutton until the spits are bare, and then pause once more to recruit their forces by listening, much moved, to a discourse on the incomparable virtues of the Georgian language. Then another course is brought in: a whole boiled shoulder of beef in a sauce of wild plum juice, highly seasoned with pepper and other spices.

Finally the guests applaud the Tamada in approximately the tenth or maybe even the twentieth toast of the day, once again draining their glasses. "With that the banquet came to an end, but only the ritual part of it. Thereafter everyone could eat (*sic!*) and drink, sing and dance just as he liked."

I would have thought this account of gluttony with musical accompaniment a mere amusing exaggeration on the author's part, like Queen Tamar's crystal teeth or the flawless skin of Princess Vis, which glowed at her birth so that it illuminated the night like moonlight, if I hadn't been to a similar banquet myself seven years ago. It was not, to be sure, held in a castle, but on a *sovkhoz*, a state-owned property not far from Tbilisi.

We sat at a long table in the manager's office. Choice specimens of the fine apples and bunches of grapes supplied by the *sovkhoz* to the capital stood on the table; on the wall hung pictures of Lenin and Stalin, the former Josef W. Dzhugashvili, who at this time had been anathematized by the Communist Party for three decades, although obviously that hadn't ruined his reputation in his native land as Georgia's greatest son.

Our Tamada, the manager of the *sovkhoz*, was called Viktor. He gave us permission to ask him questions, and for a long time he didn't fail to give answers, but then, all of a sudden, the feasting which was to leave us unfit for our study programme for the rest of the day began. When asked a question about the ratio of wages to expenses on the state-owned property, he rose to his feet, leaned his hands on the table, let his eyes, under their thick brows, wander, and explained, "The only answer to that is one hundred grams."

The interpreter translated, explaining that by order of the Tamada everyone had to knock back a shot of the amber spirit distilled from the grapes of the *sovkhoz* before he could answer the question. And so it went merrily on. Viktor kept finding new reasons to demand the consumption of another shot.

At one point he got us to drink to Dautzenbacher, who, on being commanded by the master of ceremonies to perform a

German folk song, had immediately complied with a rendering of 'At the Well in Front of the Gate' during which tears actually came to his eyes. Another shot was necessary to atone for the offence committed by the librarian Heinrich Weinzierl from Passau, who had gone looking for the men's room without asking the Tamada's permission. When he returned, relieved but visibly swaying already, Viktor wagged a forefinger at him and delivered judgement. "Cheinrich! Forfeit!"

My female colleague Dr Bender was not present when the Tamada proposed a toast to friendly German-Soviet relations that would teach President Ronald Reagan some manners. Later, when I had asked and received Viktor's permission to leave the table for a pressing reason, I found her in the back yard. She was sitting on an upturned wooden cask, her head in her hands, and shook her head mutely when I asked if there was anything I could do for her.

I walked a little way further, took a deep breath, and looked at the plain, pale-yellow prefabricated buildings in which the *sovkhoz* workers and their families lived, and the green hills behind them. I saw the bright-blue sky resting on the distant, glittering mountain ridge to the north. I looked for the pass over which the Russians had once entered the country, a winding, icy path skirting steep ravines.

Unexpectedly, I felt abandoned, lost in a part of the world from which I would never find my way back. The voices of the birds enveloped me like a flickering net dropping on me out of the air, growing denser and denser. An aroma I could not identify wafted towards me from the estate's warehouses, the strong aroma of exotic vintages that I had never drunk and didn't want to. Fear came over me, and melancholy too.

It can't have been the effect of the spirit distilled by Viktor from his grapes, although at that time I wasn't far from the limits of my capacity. And now and then on that trip, sometimes when I was stone-cold sober, I had the same sense of having lost my bearings, of being suddenly adrift in a dream world without any shore. It came over me when Ninoshvili was leading me through the streets of the Old Town of Tbilisi, and when I saw the double white peak of Mount Ararat rising above the Armenian plain for the first time. I felt it again on the shores of Lake Sevan, that huge, still expanse of water where the conquerors from Asia watered their horses before going on to Tbilisi, to leave the ruined city in dust and ashes.

So if the Georgian's visit makes me uneasy, the reason could be those half-forgotten experiences. Ninoshvili an agent? David the Avenger? Nonsense. The plain truth is that he brings back the strange sense of alienation that has all too often cast its spell over me in the same alarming way. I've had enough trouble shaking it off already.

If I remember correctly, I didn't manage it on the *sovkhoz* until the banquet had to be cut short, because one of our party dropped right out of it. It wasn't until I was helping Viktor to heave Heinrich Weinzierl, now looking pale as a corpse, onto the bus that I felt I was standing on solid ground again.

7

Ralf has indulged in a piece of incredible impertinence that I discovered only by chance. When I glanced into the spare room yesterday afternoon, to make sure it was fit to offer to Ninoshvili as accommodation at any time, I found a large map of the Caucasus fixed to the inside of the door with drawing pins. There were several stickers on the map, carefully cut out of thin card, with writing on them.

The sticker at the top, made of red card, bore the neatly printed words: *Operation Edelweiss, 1942*. Beneath it a broader red arrow shape, split into two, pointed south from Rostov on the Don. On the shaft of the arrow there was lettering reading *Army Group A (Gen. F.M. List)*. The western part of the arrowhead, stuck over the oil city of Maykop and pointing to the coast of the Black Sea, bore the legend *17th German and 3rd Romanian Army (Col. Gen Ruoff)*; the eastern part, stuck across Stavropol and ending at the mountain river of Terek, was inscribed *1st Tank Army (Gen. F.M. von Kleist)*.

Another arrow, this time cut out of yellow card and starting at the Terek, led the eye past the slopes of Mount Kasbek and down to Tbilisi. Neatly written on this arrow were the words: *Operational aim not achieved because of sabotage to supplies, 1942/43*.

I was beside myself with anger. I stormed into Ralf's room to ask him to explain himself. The wretched lad had gone, leaving his books and notebooks scattered all over the floor and the table. The cupboard door was open, with a pair of socks lying in front of it. I took the map and drove off to young Herr Gero Schumann's summer house.

It was the first time I'd seen the place. It lies behind a grand turn-of-the-century villa. Tall elms grow on both sides of the road, casting dappled sunlight and shade on the villa's two wide bow windows. There are several nameplates fitted beside the entrance porch, among them one for a firm of industrial consultants. Herr Schumann's grandmother obviously knows how to make money out of her property.

I found Herr Schumann's own nameplate, with an intercom beside it, close to a gate leading into the garden, which was more like a park. The gate wasn't locked. I tried the bell push twice; the intercom remained silent.

I hesitated. Surely Herr Schumann and his friends couldn't already be tipsy at this time of day.

After glancing around, I went in, and pulled the gate to behind me but didn't shut it. With my shoes crunching on the whitish gravel of the path, I walked past the flower beds to the back garden. There was no one to be seen behind the windows of the villa. The summer house, a single-storey but spacious building with French windows, lay quietly in the shade of gnarled old trees at the end of the garden.

I reached the terrace in front of it and tapped at one of the windows. No reply. I tried to peer in. The living room, obviously: a big sofa, armchairs. Given the dim light, I may have been wrong, but I thought that what I saw draped on the back wall, next to a bookshelf, was the flag of the Third Reich.

I knew I had already gone too far, but anger drove me on. After glancing back over my shoulder, I walked around the summer house, and started down the narrow paved path leading past the back of the building and a dense shrubbery to the garden fence. The curtains were drawn over the back windows. I found a massive wooden door, knocked at it, listened. No one answered my knock. Birds twittered. I breathed in the smell of damp earth and dense foliage.

When I straightened up and turned back, a youth of Ralf's age was standing three steps or so away from me in trainers, T-shirt and jeans, carrying a cardboard box in both hands. He put the box on the ground, never taking his eyes off me as he bent down and straightened up, then came a step closer. "What are you doing here?"

"I'd like to see Herr Schumann."

"Then why are you lurking in the bushes?"

"I'm not lurking in the bushes. I'm looking for my son Ralf Kestner."

"Ralf's not here." A second youth, also carrying a cardboard box, came around the corner of the house and stared at me. The first sniffed and spat into the shrubbery. "And anyone could say he was his dad. Can you prove it?"

"Don't make yourself ridiculous! Are you policing this place or what?"

"I can call the cops, if you want. How do I know you're not planning to break in?"

The second youth put his box down too. The first glanced at him and then back at me. "Well, *can* you prove it?"

I swallowed the insult. I still don't know what else I could have done without risking a brawl in which more than my dignity would have suffered. I produced my ID and held it under the youth's nose. He took it from my hand and studied it thoroughly before giving it back. "I'll tell Gero Schumann you've been snooping around here. I'm sure that will interest him."

"You can keep your stupid suspicions." I put my ID away and left. The pair of them didn't step aside; I had to push my way past the prickly branches of the bushes.

It took me some time to calm down. It was already getting dark when I pinned Ralf's Caucasian map to the inside of his bedroom door. And I stuck two strips of paper over the red and yellow attacking wedge formations. I had printed lettering on them first. The wording said:

And we fear that we have gone too far
Ever to see our own homes again.
Bertolt Brecht

No power in the world can wrest from the German soldier what he has.
Adolf Hitler, 9 November 1942

I left what else had to be done to Julia. When I showed her our son's handiwork, and told her where he had put it as a greeting to Ninoshvili, she reacted with obvious indignation, and I felt relieved. We were eating supper when Ralf came home. Julia rose to her feet, met him in the front hall, went to his room with him and closed the door. I even thought I heard her raise her voice, which she seldom does.

Ralf didn't reappear until I was sitting in front of the TV set with Julia, watching the news. I heard him go into the kitchen, and then a little later came the dull thud of the fridge door closing. I ignored him when he came into the living room and stood behind us, probably chewing and looking at the screen.

The culminating point of that unpleasant day wasn't long in coming. The TV news included a report from west Georgia, the once magical land of Colchis, a good minute's worth of footage showing nothing but mud and blood, the latest massacre between the troops, or rather the down-at-heel vagabonds, supporting the rival presidents Gamsakhurdia and Shevardnadze. Sub-machine guns rattled, exploding grenades sent soil spurting up, the maimed were laid side by side in a tent in their blood-soaked bandages. An old woman sat weeping outside a hut; only a few smoking rafters and the stump of the chimney were left. The body of a child lay on the bare earth beside the old woman.

Julia stayed sitting in her armchair in silence, motionless. When the news item came to an end, Ralf drew in a clearly audible breath through his nose, turned and went to his room.

8

Those German scholars of the nineteenth century who discovered Georgia, and acted as if it was their mission to civilize the barbarians there, were adept in thinking themselves better than foreigners and expressing abhorrence of other people's bad habits and misdeeds, while conveniently forgetting their own. I found one of the most absurd examples in the person of a professor by the name of B. Dorn, who in 1841 considered himself qualified to deliver a lecture on the history of the Georgians.

As far back as anyone could remember, said this historian, the Caucasus had been like "a hive inhabited by wild bees, with sharp stings designed to keep travellers in search of knowledge from penetrating into its interior". Matters were only then improving, said Professor Dorn, "now that the Russian eagle hovers over that dividing line between Europe and Asia", and "under the shelter of its pinions" interested tourists "are in a position to explore almost all corners of the Caucasus".

What this enlightened mind celebrated as the breakthrough of civilization was the bloody subjection of the Caucasus by the Tsarist empire. Under those same pinions, missionaries for German culture then came pouring into Georgia, so that in 1864 (when the Prussians were storming the Dybbøl Banker in the Second Schleswig War, and massacring Danes), the explorer Gustav Radde of Danzig was "commissioned by His Imperial Highness Grand Duke Mikhail Nikolayevich, governor of the Caucasus at this time, to carry out a biological and geographical study of that area".

We owe to Radde, for example, the discovery, so very illuminating for an understanding of Georgia, of how long *Iris caucasica* used to flower in the Botanical Gardens of Tbilisi at that time. He had this and about a hundred other flowers and plants observed daily "by Head Gardener Hinzenberg", who drew up tables recording the exact dates when they began flowering and then faded.

Similarly important discoveries about the nature of the Caucasian region were made for posterity by the zoologist Ernst Haeckel, who shrank from no expense of effort even on his journey there by the road over the pass. During the day he used every stop by the wayside, while the horses were being rested, in clambering about the mountain slopes, equipped with watercolour block and botanist's vasculum, to record their interesting features. At night he counted the exorbitant number of bugs that crawled out of the Caucasian mattresses. In Tbilisi, he was much struck by the fact that it was considerably warmer there than at home in Jena.

But undoubtedly they were all outdone by the writer and translator Friedrich von Bodenstedt from Peine, who was a senior school teacher in Tbilisi from 1843 to 1845, and in addition visited Armenia and Asia Minor. It may be that his dislike of his Georgian surroundings resulted from the fact that, on coming home from a tour of the Tbilisi taverns, he fell from the balcony of his house and was confined to a sickbed for a long time. But it's very likely anyway that only the eye of a German teacher could find as much to deplore as Bodenstedt did.

According to the observations of this educationalist, the Armenians – if somewhat dirty – are the most capable of learning among the peoples of Transcaucasia, and the Georgians the most stupid. "Taken as a whole", the latter may be physically "among the most beautiful nations on earth… but you will search in vain among the men and women here for that higher beauty where the heart, the spirit and the mind are reflected in the eye. Such supreme beauty is to be found only among peoples on a more elevated cultural level."

Herr von Bodenstedt makes it abundantly clear in subsequent passages that he himself occupies that higher cultural level (I haven't been able to find out whether he was a pop-eyed hunchback, although I strongly suspect as much). Of course he did not allow the magnificent clothing of the natives to deceive him; it stands "in no relation at all to their cramped, dirty and often disgusting dwellings".

We learn that the men of Georgia, instead of devoting themselves to serious conversation, pass the time by throwing their black sheepskin caps into the air and catching them on their heads again. Even worse, "drinking ultimately remains the favourite and principal pastime of the Georgians".

The women of Georgia, clad in the dazzling white *chadra*, are extremely pleasing to the eye, but only from a distance, and at the most until their thirtieth year; thereafter they inevitably become repellent hags, and you are advised to avoid the sight of them.

I suspect that my colleague Bodenstedt either had no success with the ladies in Tbilisi, or was doctoring his memoirs for the sake of his dear ones at home. I don't trust his indignant condemnation of the oriental woman in general for seeking "her whole happiness merely in a primitive sensual frenzy or in glittering show", nor his claim that her passion "knows no bounds but those that are imposed upon her by force". And I wonder why he doesn't reveal any experiences of his own in the bathhouses of Tbilisi, but quotes Alexander Pushkin, who was surprised but delighted when the bathhouse master, a "Tartar with no nose", admitted him to a vaulted room full of steam where more than fifty women, naked or half-naked, were amusing themselves without any inhibitions.

Herr von Bodenstedt describes other pleasures, for instance his visits to the German colony in Tbilisi, where Frau Salzmann served him her excellent Swabian omelette. And he gives an account of his sufferings: the night when he stumbled home along dark and unpaved alleys echoing with the howling of dogs, the winter morning when thick snow had fallen and the sky was so overcast that from his bedroom window the unfortunate man could see only the outline of Narikala Fortress, "the high mountain fort of Tbilisi, looking as sinister as if to veil over, with its cloak of snow, all the bloody memories left there by past centuries".

Keen as he was on culture, this idiot wrote those words in a century when the educated nations of Europe fought twenty-one bloody wars with each other. Performing a mental somersault, he attributed "the sad cultural condition" of the Caucasian peoples to the fact that murder and violence still flourished among them, which he found hard to understand, since after all, "the tree of Christianity took root among them more than a millennium and a half ago".

9

Perhaps I've become a little too heated over poor Friedrich von Bodenstedt and his like-minded contemporaries. I have remembered an incident on our journey which Karl-Heinz Dautzenbacher immediately made into a standing joke, calling it "the chicken of Ejmiadzin", adopting it into his repertoire of humorous anecdotes and citing it on every possible occasion with ever-increasing relish.

On our way to see the Catholicos of the Armenian Church we had stopped at the cave monastery of Geghard, at a height of seventeen hundred metres. The monastery, founded by two of the commanders of Queen Tamar's army, is one of the great sights of the Christian faith. It was laid waste by the Mongols under Tamerlane and later abandoned by the monks, but at the time of our visit the monastery had been restored and its churches in the rock were "back in working order", to use the Soviet expression for the practice of holding divine service.

We spent a little while enjoying the clear air and the view of the deeply fissured ravines; we looked at the porch of the main church, with its relief of a lion killing an ox, and then approached a chapel where Mass was being celebrated. Treading carefully, we had reached the entrance when out of the dim light we heard a loud, desperate cry suddenly rising in a shrill descant. It sounded like a human being in mortal terror.

The worshippers had unpacked a chicken from one of their baskets. They overcame its alarmed resistance, held it down on a stone step and chopped its head off before our eyes. Then they drew the sign of the cross on their foreheads with the creature's blood as it spurted out over the stone. The liturgy began at once.

Afterwards we asked the Catholicos, who received us in a magnificently panelled hall flooded with light, how such a heathen custom could be reconciled with the Christian faith. His Holiness, a dignified old man who spoke seven languages, replied in German, "Well – officially the Church isn't in favour of it. But as it's an old Armenian tradition, we have to do all we can to preserve it."

On the flight back to Moscow, we were served a cold supper by an Aeroflot stewardess who cast dark glances at us. Dautzenbacher heaved himself up from his seat, held a chicken thigh aloft, and looked around, grinning. "I knew it! The chicken of Ejmiadzin!" When, after landing on an airfield to the east of the capital, we were driving through the twilit birch woods, he tried cracking his joke again, swaying as he walked along the aisle of the bus, making a face as if in pain, and holding his stomach. "The chicken of Ejmiadzin! Ugh! Hasn't anyone got a shot of vodka?"

It was the only time I saw Dr Bender lose her composure. She hissed at Dautzenbacher, "Stop that, please! It's disgusting!"

I had to agree. It *was* disgusting. And perhaps I ought to revise my opinion of Bodenstedt's observations a little. Very well, it was not Georgians but Armenians who put that chicken to death so barbarously for the sake of Jesus Christ, but I'm not sure whether Georgian customs too aren't marked by such barbarity, even today.

I have read in Allen's *History of the Georgian People* that some of the injuries that one man may inflict on another affect his private life so profoundly that the pain felt, when it is a man's honour and not his material property that suffers, can be appeased only by the shedding of blood.

In the opinion of another historian, Allen's work of 1932 was already outmoded. But in a new encyclopedia I have also read that blood vengeance, as retribution not only for killing a member of a clan but also for injured honour, is a custom that has survived in some places until very recently. The encyclopedia specifically mentions Corsica, Montenegro, Albania and the Caucasus as examples.

10

Thanks to Tassilo Huber, with whom I studied for a few terms and who sits on the city council today as a member of the Green Party, I have reluctantly made the acquaintance of a secret agent, a man who works for the local branch of the Federal Office for the Protection of the Constitution, the authority charged with internal security in Germany.

It was a little awkward for me to confide in Tass, as we used to call him (partly because of his pro-Soviet contributions to discussion), but after a sleepless night I persuaded myself that it would be wrong of me to let my unpleasant experience with Ralf's friends rest at that. And one thing I knew about Tass, from the local paper, was his strong opposition to the far right. At a council meeting open to the public, he once even called Herr Schumann a dangerous rogue, and Schumann successfully sued him.

Tass didn't seem to think it very serious when I called at his office and told him about my son's friendship with Herr Schumann. He asked, "Why don't you smack the lad around the ears?" but immediately dismissed the idea sympathetically when I embarked on an answer. Stroking his beard, he told me what he knew about Herr Schumann. It wasn't much. Herr Schumann carefully avoided committing any offence that would be grounds for legal proceedings. His pamphlets and speeches always stayed in the grey area where a call for patriotic violence can still masquerade as legitimate freedom of speech.

Gero Schumann, that industrious young man, had also put his name as co-author to a historical treatise, a leaflet denouncing the Armenian massacres at the hands of the Turks and asking why, unlike the so-called Holocaust, this instance of genocide had been hushed up for decades. After Tass had also told me that, according to a credible rumour, Herr Schumann had slapped a secretary about and could keep her from going to the police only by paying a large sum in compensation, he took the latest collection of accounts of far-right violence from a stack of papers and began reading aloud to me from a study of "the onset of the new barbarism".

I'd had enough. I said that unfortunately I had to leave for home. Tass pressed the book into my hand, shrugged regretfully and said, "Ah well, this may not be very much use to you, but perhaps I can come up with some rather more concrete information. I'll see what can be done."

Two hours later my phone rang. It was a man whose name, he explained in a slow drawl, was Hochgeschurz, and Tassilo Huber had told him I was interested in anything I could find out about the lawyer Schumann. The man paused for a moment, during which I could hear him breathing, and then said he might be able to help me with one or two pieces of information.

I asked Herr Hochgeschurz who he was. He said that he had been working on right-wing radicalism for some time, comparing notes with Tassilo on that subject now and then, and he was also a personal friend of Tassilo's.

I fixed a meeting with Herr Hochgeschurz in the Town Hall beer cellar, which he suggested as a good place. As soon as I had rung off I dialled Tass's number, but I couldn't reach him either in his office or at home. When I tried his home number again in the evening a woman answered, obviously his wife or girlfriend, who told me that Tass was at a meeting of the Green Party committee and probably wouldn't be home until late.

I was able to leave school after the fourth lesson today, so I arrived at the beer cellar to meet Hochgeschurz a little early. However, Herr Hochgeschurz was already waiting. When I gave my name, the barman pointed to a niche where a stocky man of about fifty was sitting with a beer. He rose, offered me a plump hand, nodded and smiled.

Once we were both sitting down, Herr Hochgeschurz pushed a menu my way, picked up a second copy and studied the dishes available. I was still wondering whether or not to order any of the plain, fatty fare on offer when Hochgeschurz, looking at me over the top of his menu, asked, "Are you related to Dr Kestner the lawyer?"

"Yes, she's my wife." I glanced enquiringly at Hochgeschurz.

He returned my glance, and smiled. "I know her from a couple of trials." After a pause, during which he breathed audibly through his broad nose and returned to his study of the menu, he added, "I'm from the Office for the Protection of the Constitution."

For a moment I was in a state of total consternation. Then I felt angry. I had been completely taken in by my helpful friend Tass, that prominent defender of citizens' rights who spoke so tirelessly against the omnipotence of the state. Under his aggressively Green cover, he was keeping a profitable connection going with Internal Security. Now and then Herr Hochgeschurz let him into some little secret that could be politically exploited, and Councillor Huber reciprocated by drawing the snoop's attention to people from whom something might be extracted.

"Listen," I said. "I don't know what Herr Huber has told you, but he obviously entirely mistook my meaning." I put the menu down on the table. "I have no intention whatsoever of letting myself be roped in by Internal Security!"

"Come, come, whatever makes you think that was the idea? There's no question of any such thing!" Herr Hochgeschurz shook his head, rubbed his nose, and then leaned forwards. "If you think I wanted to get you to denounce your son, you're very wide of the mark. And I'll tell you why."

He looked around the dimly lit beer cellar before folding his hands on the table and continuing. "Of course we're aware who your son is. We've known his name ever since he started handing out some of Herr Schumann's pamphlets in the street. In some respects we may even known more about your son than his own parents do. I hope that won't upset you; it's what we're there for. But for that very reason I can reassure you." He smiled. "We're not worried about your son. We're worried about Herr Schumann."

The waiter came over to our table. Herr Hochgeschurz ordered eight small Nuremberg sausages with sauerkraut and another beer. I stayed where I was, I even ordered a "Bürgermeister" omelette and a half-litre of wine. I wasn't feeling good about this, but I hoped to get a few hints that might make Ralf's prospects look not quite so dark. Herr Hochgeschurz didn't disappoint me.

Gero Schumann's hangers-on, said the agent, were from sound, respectable backgrounds. A few students, a couple of schoolboys like Ralf, a candidate for an inspector's post, two bank trainees. No women. Some of them had once been in a brawl in a bar with a group of Young Socialists, and had put the Reds to flight. But there were no notoriously violent offenders among the regular visitors to Herr Schumann's summer house. The ideological and historical seminars he held there were probably too intellectually pretentious for that, the atmosphere and his grandmother's tenants too high-class.

Outside the summer house, however, Herr Schumann by no means avoided mixing with disreputable characters. On the pretext of wanting to reintegrate disadvantaged young people into society, he maintained regular contacts with skinheads and similar hooligans. He spent a good deal of money on this, as he did on his cultural seminars; he had once actually recruited a university professor to speak at one of them, and on another occasion a retired army brigadier. Herr Schumann, all things considered, was unpredictable, not least because of his intelligence and his great gifts as a demagogue. That was what made him dangerous.

Herr Hochgeschurz smiled. "On the other hand, I see your son as something of an innocent. He probably just finds it exciting to go to that summer house and hear people say that the history of the world doesn't work at all the way he's being taught at school. Of course in your place I wouldn't leave him entirely to the influence of Herr Schumann. But you shouldn't rush things. I don't have to teach you anything, you're a trained teacher yourself. However, I've had experience of similar cases. If you put him under pressure, you'll probably just achieve the opposite of what you want."

Herr Hochgeschurz refrained from asking any questions about Ralf's conduct in the privacy of our home. Instead, he brought the conversation round to Julia again, praising her talents as a defence lawyer, although professionally speaking, he said, of course he couldn't agree with the lenient sentences she got for some of her clients. He ordered a third beer and a second shot of spirits. When the waiter came to tot everything up and asked if it was to go on the same bill, Herr Hochgeschurz hesitated for a moment, as if the question had surprised him. I said I was paying, and drove home feeling greatly relieved.

11

In ordinary everyday life we're unaware of failing to look beyond our own horizons. We go about our business, dealing with whatever arises, and that gives us enough to do. The messages and images that reach us from far away lack depth; they're two-dimensional, like a newspaper page or a postcard, they don't really engage our attention. Only very seldom do they, just now and then, convey a physical sense of those distant places.

I don't know how it may be with other people, but at moments like those I have always felt mingled fascination and alarm. For instance, such a moment occurred when, many years ago, I was allowed to unpack a parcel that one of my mother's brothers – he had emigrated to South America on a coffin ship – had sent us from Buenaventura. Probably in order to give the family a good impression of his new country, he had chosen a small sculpture of some Inca god or king, I forget exactly what it was meant to be, but it was an attractive piece of craftsmanship.

I held the porous, dark-green stone in my hand, smelled it, and shuddered. That symbol of all that was distant and strange lost its aura once my mother had put it away on a shelf in the glass-fronted bookcase.

This morning at seven thirty, just as I was about to leave the house, the telephone rang. I picked up the receiver, gave my name, and instead of an answer heard a vague rushing sound, then a crackling, then two distant voices both talking at once in a language I couldn't understand, and then back came the rushing again. I felt my hand beginning to sweat on the receiver, and hung up.

Julia has told me that half an hour later there was another, similar call. She waited for a while, said, "Hello?" a couple of times, but no one replied.

I left it to Julia to make what she could of the incident, and she didn't refrain from doing so. Perhaps, she suggested, it had been my friend from Tbilisi? It looked as if his travel plans had fallen through, Julia said, and perhaps he was ringing to say that his visit to us was off.

Yes, perhaps. Or perhaps it had been Matassi, calling to find out if her husband had arrived all right, and to ask what his plans were.

12

It would be useful to be a legal expert. In a recent new edition of a work on blood vengeance and atonement, first published a hundred years ago but obviously still recognized as authoritative, I come upon the unnerving notion that blood vengeance "is to be regarded not as barbaric, but as something higher", i.e. the original form of justice. Where the state does not act, according to this theory, personal revenge is justified, for example by virtue of "the right of a husband to administer punishment". Another legal scholar, unaffected by either doubts or fears, has analysed in cold blood the significance of that idea in bringing about peaceful settlement of disputes.

In the case of injury to a husband's honour by a third party's attack on his wife's virtue, it was the duty of a husband in ancient civilizations (civilizations, this work calls them!) to punish not just his wife but also her lover. King Ibert of Sicily, catching the enchanter Klingsor in the act with his queen, castrated his rival in love on the spot. This may be a legend, but there is evidence at least of the legal custom of cutting out the kidneys of such adulterers, those organs being considered the seat of sexual desire.

In the city of Reval the law allowed an adulterer to be dragged through the streets by his penis. In Poland his testicles, or as we would say, his balls, were nailed to a board. In Spain he wasn't even granted any chance to recover from such halfway measures and perhaps repeat his offence: his entire genitals, penis, scrotum and all, were simply chopped off.

So I feel positively relieved to read that, at quite an early date, the Georgians came to the civilized conclusion of satisfying their claim to an offender's blood by taking a cash payment instead. When King David the Builder erected the main church of Gelati, he climbed the scaffolding one day, missed his footing and fell into the depths. His injuries took a long time to heal. He recovered only when a nobleman called Avshandadze recommended him to bathe in the milk of dogs, and provided a tub of that fluid, presumably by calling on contributions from all the suckling bitches in the country.

King David showed his gratitude to the nobleman by renewing a guarantee that one of his forebears had already give the Avshandadzes: anyone who killed a member of the family could, if he wanted to save his skin, get out of trouble by paying 400,000 botinauris, and anyone who seduced one of their women would have to pay half that sum. Monetary atonement could also be paid in kind, the documentary guarantee stipulating twelve white mules and twelve hounds, along with a dozen serfs. The Avshandadzes could legally cut the throat of anyone who tried to wriggle out of paying these damages.

It's interesting that not only did I gather such information, but as I studied the relevant literature horror seized upon me now and then – as if I didn't already know that murderous events had occurred throughout the history of the world. After all, I had spent years studying the subject at university. But then, so far as I remember, it left me cold. At the outside, I worried over whether some bean-counter marking my exams would want to know how many dead there were in, for instance, the Battle of Verdun (360,000 French and 335,000 German; I've just looked it up again).

My far more empathetic reaction in my venture into the study of blood vengeance could indicate an alarming imbalance in my emotions. Am I sensitive only when I'm afraid that my own skin is in danger, do I feel nothing at all so long as others alone are affected? To cap it all, when I embarked on that study I lost sight of the ridiculously banal facts. Instead of using my brain, I've been seeing ghosts.

And even my discoveries in the field of legal history show me no cause for that. I am not a case for blood vengeance. I didn't kill Matassi. I didn't commit adultery with her either, because presumably even in Georgia *immissio penis in vaginam*, full consummation of the sexual act, is necessary for that. I just put my hand under her skirt, and very likely Ninoshvili never even heard about it.

Yes, well, I can't rule out the possibility that Dautzenbacher, who was standing around with Ninoshvili for a while at the time of our flight to Yerevan before he went to stand in line for passport control, dropped some remark about Matassi's visit to my hotel room; in fact it would have been rather surprising if he'd failed to make use of this opportunity for an insinuating joke. But neither then, when my Georgian friend waved to me, smiling, nor later, via the New Year cards he's sent me since, did Ninoshvili show that he knew anything. Instead, he regularly sent me warm good wishes from Matassi, who added "A Happy New Year!" in her own hand, in English, with her signature.

If the couple had been involved in a plot against me in Tbilisi, then if the sin was nipped in the bud it might at the most rankle with Ninoshvili. But if they were not agents, just a perfectly ordinary couple, then I'm as good as sure that Matassi said nothing to her husband about our little flirtation. And then she won't have admitted it to him even if, prompted by Dautzenbacher, he had asked about it.

It may be that Georgian society, as the historian Suny wrote in 1989, is still ruled entirely by men; it's not so very different even in our own enlightened culture. But I have well-founded doubts of Professor Suny's sweeping statement about Georgian women. I don't think they observe their

50

traditional rules of behaviour just as they always did – according to Suny they are still subservient to men, devoted to domesticity and sexually demure.

Perhaps Matassi was an exception. She wasn't demure, anyway. If I didn't still have her beautiful, immaculate face before my mind's eye, I'd even call her a hussy. She didn't reject my advances, she even offered provocation.

Well, here I close my studies of blood vengeance and put them away in the files. They have been a ridiculous waste of my time.

13

Perhaps it was because of being under strain for so long, but anyway, I misinterpreted my strange experience on Viktor's *sovkhoz*. That sense of losing the ground underfoot, of un-expectedly finding ourselves in another world, doesn't just happen when we're travelling abroad. It sometimes comes over us even in familiar surroundings, as I would probably have remembered if my hysterical fears hadn't blocked the idea.

I had an experience of that kind yesterday afternoon when I'd gone to the university to get hold of some material on the legal situation in cultures where blood-vengeance killings are common. I joined the young people standing in a queue slowly moving closer, at a snail's pace, to the lending desk in the library; other young people followed me. Rain had been falling from a sky of ragged clouds that let the sun shine through now and then. The students' anoraks hemming me in smelled damp and a little musty, and so did their sweaters and jeans. Straggling hair, a few beards that could have done with a comb.

Suddenly I was filled with melancholy. A memory had surfaced in me, vague, yet perceptible by all my senses. The bleak, desolate mood of an afternoon many years ago, in a German or History class when I had spread out half a dozen books around my workplace. I had to study them, but I couldn't. The strong smell of the old papers. Muted voices in a corner behind the shelves, the faint rustle of a page being turned, no other sign of life. The autumn sun came out, tinged the edge of the roof of the lecture hall opposite with colour, and then went behind the clouds again. I wanted to get out of there, but where could I go?

And it's not just melancholy that overwhelms us at such moments, irresistibly transporting us into another world. Again, when I saw Mount Ararat for the first time I lost all awareness of my present existence, of the moment in space and time where I now was, something to hold to, but at the same time my heart expanded. I felt blessed.

It was an experience like Pushkin's when he pitched his tent in the dark on his journey to Erzerum, came out into the fresh air next morning, and was overwhelmed by the view of the Biblical mountain. He thought he saw, with his own eyes, Noah's ark coming to rest on the peak of Ararat on the seventeenth day of the seventh month of the Deluge; he saw the raven and the dove flying, the symbols of punishment and atonement sent out by Noah to discover whether the water had gone down.

And these moments are enough, as at the library borrowing desk and indeed on far lesser occasions, to remove us from space and time. The church bells on a Sunday morning bring to mind the aroma of the Sunday roast and my father's cigars, they show me freshly swept streets with windows flashing in the summer sunlight, or sometimes the snowstorms when I looked out of our warm living room. Admittedly, the happiness we feel at such times is only borrowed. We have lost the real thing, and what goes to our hearts is more like our longing for it.

I am almost sorry that Ninoshvili probably won't be coming after all. Three weeks have passed since his letter arrived, twenty-one days during which there have been some considerable upheavals in the Republic of Georgia. I'm assuming that he must have given up his plans to travel, and I feel that like a loss, quite apart for my fear that something may have happened to him or Matassi or even both of them. I would have liked to discuss the matters on my mind with him.

I would have liked to ask him what he felt about my own native land, the foreign land he would have been seeing for the first time. And I would also have wished to hear more from him about his own country, which unexpectedly has come closer to me in the last few days. I have been continuing my reading of more recent Georgian literature, since such books were still lying around on my desk, and I find them – presumably because the tension upsetting my perception has finally worn off – interesting and stimulating in a way that I hadn't been able to feel earlier.

I found in a novelist called Otar Chiladze, born in 1933, an almost alarming echo of my occasional loss of my hold on reality. In a novel set at the turn of the century, Chiladze describes Batumi, the Black Sea port captured by the Russians from the Turks in 1878, as vividly as if he had been living there. Dimitri, a young lawyer who has studied for several years in Odessa, where he married a shy girl called Daria, returns with her to his native city of Batumi. But the wild parties that his parents once held in their house behind the green garden gate are over now. His parents themselves, buried long ago, look down on the young couple in silence from their black picture frames.

Silence develops between husband and wife, and when they lie side by side at night, mute and still in the marital bed, they are both overcome again and again by images from their past, which is stronger than the present. Daria feels that she has suddenly turned back into the little girl whose grandfather used to bring her a bunch of grapes from the vineyard, with spider's webs clinging to it, or a downy-skinned peach. Dimitri sees himself sitting as he did in his childhood, on an officer's lap amidst his parents' merry-making guests, and hearing the crack of a pistol shot. Yet again someone has fired a gun purely for fun, but this time the bullet misses the ceiling and grazes the officer's hand; no great harm done, no, and Dimitri watches as the ladies, laughing and crowing, bind up the officer's bleeding hand with his mother's veil.

One day a stranger erupts into Daria and Dimitri's moribund relationship, an actor from Tbilisi whom Dimitri, never guessing what complications he is bringing down on himself, invites to the house. "Come in, come in, guests are sent by God." And the Georgian author's novel begins to brim over with images, characters, aromas and sounds. It doesn't stop at the melancholy whistling of the locomotives pulling carriages along the Transcaucasian Railway from Tbilisi to Batumi, or the distant wailing sirens of the soot-encrusted pilot steamboats escorting gigantic ships into harbour to take on board the ever-richer flow of oil in the form of naphtha.

The local whores turn choosy; as soon as a British ship comes into harbour they despise the Turkish lira and sell themselves only for sterling. The coffeehouses of the city begin to swarm with Turks wearing the fez, Germans in leather gaiters, Scotsmen in tartan kilts. Night after night the actor knocks on Dimitri's door, hammers away on the piano, quotes *Hamlet* and holds forth, spouting revolutionary monologues. Dimitri is afraid that the police are listening and will deport them all to Siberia. The workers go on strike and storm the prison. Cossacks gallop along Marine Prospect, leaving the street smelling of weapons, leather, sweating horses. Thirteen workers are shot.

Yes, I'd have liked to know more about the country. But that's all over now. I shan't be invited to Georgia again in a hurry. Perhaps I could book a voyage from Odessa to Batumi with Inturist, if the agency still exists in the new republic. I imagine approaching the land of Colchis in the light of dawn, like Jason, seeing the snow-crowned peaks rise halfway between the sea and the sky. Yes, if the land of Colchis still existed.

14

David Ninoshvili has arrived. I found him in the kitchen with Julia late in the afternoon when I got back from a rehearsal with my drama group. He had tied one of Julia's aprons round his waist and was chopping parsley. He put the knife down, flung his arms around me and kissed me on both cheeks. Julia poured me a glass of the Kakheti wine brought by Ninoshvili as a present to the household. They had already opened it to taste it.

Ninoshvili is a little stouter than I remember him, but he's still a youthful-looking, well-built man, a handsome specimen of the race that even Herr von Bodenstedt thought one of the best-looking peoples on earth. I was reminded of Grigol Robakidze's description of typical pure-bred Georgians: tall and strong, broad-shouldered with a slender waist, a shapely aquiline nose, chestnut hair and a pale gold complexion.

The only difference is that his eyes are not honey-coloured but very dark.

They were shining as he drank a toast: "To the renewal of our friendship!" He didn't leave Julia out either, but turned to her: "And to Dr Kestner, hoping she'll be part of it! Or may I say Julia?"

15

It took me a good fifty minutes to pacify my drama group at midday today. Yesterday afternoon I had thrown Micky Rautenstrauch out because, yet again, he hadn't learned his lines and was brazenly trying to carry it off by improvising. The stupid oaf really seemed to think he could fool me that way.

But as soon as I had sent him packing there was vigorous protest: Jürgen Dahlmann, playing Romeo, even claimed that the whole production would fall apart without Micky, and Günsel Özcan, our Juliet, who doesn't appear in the scene we were rehearsing and until then had been sitting chattering and giggling in a corner of the hall, started protesting more and more vigorously. When I asked what useful arguments she could contribute, she actually said well, after all, Brecht had called the play a practice piece for actors, so it was fair enough to ask for Micky to be allowed to practise.

I put an end to the argument by sending Günsel and Valerie Müller up on stage to rehearse the scene between Juliet and her nurse. But the whole thing had gone flat, the two of them just reeled off their lines, and were obviously keen to prove that with my expulsion of Micky Rautenstrauch the heart had gone out of the drama group. I had also realized that I was going to have trouble finding a replacement for

Micky; although he was only seventeen the boy had caught exactly the air of ponderous desperation necessary for the part of Romeo's tenant Gobbo, as presented by Brecht in an additional scene to go into Shakespeare's play, which we were including. But I wasn't giving in so quickly.

At noon today, when the last lesson was over, I asked Christian Berkhan whether I could have a word with him. Romeo and Juliet were instantly suspicious, exchanged glances, and Günsel put up her hand. If it was something to do with the drama group, she said, she and Jürgen would like to be in on it. That dream couple, self-confident as they are, know exactly what liberties they can take, so I shrugged my shoulders and agreed.

Poor Christian, who had tried in vain to get a speaking part a couple of times, was obviously much alarmed. As the classroom emptied, he stayed sitting as if nailed to his chair, and looked at me as though he expected me to tell him to jump off the roof just to see what it was like. He cast just one quick glance behind him, to where Romeo and Juliet were sitting side by side at a table, Jürgen leaning back with his arms crossed, Günsel propping her chin on one hand, the fingers of the other drumming on the table top in a way that boded no good.

I explained the part of Gobbo to the offender and asked if he thought he would be able to take it on. He began to stammer, yes, of course, he'd be happy to, he was sure he could do it, but the rehearsals were quite well advanced, the cast were used to the play now, and so on and so forth. The little coward was afraid to cross any bridge I built for him. When words looked like failing him entirely, Jürgen suddenly cleared his throat: maybe Günsel and he could make a better suggestion, he said. Oh yes? I couldn't wait to hear it, I told him.

Günsel stopped drumming her fingers and took over: we probably needed an understudy for Mercutio anyway, in case Max Blümel had to move to Hamburg with his father. And she could really see Christian as Mercutio. So could he, agreed Jürgen, and if we restored the passages of text that I had cut only because Max couldn't get them into his head, then Mercutio would be a great part for Christian.

I wonder when those two thought up that manoeuvre to outflank me. Anyway, they performed it at a moment that not even the Prussian general staff could have picked better. As I was pointing out to them, in some annoyance, that we were not discussing an understudy for Mercutio but the part of Gobbo, there was a knock on the door, and Micky Rautenstrauch looked in, smiling and nodding. He said he didn't want to disturb us, but it was important to him to settle something urgent for what might be called personal reasons; he wanted to explain... It wouldn't take long, he said.

He was undeterred by the look I gave him... He came in, closed the door behind him, and said he wanted to apologize. Of course it was bad that he hadn't known his lines, but there'd been stand-up rows going on at his home, not a moment's peace for days. He'd spare me the details, he added, he just wanted to say that he'd gone right through his part last night and knew it perfectly now. But he was only telling me, he said, so that I'd know he really was sorry.

Günsel played a lively rhythm with her knuckles on the table, and Jürgen joined in. Poor Christian crumpled entirely. He said he'd be happy to understudy Mercutio, that part was probably more his kind of thing. I beat a retreat in good order by stressing the merits of good teamwork, and finally said, raising my voice, that this was definitely Micky's very last chance, and if he didn't toe the line he was out of the drama group for good. Micky nodded. "Yes, sure, that's fine." Günsel batted her eyelashes at me in her most fetching way, and I set off cheerfully for home.

That impressively capable trio with their victim, a kind-hearted dimwit who was past helping, had put David Ninoshvili right out of my mind.

When I got home the house was empty. I called, "Hello?" but there was no answer. On my desk I found two pieces of paper with numbers and a few words in Georgian written on them. Apparently he'd been telephoning and making notes. I took the pieces of paper into the kitchen and studied them while I ate a pot of curd cheese.

In his handwriting in Georgian, Ninoshvili uses the international transcription alphabet, Roman letters complemented only here and there by unusual signs. But I thought that in what he'd written here I also detected the look of the original Georgian characters, like hieroglyphs that are drawn rather than written. Curves breaking midway and ending in pointed wedges. Crossways lines and pendants. The Hebrews wrote something like that, or no, it was the Persians. It's the handwriting of the Orient, anyway, not of Europe.

I put the scraps of paper down on a corner of my desk, and unpacked the essays that I was going to read and mark. After the first three I got to my feet, slowly climbed the stairs, opened the spare-room door and looked in. He hadn't brought the small, shabby case I'd imagined in my fantasies. A large brown leather suitcase in good condition, with heavy metal clasps, stood on the chest under the sloping ceiling.

It had begun to rain, and drops were pattering against the window. I hesitated for a moment, then went up to the case and tried to lift the lid. The case was locked.

A car started out in the street, and the sound of the engine moved away. I listened. There was still nothing to be heard but the pattering of the raindrops. I cast a glance around the room, struggled with the temptation to look inside the wardrobe, which had its key in it, and inside the drawer of the bedside table. Finally I overcame myself and went back to my desk.

After looking through another three essays, I reached for one of the scribbled notes, picked up the phone and dialled one of the sequences of numbers written on it. The call went through, but I heard only the ringing tone for an endlessly long time. Suddenly a man's voice answered. "Hello?" I hung up.

Ninoshvili had seemed slightly annoyed yesterday evening when we told him about the two mysterious calls before he arrived. No, he said, it hadn't been him, and he didn't imagine that Matassi already wanted to call and ask how he was. Were we sure it was someone calling from Georgia?

He has brought me a present from Matassi. He disappeared into the spare room before supper, and returned with a flat, round package that he handed to me in front of Julia. When I asked what was in it he said he didn't know, Matassi had put the little package in his case at the last moment. I unpacked the present. It's a small glazed earthenware plate, obviously a replica of an old work of art. The rim is brightly patterned, the plate itself shows a man and a woman in colourful Caucasian costume. They are turning to each other, and the man is smoking a long pipe. Matassi has added a pink card on which she has written, in English, "In remembrance and with my best wishes! M."

Julia said oh, what an exquisitely pretty thing, and Ninoshvili nodded with a silent smile. I stood the plate on my desk and put the card in the drawer. One or two hours ago, in the middle of my work, I touched the plate, smelled it, and then, because the glaze was giving nothing away, I smelled the card too. The Orient. Myrrh, what else, or at least what I think is the fragrance of myrrh. Perhaps she let a drop of her perfume fall on the card.

I found it hard to concentrate on the essays again, and not just on account of Matassi. I couldn't decide whether it was a good sign or a bad sign that Ninoshvili was staying out so long. Absurdly, I thought of his expedition to the confectioner's, and I was all but on the point of getting to my feet to go and make sure he hadn't concealed himself somewhere about the house.

After all, so far as I was aware, he didn't know anyone but us in this city. And I couldn't think that among the publishers he was planning to visit here he had instantly found someone interested in bringing out Georgian literature in German translation, and they had already entered into negotiations that were going on until evening. Was he using his commission from the Georgian Ministry of Culture and his travel expenses to loaf around town somewhere?

My speculations were resolved in a surprising way. At about six thirty the front door was opened and I heard the voices of Julia and our guest. They were engaged in lively conversation. It turned out that this morning, when I had already left the house, Ninoshvili had asked Julia where he could find a copy shop. For the sake of simplicity she offered to get her secretary to photocopy his manuscripts. So he visited her in her office in the afternoon, and when she had finished work the two of them went to several shops where Ninoshvili found ingredients for a Georgian supper.

I don't know whether he also paid for them. Anyway, this evening we're starting with *pkhali*, which as our Georgian friend explained to me is chopped cabbage with walnuts, pomegranates and red peppers, and as the main dish we're having *chanakhi*, apparently a delicious dish made of mutton, aubergines, tomatoes and potatoes cooked and served in an earthenware casserole.

For some minutes now there's been a spicy aroma in the house. I can hear the two of them talking in the kitchen, and laughing now and then. When I passed the kitchen door on my way to fetch today's paper from the magazine rack in the living room, I heard Julia talking broken Russian. Or anyway, it sounded like Russian. Evidently she's trying out her linguistic knowledge on David Ninoshvili, a skill gleaned from when she was at Halle Polytechnic High School in the Democratic German Republic.

16

I've looked up a couple of sentences that I noted down rather absently, shaking my head over them, when I was reading Robakidze, but which have appeared to me in a rather dubious light since yesterday evening. That twentieth-century Georgian man of letters, an upright democrat and an enemy of the tyrannical Bolshevist rule of his native land, described Alexander Pushkin's visit to Tbilisi in a historical excursus in one of his novels, and wrote this rather offensive passage: "The Slavonic steppes could not satisfy his Negro blood. Only in Tbilisi did Pushkin feel at ease…"

Well, Robakidze would have been referring to the fact that on his mother's side Pushkin was descended from Peter the Great's Moorish godson Ibrahim, whom the Tsar generously sent to a military academy in Paris, where he did Peter great credit. The Moor left the academy with a commission as a captain in the artillery. And in the 1920s it may not yet have seemed incorrect to anyone to call a Moor a Negro, or assume that his blood made him particularly excitable.

But it was not just Negroes on whom Robakidze the Georgian looked down with obvious distaste. He has his hero flee from the streets of Tbilisi, where the Kurds' smell of sweat takes his breath away, to Kashveti Cathedral, at the sight of which he receives an insight into the Iberian, meaning Georgian, nature. "Every stone of the temple is a virgin… the temple itself is a virgin, a pagan virgin offering herself as a sacrifice…" Here again, the forecourt of the cathedral is crowded with evil-smelling, degenerate figures, but "suddenly eyes are shining, eyes that one would recognize among thousands, the eyes of the virgin Iberia. A pure, unmixed race. Pride and modesty in one."

I remembered this hymn of praise when at Julia's request Ninoshvili tried, over our Georgian meal yesterday evening, to explain the reasons for the constant bloodshed in his native land. Ralf, who had avoided spending much time with our guest on the first evening, had come home hungry, was obviously unable to resist the smell of supper, even though the wop had cooked it, and sat down at the table with us. As he consumed large quantities of *pkhali* and *chanakhi*, he listened, clearly with growing interest, to what Ninoshvili told us.

The civil war, our guest explained, would not have broken out but for the attempt of a couple of recalcitrant tribes to break up the unity of the Georgian Republic. They were the Abkhazians in western Georgia, and the Ossetians, a mountain-dwelling people descended from nomads who had set their faces firmly against civilization. The cultural and political level of these tribes, who had settled on Georgian soil over the course of time, was pathetic compared to the Georgian people themselves, but they refused to recognize the fact and instead had always been inclined to bloodshed, all the more so now that Georgia was a sovereign state again.

For instance, said Ninoshvili, masked Ossetians had hauled thirty-two of their own countrymen out of a bus and massacred them, laid the blame on the Georgians, and then tried to show that Georgia was intending genocide, a kind of Holocaust of the Ossetians. As for the Abkhazians, they had planned, he said, to increase their influence in Georgia by turning to their fellow tribesmen who emigrated to Turkey centuries ago, appealing to them to return, as genuine Turks, or at least citizens of a state that had been hostile to the Georgians over a very long period.

Ralf asked whether you could say that Georgia was threatened by foreign domination. Ninoshvili smiled. "Not yet. And we shall oppose any such thing." In this connection, he explained the concept of the Caucasian race, a term which had been taken as meaning white people in general in the nineteenth century. The half-savage tribes who had made their way into the Caucasus as newcomers, or more precisely as an occupying force, could not of course have been regarded as the prototype of that race, only pure-bred Georgians. In Germany of all countries, we should understand that those Georgians were unwilling to dispute their claim to leadership with other inhabitants of the country originating outside it.

At this point, to my own satisfaction, the argument obviously became more than Julia could stand. She ended the conversation by starting to clear away the dishes. Ninoshvili rose from the table at once to help her, and would not be dissuaded. Ralf said good night and went to his room. I switched on the TV and watched the screen without really seeing what the programme was about.

17

It was not the kind of relief you might hope for in an unpleasant situation, but it did boost my ego, and that, I won't deny, did me good.

Elke Lampert, who had been wandering around the corridors for days looking lost, told me her troubles. When I came into the staff room this morning to kill time, having an empty period in my timetable just then, she was sitting alone in a corner by the window with an open book in front of her, staring out of the window at the chestnut trees. Their golden leaves were gradually falling and drifting to the ground.

I poured myself a coffee and picked up a newspaper that someone had left lying around. Heavy fighting in Abkhazia. The headline was enough to make me go on leafing through the paper. When I had reached the arts section I unexpectedly heard a slight sound. I glanced at Elke. She had turned her back to me, but I could tell that she was mopping her eyes with a handkerchief.

I tried to concentrate on what I was reading. After a while I heard another sound, this time clearly a suppressed sob. Elke's shoulders were bowed, she seemed to be doubling up. Alarmed, I went over to her and asked if there was anything wrong. She turned away from me, the handkerchief to her mouth, and shook her head in silence. I sat down beside her and touched her arm with my fingertips. She looked at me with brimming eyes. Next moment she could no longer control her sobs, and her tears began to flow.

I had expected various reasons for her distress, but not what I now heard. Her husband, small, unprepossessing Kurt Lampert, had found himself a girlfriend twenty years his junior. I know the man, I have even – reluctantly – been on first-name terms with him since Elke brought him with her to the skittles evenings so tirelessly organized by Brauckmann to encourage friendly social relationships among the staff. On these occasions I had noticed Kurt Lampert, if at all, only because in spite of the amount of beer he poured down his throat, his unerring aim could always knock down both the left- and the right-hand corner pins.

His intelligence is nothing out of the ordinary. He works as a manager or head of a department in a pharmaceuticals firm, maybe he supervises the pill-rolling machines. What clever, sensitive Elke sees in her husband I don't know. It's my impression that he isn't even very easy to get on with, or so I conclude from the unpleasant way he crows when he himself or his team win at skittles.

He is also, obviously, an unscrupulous liar. When Elke found out that he was sleeping with this girl from the office, he swore blind that he'd already broken it off with her. Last week she caught him in the act with the girl, on the back seat of his car.

I didn't ask Elke how she'd found the car. I tried to cheer her up. These things, unfortunately, were happening all the time, I said. Maybe he'd had good intentions but had weakened once again. She shouldn't let jealousy consume her, I told her; that would only make it all seem worse. And so on and so forth. As I talked Elke stared straight ahead of her. I was suffering from an awkward feeling that I had put forward more convincing arguments on other occasions. In the end I ran out of words and just patted her arm.

After a while she looked at me. "Has anything like that ever happened to you?"

"What, on the back seat? No, I probably wouldn't feel very comfortable."

"I didn't mean that. I mean, has your wife ever cheated on you?" Then she immediately apologized; it was none of her business, she said, but she really was so upset.

I shook my head, said there was no need to apologize. And it wasn't difficult for me to answer her question, I added: no, Julia had never cheated on me. At least, I'd never had the slightest cause to suspect such a thing. Elke nodded.

As we both sat there in silence again, I realized that my marriage is very enviable compared to other people's. In nearly twenty years, of course, there's been a cloud in the sky now and then, even a quarrel, for instance over pushy Erika and the trouble that brash female from Halle makes in our household every six months. But when that happens I've always taken back anything hasty I said, because I am also impressed, even pleased, by the way Julia stands so firmly by her school friend.

And of course from time to time some impertinent goat has come along thinking Julia might fancy him and has tried to ruffle her feathers. I remember a lawyers' ball where a provincial presiding judge with pepper-and-salt hair and a deep-black moustache, a former hockey player said to have been almost picked for the national team once, attached himself to Julia – not so much a cockerel as a polyp, a bloodsucking jellyfish. He put both his arms around her when they danced, rubbed his moustache against her ear. Julia kept still and smiled; I don't know, but perhaps she had to appear before the man in a court case, and wanted to lay the foundations for a verdict in her client's favour.

When she had gone out for a moment, I managed to clink glasses with the judge when I was holding a glass of red wine, which spilled over his dress shirt and dyed it red down to his cummerbund. I apologized, although I did tell the judge he hadn't been entirely in control of his movements. For a second I was afraid he was going to throw a punch at me. But then, still scrubbing vigorously at his dress shirt with his handkerchief, he left the hall and wasn't seen again.

When Julia came back with fresh make-up on, I told her that unfortunately the judge had had to go, and why. She laughed and kissed me.

And in the long years of our marriage her physical desire for me hasn't worn off, any more than mine has for her. My occasional lapses – all things considered really very rare – haven't been because of sexual frustration at home; if anything they have not diminished but intensified my feelings for Julia. And they have done our relationship no harm because, of course, I successfully concealed them. I shrank from the complications that might ensue after a confession. Julia is jealous. But then again, if that can sometimes be a nuisance, it's just one more reason for me to think myself lucky in my wife.

When we had gone to bed on the night of Ninoshvili's arrival, and were lying side by side, each with a book, she suddenly asked me what Matassi looks like and what kind of woman she is.

I'd never shown her – probably because of my guilty conscience – the New Year cards with Matassi's warm greetings, but I had purposely let her see the letter in which Ninoshvili announced his forthcoming visit and wrote that, unfortunately, Matassi couldn't come with him. After all, I must assume that my Georgian friend would mention his wife in front of Julia at some point. As soon as she had read the letter she asked who Matassi was. I shrugged and said it must be the name of Ninoshvili's girlfriend or wife, I'd met her once or twice in Tbilisi, although I had forgotten her name.

She was satisfied with that, for one thing probably because at this point she didn't feel like bothering more than absolutely necessary with our unwanted visitor, who threatened to divide our family. But now Matassi's present to me had aroused her suspicions.

"Is she pretty?" asked Julia. I muttered something, put my book down, switched off my reading light, turned on my back, shook my duvet into shape and looked up at the bedroom ceiling in the dim light, as if I had to search my memory. "Well, what exactly does pretty mean? So far as I remember she was quite... quite tall. Almost Ninoshvili's height. Sorry, I can't tell you any more about what she looked like. I think I hardly noticed her."

"Just what I'd have advised." Julia put her own book down, switched out the light, snuggled close to me and started petting.

If all that ought to have made me feel guilty, poor Elke Lampert did a great deal to ease my conscience. She went on sitting quietly there for a while after I'd answered her question about Julia's fidelity. Finally she looked at me, nodded again and smiled. "Yes. Why on earth would your wife cheat on you?" I looked enquiringly at her. She said, "You're such a nice man. A good person." And she kissed me on the cheek.

18

Julia did not mention Ninoshvili's remarks about the Caucasian race and the barbaric tribes sabotaging peace in Georgia again. Presumably his account of it had embarrassed her as much as it did me. At the most, I did feel an urgent need to make it clear to our guest that civility, which had required us not to start arguing with him over our Georgian meal, has its limits. I spent a little time preparing what I had to say, and then spoke to him about his remarkable discourse on Georgia.

The opportunity unexpectedly arose when I came home at midday. He was sitting in front of the TV set watching the repeat of a soap about a German family. I asked him if he'd had any lunch. Yes, he said, he'd made himself something from the freezer. I don't know whether I showed surprise, but anyway he added that Julia had kindly said he could help himself from the freezer if he needed to. Of course, I said, that was what its contents were there for, he must make free with them.

I fetched myself some curd cheese and sat down with him. He obviously found it difficult to tear himself away from the stirring story of the TV family. Smiling, he let his eyes wander between me and the screen. Perhaps he was wrong, he said, but he thought that very likely he could learn more about Germany from what went on in a programme like this than from half a dozen books. Well, I said, some might doubt whether life in German families was really like what happened in this soap.

Of course, of course, he agreed, naturally everyone knew these incidents were adjusted to the audience's taste for commercial reasons, but on those very grounds… And he let his gaze return to the screen.

I was already wondering whether he really intended to continue the conversation with the television still on, but then the programme came to an end and he switched off, leaned back in his armchair and sighed. I said he was welcome to watch any other programme that interested him, but he dismissed the idea. No, no, he had to go out soon anyway. He had an appointment with the director of a publishing firm. Oh, indeed, I said. What firm was it? It was called Lyra, said Ninoshvili. I'd never heard of this outfit, but I nodded knowledgeably. So did that mean, I asked, that his project was getting somewhere? Oh yes, oh yes, although it wasn't easy. He hadn't signed any contractual agreement yet, but the prospects already looked good.

I nodded. Silence fell. I used it to say that since the opportunity arose, I had a few more questions to ask about the causes of the Georgian civil war. Go ahead, he said, what did I want to know?

I said his explanation had been very interesting. All the same, I'd been slightly surprised by the uninhibited way he had spoken of the concept of race. He looked at me enquiringly, as if he were surprised.

Well, I said, for a start, and to take just one example, the idea of the white Caucasian race was absolutely obsolete, no reputable anthropologist used it these days.

No, of course not, of course not! It looked as if he didn't take offence at my objection, indeed it set him off on a critical digression about ethnology. He quoted Johann Friedrich Blumenbach, the German naturalist, who – as of course I knew much better than he did – taught in Jena in the eighteenth century and was the first to divide mankind into the Caucasian, Mongolian, Ethiopian, American and Malayan races or varieties. He also quoted Baron Cuvier and his system of distinguishing between only three main races, the white, the black and the yellow.

Before he could turn, as it seemed he might, to the sub-divisions of Cuvier's system, I interrupted him. "Yes, that's all true as far as I know. But I'm sure you are also aware that in Germany the concept of race is particularly loaded. You must know that, for us, it evokes the memory of a shameful, catastrophic phase of our history. The memory of the Holocaust in which the Jews perished."

He turned his dark eyes away from me and sat there in silence for a while. Then he said, "My friend! I do most sincerely beg your pardon! I spoke without thinking, and in front of your wife and your son too. Will you accept my apology?"

71

I said it was nothing to do with that, he didn't have to apologize. He replied, "Thank you, my friend. And I will just add, to help you to understand me better, that anti-Semitism is foreign to the Georgians. For a long time, many Jews have lived in our country as highly regarded citizens. Perhaps that is why I spoke so thoughtlessly."

I wasn't letting him get away with it so easily. I said perhaps I had also misunderstood his remarks about the Abkhazians and the Ossetians. Fair enough, all I knew about the Ossetians was that their customs are rough and ready, like those of all the mountain-dwellers of the Caucasus. But Abkhazians had already been living in the land of Colchis and participating in its culture, according to old sources anyway. And that wasn't all: I had read, at some time, that they used to govern the old kingdom of Georgia along with the Georgians, as a kindred people with equal rights. Or was it not true that in the list of his titles, David the Builder had even described himself first as King of the Abkhazians, and only then as King of the Georgians?

He nodded emphatically. "Right, quite right! But unfortunately the Abkhazians were unworthy to be singled out for such praise. They didn't want to be our kindred people, they separated from us. And what happened? They returned to savagery. They reverted to what they had been before. No culture." He smiled. "Do you know, the Abkhazians don't even have their own alphabet! No literature. Their liturgical language, their official language – all borrowed from the Georgians. No one has to tell an educated man like you what that means."

I felt as if I were banging my head against a brick wall. While I was still searching for another argument, he looked at the time and got to his feet. "I'm afraid I must go now, but we should explore this subject further. I came here to learn, and you're helping me. Very clever questions." He came over to me, clasped my arm in both his hands, and looked me in the eyes. "My friend, what I said at supper… let me ask you again to forgive me. And thank you."

He turned his handsome face with its regular features away, shook his head silently as if he could say no more without bursting into tears, let go of my arm and left the house.

19

I don't believe that Fate corrects our self-confident but mistaken judgements by instantly teaching us a lesson. All the same, pride comes before a fall, and sometimes surprisingly quickly.

This morning there was a punch-up in the school yard during break, worse than anything we've seen before for violence. There were two Turkish pupils involved, but they were fighting on opposite sides. It wasn't a case of race or nationality, just plain ordinary human antagonism.

Four eleventh-year students, one of them a girl, were sitting on one of the benches lining the path from the street to the school yard. Five others – out of a party of twelve on their way to the kiosk by the bus stop to stock up on something indispensable for the day's remaining lessons, such as jelly babies or coconut bars – were walking past the first four. Among those five were Christian Berkhan, his Turkish friend Hasan Ileri and plump Natascha Schmidtlein.

According to the unanimous accounts of Christian, Hasan and their two male companions (at this point Natascha was unwilling to say anything at all about it to the principal), one of the boys on the bench shouted after them, "Hey, where're you guys off to with Fatso there? Going to show you her big arse, is she?" The girl sitting on the bench is said to have laughed.

It wasn't Hasan or either of the other two boys from Natasha's class who reacted, no, it was easy-going Christian who turned and planted himself in front of the bench. He apparently asked the four, in threatening tones, "Want us to smash your faces in?" Thereupon, according to the statements given to the principal, the boy sitting in front of him kicked him in the balls. Christian went for the boy's throat, Hasan and Natascha's other two swains were quick to join the fray, and a fracas ensued, after which my colleague Frau Müntefering, who is trained in first aid, had to patch up nine of the combatants. Then Kubicki, our trainee teacher, drove two of them to Accident and Emergency at the hospital, because Frau Müntefering had diagnosed possible concussion.

The girl who had been sitting on the bench suffered injuries too: a thick lip and a cut in her earlobe, which was bleeding. One of the boys with Christian, the lad who blamed her for causing the whole thing, stated that she had previously torn out a tuft of his hair. Hasan Ileri, when asked who gave him his black eye, replied, "The Turk." Natascha Schmidtlein had not taken part in the hostilities, but by general agreement of the others she tore a loose slat out of the fence around the school grounds and handed it to the gallant Christian, who hit little Rudi Ballensiefen on the head with it, drawing blood.

I can guess what would have happened if Natascha, or the girl who laughed at her fat arse, had happened to have a Kalashnikov ready to hand instead of a fence slat. If I'd thought that to forget all the commandments of peaceful human co-existence, you had to be a Georgian, or a Serb or a Croat, I'd have been taught a lesson there and then.

74

I'm considering incorporating some lessons on the Georgian civil war and its causes into my history course, maybe a four-part series. It probably wouldn't do much good. But surely we must at least keep some hope going; what else can we do?

20

The publishing offices of Lyra and one Dr B. Unger occupy the first floor of an apartment building in a remote suburb. I looked up the address in the phone book and went to see the place. Even if Dr Unger is a bachelor and lives in one room, the publishing firm can occupy at most three rooms on that floor.

To glean more information I called Gerd Buttgereit, who is commissioning editor at Grabosch & Haumann. He knew the name of the firm, but after looking up some details told me that its main offices were in Leipzig. Dr Unger, named as head of the branch office here, opened it a year ago. Lyra publishes poetry, as you might conclude from its name, but also has a list including translations of a dozen or so novels and collections of short stories from the eastern European languages.

I wouldn't have made these enquiries if I hadn't come to feel serious doubts about Ninoshvili's commitment to his cultural project. For instance, when I came home in the afternoon of the day before yesterday he was sitting in Julia's study (she had said he could use it now and then), telephoning with the door closed for almost two hours. However, his various conversations didn't sound at all as if he were making contact with German publishers. I kept hearing him laugh as I passed the door. Twice I thought he was speaking Russian.

After he had finished phoning he took up his position in front of the TV set. Watching television was obviously becoming one of his favourite occupations here on German soil. Besides his claim that he learns from what he sees there, he has come up with another argument, one that can't be dismissed out of hand: he has to keep up to date with what's going on in Georgia, he says. However, he is glued not only to the news but to any kind of trash, not least the ads whenever they pollute the channels.

A couple of days ago in the afternoon, as I looked in through the living-room door, he was singing along with the Maggi soups jingle – "Mag-gi… such good soup!" Then he burst into laughter. I asked what the joke was, and he gave me in all seriousness an analysis of that intolerable nonsense: the melody is catchy (for God's sake, you wonder why he thinks such stuff is typically German!), you can't forget it, but even better is the picture of the soup spoon suddenly tying itself into a knot – very clever, very amusing. The advertising people really know how to fascinate the public and "…how do you put it? Get their product to stick in the mind."

Yesterday afternoon, when I suddenly realized as I was working that I hadn't heard a sound anywhere in the house for some time, I found him in Ralf's room. Ralf, who hadn't played chess with me for over a year, was sitting at the chessboard with him. In between two moves he explained to me that chess was particularly popular in Georgia, and Georgian players were phenomenally successful, as the two women world champions Nona Gaprindashvili and Maia Chiburdanidze, among others, had shown. He was sure I'd know those names.

I did know them, or at least I'd read them once, but I said briefly no. He smiled. Ah, well, that was the fate of the Georgians, he said. Nana Ioseliani, now preparing to take the title back from Xie Jun of China, was a world-class player, although the war had cramped her style. However, the Western media obviously preferred the Polgár sisters, although Ioseliani was a considerably stronger player than those three Hungarians.

After imparting this information, he checkmated Ralf in four moves. Neither Ralf nor I could work out the combination he was using from the position of the pieces on the board. It would have been worth a hundred marks to me, maybe even two hundred, if I could have shown him that he'd made a mistake. But he sacrificed two pieces, one of them his queen, and drove Ralf's king into a corner. It was a conclusive combination. Our guest smiled and put the pieces back on the board for another game.

The two of them played until supper. I was already feeling this was as much of an imposition as a man in Ninoshvili's position, here on a mission like his, could allow himself. But at noon today he made use of his time and exploited our hospitality even more outrageously.

I came home around twelve, probably earlier than he had expected. When I didn't find him either in the living room or in Julia's study, I called, "Hello?" There was no reply. I assumed that he was out and felt a certain relief, because I still wanted to believe that his intention of opening up Georgian literature to German-language readers was more than just a smokescreen. But as I climbed the stairs to my study I heard rushing, glugging sounds coming from the bathroom. I stopped outside the door. No doubt about it, water was running into the tub.

I knocked on the door and called, "David, are you in there?" He replied, "Hello, Christian! I was just running myself a foam bath." I heard water splashing. "Do you want to come in at the moment?" he called.

I gasped for breath. Then I called back, "No, no, I wouldn't like to disturb you."

Sitting down at my desk, I tried to recover my composure. The top floor of the house has a spacious, comfortable shower in between Ralf's room and the spare room. Until now, all our guests had been perfectly happy with it, even Erika. At least, none of them has ever expressed a wish for a foam bath in the tub that Julia and I use in the first-floor bathroom.

Perhaps he asked Julia, and perhaps she said it was all right. I don't know, maybe I don't want to know. One way or another, that man is intruding upon my private space in a way that brings me out in a sweat.

I spent about ten minutes sitting at my desk, and I still couldn't master the turmoil of my feelings. Suddenly I had an idea. I rose to my feet and moved cautiously to the bathroom door. He had turned the taps off, but the water in the tub was splashing slightly. I heard his voice as he hummed to himself, and all at once he burst into song. This time it wasn't the Maggi jingle. He was singing a Georgian folk song, or at least it sounded as melancholy and heartfelt as I imagine the songs of Georgia must be.

Stepping quietly, I climbed the stairs to the top storey and opened the spare-room door. I stood listening, and then went over to the leather case. The clasps were closed but not locked; they could be opened. I lifted the lid of the case.

I had already been surprised that he hadn't yet shown me any of the manuscripts he said he was trying to sell in the Federal Republic of Germany. What I found in his case was far from impressive, at least in terms of quantity. One quite thick manuscript of about three hundred pages, and a bare half-dozen shorter texts. Under them, in a folder with the stamp of Julia's law practice on it, were the copies she had had made by her secretary.

Two books and a newspaper in the Georgian alphabet, a Georgian-German dictionary. A document case with which I had once seen him leaving the house: it was empty. A notebook containing telephone numbers, most of the names also written in the Georgian alphabet. Otherwise just bits and pieces: a chocolate bar, empty envelopes, a well-worn knitted waistcoat.

On a sudden impulse, I leafed through the book. I found four medium-sized photographs between the pages of one of them. Three of the photos showed men, the fourth was of a blonde woman. There were notes in Georgian on the backs of the photos.

I felt a drop of sweat running down my temple. I went through the suitcase again, this time more thoroughly. I found a pair of thin, black leather gloves tucked into a side pocket, and a flick knife with a decorative handle in another.

After I had stood there for some time as if dazed, bending over the suitcase, I pulled myself together, put the lid of the case back and shut the clasps. I had already left the spare room when I turned back. I opened the wardrobe door, felt around in the underwear and shirts that he had stacked neatly on the shelves, searched the pockets of his suits. Nothing of interest. I opened the drawer of the bedside table. Underneath a street map of this city I found a photograph of Matassi.

She was leaning on the balustrade of a lookout platform, smiling, her shadowed eyes looking at the photographer. In the background, I could make out the Kura Valley and the higgledy-piggledy houses of Tbilisi. I thought she didn't look a day older. She was as beautiful as I remembered her.

Ninoshvili spent almost an hour in the bathroom, and after that another half-hour in the spare room. It was nearly two when he knocked on my door. He looked splendid, tall and strong, broad-shouldered, narrow-waisted, a supple figure. His chestnut-brown hair shone. He was wearing a tie with a discreet red-and-blue pattern and a pale-blue shirt. The document case was tucked under his arm. "I must be off now," he said. "I have an appointment."

I nodded. "Good luck, then." He said nothing for a moment; he did not take his dark eyes off me, but was looking at me as if he had to think about what I had wished him. Then he said, "Thank you. I thank you, my friend." And he closed the door.

21

In all times allowances have been made for youthful high spirits, and so today there are still many who think our young people no better but no worse than the young have always been. But even without looking on the dark side too much, even if we try to judge with leniency, it will not have escaped the watchful eye that there is little for the heart to rejoice in as we contemplate young persons today. We hear new complaints about the younger generation daily, and only too often we read newspaper reports of serious crimes and misdemeanours committed by young people. Criminal statistics showing that the number of youthful offenders found guilty in the courts has risen by over fifty per cent in the last twenty years… give us grave cause for concern.

This quotation is not from any of the articles in Tassilo Huber's collection on the onset of the new barbarism, although only its style would mark it out from those modern studies. I copied it from an heirloom, a yellowing paper that I have kept for years in my collection of educational memorabilia. It comes from a teachers' journal published in Rhineland-Westphalia and is dated 22 June 1906.

I had intended, as something of a joke, to duplicate this gloomy account of the condition of society, and hand it out to the staff before the meeting that was to deal with the battle of the school fence and the disciplinary measures to be taken. I could also have added to my flyer the five reasons for the decadence of modern youth as succinctly analysed by the writer of this piece, a school headmaster, not last week but almost a century ago. They were the break-up of the family unit, inadequate living conditions, alcoholism, loss of religious faith and unrestricted freedom of the press. I was going to mention the source and the date of my material only on the other side of the flyer.

But then I refrained after all; more likely my little joke would just have made the situation worse. Brauckmann had already gone public with his demand to have all nine combatants, without exception, excluded from the school on the grounds that they were all lying through their teeth. Poor Christian humbly approached me later, asking if I thought it would be a good idea for him to visit Rudi Ballensiefen at home, although Rudi was already back in training for his football club, and apologize to both him and his parents, maybe also bringing Rudi a present. I told him he'd do better to stay put in school learning his lines as Mercutio.

It was not exactly easy, however, to get that idiot out of trouble, along with a few of the others whom I felt sorry for. I can't deny that Natascha Schmidtlein, who is not only plump but also bone idle, had already prejudiced her teachers against her so much that most of them secretly thought it served her right to be called Fatso by the boy who started the trouble. A certain amount of resentment came though in the discussion, anyway; it was chiefly Natascha's teachers who claimed that Christian Berkhan had no conceivable reason for threatening to smash in the faces of the four students sitting on the bench, certainly not for hitting little Rudi Ballensiefen so hard on the head.

At the beginning of the meeting only Elke Lampert was on my side (she's been feeling better since her husband showed her a succinct letter dumping his lover, which he then posted before Elke's eyes). Initially she confined herself to the sensible and moderate comment that while this outbreak of violence was certainly both regrettable and disturbing, there was no need to make a great song and dance about it. That wouldn't do anything to improve the atmosphere in the school, said Elke. However, when our maths and physics teacher Philippovich, who is known to think poorly of the intelligence of the female sex, was the first to say roundly that Christian Berkhan had run amok for no reason at all, Elke got into her stride.

She protested indignantly against any attempt to make light of the injury to Natascha's feelings. It wasn't unknown, she said, for such obscene aggression to be tolerantly regarded as a trifling offence and played down. But anyone thus inclined might stop to think what lasting hurt that remark, which was of course going the rounds of the whole school, had inflicted on Natascha Schmidtlein. And perhaps we all ought to ask ourselves whether there wasn't a positive side to it when a boy like Christian wouldn't let malicious abuse of Natascha pass, not of course that Elke meant to excuse his part in the fracas.

I thought her plea was well phrased, although I have some doubts whether Natascha's well-upholstered nature had suffered very much from the insult. At an appropriate point I put forward another argument, which I would have done better to discuss with Christian first. I said that from my own observation I could see he was still feeling pain in the genital area, and if he hadn't said so explicitly, his reticence was certainly thanks to his usual inclination to settle quarrels

82

peacefully, even if that meant that he came off worst. At least the second part of my argument was perfectly true.

The tribunal came to a satisfactory conclusion. The meeting decided that the evidence hadn't shown clearly whether one or another of the participants in the fray was particularly to blame. On these grounds the principal gave all nine involved a stern warning. I quoted the final passage of our conclusions in Christian's German lesson, raising my voice: any repetition of the incident would lead to the instant exclusion of the guilty parties from school, without any right to appeal. That skunk Oliver Zacher grinned all over his face, and I sent him out of the room for ten minutes to try working out what was so funny about this announcement.

After the meeting, when my colleague Brauckmann congratulated me with a nasty smile on the great success of my lessons on peacekeeping, I said well, he knew me. Of course my colleagues are keeping a close eye on my series of lessons on the Georgian civil war. I've no objection. I just have to make sure that it furthers the ability of my students to think creatively, more so than the material that it replaces on the timetable.

At first I had considered opening the four lessons with a digression on the mythical phase of the history of Georgia, since it was possible that the Argonauts' adventurous voyage to the land of Colchis might stimulate the students' imagination and arouse their interest. However, I had my first doubts when I looked up Gustav Schwab's book *The Finest Legends of Classical Antiquity* and read his preface, written in 1837.

Of course it didn't surprise me that the good Stuttgart schoolmaster wanted his work to serve a useful purpose in the education of young people in our fatherland, and therefore made sure that "everything offensive" was removed from his

83

retelling of the violent deeds of the heroes. And it amuses me that he finds himself in some difficulty because certain subjects "contrary to our higher concepts of morality, and even in antiquity recognized as unnatural (for instance in the Oedipus legend)... cannot be ignored". But I'm rather afraid that Pastor Schwab's efforts to bowdlerize such scandalous stories so as "to cause young people neither to pursue unedifying ideas nor to indulge their curiosity" are a waste of time today.

My bright sparks here don't need to indulge any curiosity; they know the facts. If I were to teach them about Oedipus and ask how they would describe his character, some wit would probably whisper audibly to his neighbours, "Motherfucker!" Perhaps one or two of the more sensitive might be impressed by the story of how the Argonauts' sails began to flutter as if in a storm when the great eagle flew over them on the way to torment Prometheus. But the fact that the Colchians hung up their dead heroes to dry in the air, while they buried the women "so that the earth would have its part in them" would certainly be greeted by merriment. "Only the *dead* women, Herr Kestner?" "Didn't they have any better fertilizers?"

No, I shall probably start by giving them two texts, a speech made by President Gamsakhurdia and one made by President Shevardnadze. Their exactly identical arguments are the best way to convey the absurdity of the civil war: each of the presidents accuses the other of planning to hand over the fatherland to the Russians, and making a pact with the KGB to that end.

The KGB, incidentally, and not just according to these sources, seems still to play a considerable or at least an ominous part in events in the Republic of Georgia.

Yes, and the Georgians still cut their enemies' throats as they did in King David's time!

84

But no, really, on the basis of what little I know, isn't it equally possible that our guest brought gloves because an elegant man always sports such accessories on special occasions at home in Georgia, so Ninoshvili thinks they're de rigueur in Germany too? And perhaps he carries that flick knife around with him just because he's read that you have to expect to be attacked at any time on our streets in Germany. What do I really know about the man, after all?

22

It may have been meant as an act of reparation, but anyway Tassilo Huber has fixed it for me and Julia to be invited to an evening reception in the Town Hall. I didn't feel particularly keen to attend this social event – it was being held to welcome the new Town Clerk – but Julia seemed interested, and so did Ninoshvili as soon as he heard about it.

Julia asked me in private if I'd call Herr Huber and ask him for an invitation for David as well. It would give our guest a chance of getting to know people who might be useful for his project, she said. So I phoned Tassilo Huber. "By all means," he said. "And there's a woman on my Party committee who runs an aid programme for Georgia, she'd be very interested to talk to your guest."

The three of us took a taxi to the Town Hall. I sat in the front passenger seat, which Ninoshvili had left for me, while he opened the door to the back seat for Julia and got in beside her. He was wearing his dark-blue suit, a white shirt and a striped dark-blue tie, but not the black gloves. He looked very handsome.

In the turmoil of people talking at the top of their voices, Tass introduced me to the head of the education authority, a gaunt-faced bore who tried to make conversation by asking me about our school sports hall, which needs renovation. I haven't seen the inside of the sports hall for years, but I did my best for the school by describing the deficiencies I'd sometimes heard mentioned at staff meetings, just as if I had come to the Town Hall straight from a depressing survey of the place. The head of the education authority showed no understanding and indeed no interest, although he had raised the subject in the first place. He seemed to find me as tedious as I found him.

Meanwhile Tass had led Ninoshvili further on. Julia followed them after giving the head of the education authority a friendly nod, to which he responded with a little bow. While I was still occupied with the holes in the flooring of the sports hall and the danger to life and limb they represented, I saw Ninoshvili and Julia in conversation with a curly-haired young woman who kept nodding and frowning earnestly while Ninoshvili talked to her. Another rather older woman in a black trouser suit joined them, and Ninoshvili bowed to her as if to kiss her right hand.

I concluded my report on the state of the sports hall, thinking that I might get rid of the head of the education authority by preserving a dogged silence. But he didn't seem to know any of the many other guests at the reception, and remained rooted to the spot, now and then casting a fleeting glance around but then turning his hollow eyes on me again and murmuring, "Ah, yes," as he sipped at his glass. I wondered how he would react if I asked him, "Why don't you just go home?" But before I could bring myself to try it, the Mayor began his speech.

He stepped up to a microphone, his chain of office hanging around him; a man of about forty-five with a crew cut and rimless glasses followed him, placed himself on the Mayor's right and two steps behind him, and folded his hands in front

86

of him. The Mayor tried out the microphone a couple of times and then began, "Your Eminence, Your Excellencies, ladies and gentlemen."

I couldn't see Julia and Ninoshvili any more in the crowd turning towards the microphone in a semi-circular formation. The Mayor's voice was soothing; I felt myself becoming drowsy, closed my eyes, managed to open them again with an effort but let my eyelids sink once more. I fell into a doze in which tiny yellow points of light appeared on the reddish background of my closed lids, moving gently like candle flames seen burning in the distance by night.

The smell of the candles reached my nostrils as well, I breathed it in, assessed it. It wasn't the smell of church, of the cool cross-vaulting there. Or of the graveyard and the moist breath of All Saints' Day. No. Christmas time. It wasn't just the candles I could smell. Gingerbread, spice biscuits, oranges. The resin and needles of a Christmas tree. The fresh paint of my new toy. Still in my pyjamas, I crawled under the tree early in the morning on the first day of Christmas and brought out the red omnibus that I had put there after the present-giving on Christmas Eve, in case anyone carelessly trod on it.

I woke up as the people around me began laughing and clapping. The new Town Clerk was at the microphone now. He had probably just cracked a little joke. "It's clear to me that as an outsider, I shall have to consider myself on probation among you at first. I've been told that it took even the Archbishop twenty-five years before he could say, without fear of contradiction, that he was a citizen of this place."

Once this speech too was over, and the noise and chattering broke out again, I nodded to the head of the education authority, who was clearly about to ask me for my first impressions of the new Town Clerk, moved a few steps away and looked for Julia and Ninoshvili. I couldn't see them. But unexpectedly Herr Hochgeschurz came up to me, carrying a glass of beer. "Good evening, Herr Kestner," he said, offering me his fat hand. After he had drunk some beer, he smiled and asked, "How are you?"

I said I was all right. Herr Hochgeschurz nodded, reached for a tray being carried past by a waiter, and helped himself to another beer. Having taken a sip of this one, he asked, "Have you actually met Herr Schumann?" No, I said, I hadn't yet had that pleasure. The agent raised his chin and jerked it sideways. "That's him. The young man in the bow tie."

Herr Gero Schumann looked even more stylish than I had imagined him. As well as his dark-red bow tie he wore a dark-red blazer with gold-coloured buttons and black trousers. His fair hair was cut short and neatly parted in the middle, he had pale-blue eyes behind gold-rimmed glasses. He was engaged in lively conversation with two ladies, both of rather mature age but elegantly dressed. Herr Schumann burst into laughter and threw his head back; the ladies, also laughing, showed their gleaming crowned teeth.

Herr Hochgeschurz said, "You might not believe it, but he gets on particularly well with women of that age."

"Well, why not?" I said.

I saw Julia and Ninoshvili behind Herr Schumann and his motherly admirers. They were talking to a bald man who seemed to be explaining something to Ninoshvili; he kept prodding his forefinger in the direction of the Georgian's chest. Ninoshvili was listening attentively, his face turned slightly away, and nodding at every third word.

Herr Hochgeschurz followed the direction of my glance as he breathed in audibly through his broad nose. I asked the agent, "Do you know the gentleman standing there with my wife?"

"The bald man?"

"That's right."

"He's head of the Political Asylum Authority."

I tried to preserve my composure by draining my glass, almost choked, beckoned to the waiter and took a beer. Hochgeschurz told the waiter, "Just a moment, please," emptied his own glass and took a new one. He drank and wiped the foam from his upper lip. Then he asked, "Is the gentleman from Georgia your guest?"

I had a presentiment that Hochgeschurz had not met me in this large and confused crowd purely by chance. "Yes," I said. "Do you know him?"

"Herr Huber introduced me to him in passing." The agent was breathing heavily and looked at Ninoshvili, the head of the asylum authority and Julia, who was speaking now and turning to the bald man. As I raised my glass again, Herr Hochgeschurz added, "But I met him again the day before yesterday."

I looked at him over the rim of my glass. "In the court-house," he said. "Your wife had brought him to a trial with her. He spent all morning listening in the public gallery." Hochgeschurz smiled. "He seemed fascinated by the proceedings." After a couple of noisy breaths, he asked, "A lawyer himself, is he?"

"No." I think I can be sure of that at least. David Ninoshvili may be all kinds of things, but as far as I'm aware he's not a lawyer. And God knows what he was doing in that courthouse.

On that very day, the day before yesterday, he had told me in front of Julia before I left the house that he had an appointment with a publisher's commissioning editor that morning.

23

The trial was nothing to do with agents. The proceedings had involved a nineteen-year-old hairdresser who had refused to dance with the driver of a beer-and-spirits truck in the Blue Moon disco. Thereupon the truck driver and two of his friends had pushed the hairdresser up against the bar and indecently groped her. She had freed herself by throwing her whisky-and-coke into the truck driver's face, and the glass had broken and cut her rejected suitor's upper lip. The three men had caught up with the hairdresser as she tried to get away through the back entrance, and one of them, a man of twenty-two living on benefits, had grabbed her long blonde hair and slammed her face several times against the drinks dispenser in the passage leading to the Gents and the Ladies.

The trial had lasted from nine in the morning until lunchtime, because there were a number of witnesses giving evidence, including the barman and the attendant in the Ladies, the crews of two police patrol cars and a couple of civilians who had helped to overpower the twenty-two-year-old when he tried to resist arrest. Julia, who was appearing for the defence, had argued that the hairdresser should have known and did in fact know that the Blue Moon was a place of disrepute where sexual molestation was more or less the norm. She at least got her client spared a custodial sentence, although he was fined to the amount of twenty times his daily wages plus compensatory damages.

I would probably never have heard about this real-life drama if I hadn't asked Julia, as if casually, when we had come home from Town Hall and gone to bed, why Ninoshvili had gone to the courthouse with her. She lowered her book and looked at me.

"Where did you hear about that?"

I told her Herr Hochgeschurz had told me at the reception.

"So how do you come to know *him*?" I replied that Tassilo Huber had introduced us at the reception. Herr Hochgeschurz was obviously very loquacious, I said, and he had confided to me that he works for Internal Security.

She said nothing for a while, and then put her book aside. "Of course I ought to have told you. But I was sorry for David. He asked me not to say anything about it."

David, I now discovered, isn't feeling at all happy. He's encountering serious obstacles in his attempts to find a German publisher for Georgian literature. There's obviously not much interest in what he has to offer. He has already had three rejections from the addresses suggested to him as hopeful prospects by a Hamburg journalist who visited Tbilisi. The journalist was just making empty promises, and didn't even mention David's forthcoming visit to those publishers after he returned to Germany.

"Is Lyra one of those firms?" I asked.

She was silent for a moment and then enquired, "You haven't been snooping around after him, have you?"

"Snooping around? What do you mean?" I shook my head as if her question verged on the insulting. "He told me its name himself."

She nodded and plumped up her pillow. "Lyra is not a publishing house to be taken seriously. The books they bring out are hardly ever designed to appeal to the general public. What's more, they pay peanuts."

She fell silent. I said, "But I still don't know what Ninoshvili was looking for, going to that trial. And why did he tell me an hour earlier that he had an appointment to see a commissioning editor?"

She sighed. I now found out that David feels… well, you'd have to call it ashamed when he talks to me. His pride won't allow him to admit his failures to another man, and one who is his host as well. Maybe that kind of pride is a Georgian characteristic, she doesn't know, she understands so little about the Georgians. Anyway, he's ashamed, and he's also ashamed because I've already caught him once idling about during the day.

I said, "I'm sorry, but I rather got the impression he enjoys idling about."

She shook her head. "You're not doing him justice." And she told me that on the morning in question, as soon as I had left the house, David told her his troubles. He confessed that he didn't have an appointment at all, and once that was out he obviously couldn't keep any of the rest of it to himself: his disappointments, his humiliating experiences. As he told her all about it, the tears kept coming to his eyes. "It was really dreadful. I felt so sorry for him." She wanted to spare him having to hang around town somewhere to kill time while he was supposed to be keeping his appointment, she said, so she offered to take him to the trial with her.

Apparently Julia didn't want to give me the impression that David Ninoshvili had been doing nothing but killing time in the courthouse too. She mentioned the intelligent questions he had asked her afterwards, during lunch, and that's how I came to hear all about the hairdresser's little run-in with the driver of the brewer's truck.

At the end of her story she turned to me and put her hand on my arm. "Will you do me a great favour?" I looked at her in silence. She said, "Please don't let him know I told you all this."

I shrugged. "Well, fine, if you think it's so important."

She switched off her reading lamp and moved closer to me. "Is he going to ask for political asylum?" I asked.

She raised her head and looked at me, wide-eyed. "What makes you think that?"

"The two of you spent rather a long time talking to the head of the asylum authority."

"Yes, but that had nothing to do with David personally! The problem interests him. I should think anyone from abroad would be interested to observe what goes on in this country." She shook her head. "That doesn't mean he wants to settle here himself. He's anxious to get back to Tbilisi as soon as possible. After all, he has a wife there."

I switched off my own reading light. Julia kissed my ear. "You of all people ought to understand why he wants to get back to his Matassi as quickly as he can."

"Why me of all people?"

She laughed. "You've been telling fibs, darling. You certainly haven't forgotten how beautiful she is. David told me how you made eyes at her. And he said the two of you got on very well together."

24

If Elke Lampert were to hear of my latest exploit she'd probably feel confirmed in her view that I am a good person. But I'm not about to pretend to myself: I did only what seemed advisable, so as to bring this macabre guest performance in my house to an end as quickly as I can and be rid of the lead actor.

This morning, when Ninoshvili appeared at breakfast (in good spirits, or that was my impression), I asked him whether he'd like to give me one of his manuscripts to read. He acted as if there was nothing he'd rather do. Yes, of course, my opinion would matter a lot to him and would certainly be very helpful. As he was obviously aware of the awkward fact that he had so far kept his pearls of Georgian literature locked away from me, he added that if he hadn't asked me to do this very thing before, it was only because he didn't want to impose on my valuable time.

When I came home at midday, I found the thicker manuscript – a novel – and two stories on my desk. I speed-read the novel and read the stories in full. The German of the translations (which Ninoshvili didn't do himself) would need revision, and the novel strikes me as rather too heavily weighted with reflections, but the two stories aren't at all bad. One of them even impressed me, for instance in vividly conjuring up old Tbilisi waking on a summer morning: we hear the cries of the tradesmen in the streets, milkmen, men delivering paraffin, bakers, all fervently praising their wares, their trades and their way of life.

That afternoon I phoned Gerd Buttgereit and asked if he could suggest a publisher who might be interested in such works, because they were definitely unusual. And the public knew a little more about Georgia these days, I pointed out, although unfortunately only because of the war. Gerd said, as I had expected, that he was afraid he couldn't see any opening for them on his own list just now, but he gave me the names of three publishing houses, two in Frankfurt and one in Darmstadt, and also the phone numbers of people there with whom I could get in touch. I was to give them his regards.

Ninoshvili, damn him, did his best to blunt any idea I might entertain of having done a good deed. He came back from town late in the afternoon, after a heavy shower, wet through, his hair dripping, his shirt sticking to his skin, his

94

trouser legs stiff and soaked with rain around his shoes. He said the storm had taken him by surprise in the street. Maybe, in his desperation, he had gone to see Dr B. Unger in his suburban office again, and preferred to save the taxi fare back.

He was a pitiful sight. Nothing was left of the handsome man of the reception. He unbuttoned his jacket, flapped it in the air as if he could get it back into shape that way, looked down at himself, glanced up, and smiled with some embarrassment.

I told him I had spoken to three publishers who might be interested in his manuscripts, and had said they were willing to see him. He looked at me incredulously, then began to beam like a child who has felt outcast and now receives unhoped-for comfort. "My friend! You did this for me?" He came closer to me, spread his arms and hugged me to his wet chest. After kissing me on both cheeks, he put his head back and looked at me in expectant suspense. "Did you really think those three manuscripts were good?"

I said I thought them very interesting. He said, "Thank you, my friend!" and shook his head in silence, as if he were too deeply moved by my friendship to utter another word. Then he turned away and climbed the stairs, stiff-legged.

I felt sorry for him. I almost offered him a foam bath in our tub on the first floor to refresh himself.

God knows, all I needed was to give way to such mawkish emotions. I could hardly commit a greater folly than to take Julia's version of events on board without querying it. So Ninoshvili is suffering in secret, is he? He needs and deserves help, proud man that he is, holding his head high by day but weeping into his pillow by night because he doubts himself?

Well, David Ninoshvili is not so much in need of help as all that, or so noble and so deserving of sympathy. It struck me only later that I hadn't found his passport during my researches in the spare room, or his purse or wallet. Either he took them into the bathroom to share his foam bath, in which case he harbours suspicions which would be unfounded if he had nothing to hide, or he has actually hidden those items in the spare room in some safe place that won't be easily found. In that case I certainly ought to ask myself what else he keeps there, ready to be brought out at a given time.

25

I have always been sensitive to close contact, to people's physical aura, that almost indefinable mixture of body aroma and warmth and something that can't be pinned down. In women I usually find it stimulating, in men it often repels me.

That provincial court judge, for instance, the one who tried to get his paws on Julia until I warned him off – I disliked him, and not just because of his sheer effrontery or his penetratingly astringent perfume, presumably concocted using the sexual secretions of animals. Even before I knew what part the man was playing and what he was trying to do, I had noticed his aura. It forced itself on you even from a distance.

Maybe it was to do with his body language: the way he moved his greying head and looked around the hall. At least, I felt I could see the tanned skin not just of his face but his chest and stomach too, still taut over the beginnings of love handles; his pubic hair, as black as his moustache; his prick and balls. The man's aggressive virility seeped out of every pore. As soon as I saw him he made me want to puke.

Of course it could be claimed that I worked all this out only later, and my dislike was the result of plain jealousy when this brute tried to fascinate Julia. But I've had similar experiences of insuperable physical antipathy before, for instance with my colleague Philippovich, who could never appear to me a rival for the simple reason that he's never met Julia.

I can't cite any rational grounds for disliking Philippovich, I can't even say he annoys me or gets on my nerves; I often even think the malicious remarks he regularly makes about our women colleagues amusing. I suspect him of thinking of his comments in advance and polishing them up at home. But whenever I see him, I seem to catch a sour, cheesy smell, I see his feet with their long, bony toes as he moves them about in his shoes, I notice the sharp hipbones standing out under his white skin. I've never seen Philippovich naked, and my suspicion that he doesn't wash his feet is entirely unfounded. I just find him physically repellent, and there's nothing I can do about that.

I assume that this sensitivity of mine comes from the sexual area. Perhaps my disposition is over-heterosexual. The fact that I have equally intense feelings, although most of them of a contradictory nature, with women would back up that theory. Erika, for instance – if only she'd stop wearing her cloying perfume I might possibly feel tempted, in spite of the hectic way she behaves. She gives off unmistakable sexual signals even at a distance, just like the provincial judge, and what puts me off *him* could attract me in Erika – yes, even in her.

I am afraid I shall not succeed in playing down my prejudices against Ninoshvili by classifying them with such experiences. It's certainly obvious that I felt distaste at the sight of his strong, bare knees and muscular hairy calves, as glimpsed yesterday evening when he had showered and was indulging himself with a little time spent in front of the

TV set wearing his dressing gown, his hair freshly washed and combed – those knees and calves, and I feel distaste for the evident signs of his virility too. I freeze at his hugs and cheek-kissing. Yes, no doubt about it, David Ninoshvili's masculinity repels me.

But I won't make it so easy for myself. Don't I also dislike the idea of having a Georgian living in my house with me? A foreigner anyway.

A foreigner who seems to me a barbarian because his background is not the same as my own. A foreigner who challenges me to concern myself with his existence, just as asylum seekers, the disadvantaged and those on the margins of society also do. Someone different who disturbs my peace and quiet, my self-satisfaction.

I have tried to establish an easier relationship with Ninoshvili. Today, on a cool Sunday morning, I asked him if he felt like a good walk. He was enthusiastic, disappeared into the spare room at once and came back in a smart casual sweater. I drove to the Katharinenforst, where we parked the car and set out on a woodland walk of about ten kilometres. It's ridiculous, but I deliberately chose a way-marked round route which I knew is busy at weekends with people out for the day.

Ninoshvili was in cheerful mood. He had me in difficulties once or twice by asking what the name of this tree or that grass was, but he laughed when I confessed that botany wasn't one of my strong points, and even excused the gaps in my general knowledge by saying that the same thing often happens to him when he is showing a guest around at home, it's only such incidents that show you don't know all about everything, even in your own country.

I asked him if he knew the work of Gustav Radde, and he surprised me by delivering an extensive and knowledgeable encomium on the activities of "that great German explorer" in Tbilisi. "He taught the Georgians a great deal, my friend, we're grateful to him." He had never heard of Herr Hinzenberg the head gardener and his botanical tables recording the flowering of *Iris caucasica*, but he thought what I said about him was very important, "very instructive for a nation that – as you know – was sadly neglected by Europe for a very long time, and so in the past people couldn't learn from the rest of the continent, although they always wanted to know more".

I refrained from asking whether he knew about Herr von Bodenstedt and his contributions to the study of the phenomenology of the Georgian people. Instead I asked him how he felt here in Germany, and what his strongest impressions had been to date.

He stopped, smiled at me. "You really don't know that, my friend?" No, I said, unfortunately I hadn't found enough time to look after him. He shook his head. "You're too modest, my friend." Then he said, "I feel very comfortable in your country. And my strongest impression has been of all you've done for me. You have opened doors for me that I couldn't open for myself." I said it was nothing worth mentioning, it had cost me only a few telephone calls.

"No, no." He shook his head and walked on. I hoped he wasn't going to pursue this subject, which was a little embarrassing to me. However, he had more to impart. He said, "I couldn't ask you for such a service. A guest is sent by God, but he must not abuse the laws of hospitality. You did me that service of your own accord. You owe me nothing, so you did it out of friendship." He looked at me. "Or were you thinking you *did* owe me some kind of debt?"

I felt hot under the collar. I said it was nothing to with owing a debt, but after all, I had enjoyed his own hospitality in Tbilisi. He didn't reply to that.

All of a sudden he stopped, picked up a branch that had broken off a tree, and looked at the wood where the break showed. I didn't know what kind of tree the branch came from, but he told me its Georgian name and said that very elaborate carvings were made from this wood in Georgia. While I was still looking at the yellowish wood where it had broken off, he put his hand in his trouser pocket.

He took out the flick knife and made the blade spring out. I took a sudden step backwards. There wasn't a soul in sight on the woodland path either ahead of us or behind us. He looked up, glanced at me, then turned back to the branch and began whittling away at the broken surface. He carved it until it was pointed, and held it critically up to his eyes. "Very good wood." Then he threw the branch away and put the knife back in his pocket.

Later, after we had walked on for a while in silence, I forced myself to ask whether he always carried that knife about with him. "No, no." He smiled. "A legacy, you understand. From my great-grandfather. A valuable work of art." He took the knife out again, flicked the blade out once more, and showed me the ornamentation on the handle. "You know superstitions? I have a superstition that this brings me luck."

26

Ten minutes ago, at three fifteen on Monday afternoon, Herr Hochgeschurz rang. He asked how I was, and when I said I was afraid I was in a hurry he apologized. He'd only wanted to give me some information that might interest me, he said. Yes, well, I said, what was it about, please?

The agent told me he had found out that Herr Ninoshvili had given a lecture on the Georgian civil war in Herr

Schumann's summer house. The occasion had been well attended, and there had been lively discussion afterwards. Herr Schumann and his young people, as well as some older guests, had obviously been greatly impressed by Herr Ninoshvili, said Hochgeschurz, and he was warmly applauded.

I forgot to ask the agent the date of this talk. It must have been the evening when Ninoshvili and Ralf had apparently gone to the cinema and then to a bar – "very interesting atmosphere, very folkloric", I'd been told.

Now I have to go to my drama group. Max Blümel is indeed moving to Hamburg with his father, so Christian Berkhan has to get through his first rehearsal in the part of Mercutio, and Günsel Özcan called in sick just now.

I feel like flailing out all round! I'll turn that sly Georgian out this very evening. It has nothing to do with racism or Julia, or Matassi, or the KGB. The man thinks he can play games with me!

27

When I got home Julia was sitting in her study with Ninoshvili, who was at her desk with the phone receiver to his ear while she sat in the chair beside the desk. She gestured to me not to disturb him. I stood there for a while. Ninoshvili said, "Hello? Hello?" and then put the receiver down on its rest. "Call interrupted again." He picked the receiver up once more and began dialling a long number, pausing after each digit.

I cleared a chair and sat down. Julia came over to me and whispered that the war in Georgia had taken a dramatic turn for the worse; David had been trying to reach Matassi for the last hour.

The Abkhazian separatists have taken the harbour town of Sukhumi on the Black Sea. President Shevardnadze, who directed the defence of the city himself for twelve days, has fled. He has said, speaking from an unidentified place, that "Russian, Chechen and Abkhazian soldiers armed to the teeth" killed hundreds of people in Sukhumi.

It was being said in Tbilisi that Sukhumi fell only because the Georgian reserve troops, who had been stationed in the town of Otshamshira ready to hurry to the president's aid, turned traitor and refused to leave their quarters. These double dealers were supporters of former President Zviad Gamsakhurdia, now overthrown, who was planning to seize back power with the help of the Abkhazians.

It's said that a hundred thousand of the Georgian inhabitants of Abkhazia are on the run. The TV news showed pictures from the region at the centre of the fighting this afternoon: women and children, frail old people going down a road with their bundles while jets of mud shot up in the air behind them as shells landed. In an interview, Shevardnadze has called the Abkhazians "murderers and Fascists".

While Julia tiptoed back to her chair Ninoshvili, listening intently to the receiver, raised his head. "Hello?" he called, and then suddenly began to speak Georgian. He talked fast, pausing again and again to nod, his brows drawn together. Julia stood up, took the tea glass standing in front of Ninoshvili, went out to the kitchen with it and came back with the glass refilled.

I stayed where I was. This phone conversation did not sound to me like a man conversing with his beloved. I hadn't heard Matassi's name at the beginning of the phone call either. I was going to wait and see if I could catch it later. But I didn't understand a word.

The conversation lasted almost ten minutes. When Ninoshvili had put the receiver down he rubbed his forehead with both hands and stared absently at the desk for a while. Then he looked up and saw first Julia, then me. He nodded. "Matassi sends her regards. She says she's all right, nothing has happened to her. But a bad situation. Very bad situation."

I tried to find out details of the very bad situation. I asked whether there was fighting in Tbilisi as well. Julia said, "Give him a little while to calm himself. Would you like a glass of wine now, David?" He nodded, his mind obviously elsewhere.

We moved to the TV set. Julia brought in a bottle of wine and poured a glass first for our guest, then for me. She sat down with us until the next news programme was over. Georgia had already dropped to number three in the bulletins; there were no new developments. Julia rose and went into the kitchen. She was obviously trying to move with care. Ninoshvili picked up the TV magazine and studied the programmes in silence. I assume he was looking for the time of the next news bulletin.

I heard clattering from the kitchen. Julia was evidently making supper. I stood up and went to join her. "Can I do anything?"

"No, thanks. I'm just going to put something cold together. Or are you very hungry?"

"No." I watched her for a while.

"Won't you keep him company for a bit?" she asked.

I said no, I wouldn't, and she looked at me in surprise. I asked, "Did you know he let Herr Schumann hire him to give a lecture? In that summer house, to Schumann's followers."

She put down the fork she was using to arrange slices of cold meat on a platter, passed her hand over her forehead, lowered her head and sighed. "Well, did you know?" I asked.

"No."

"It was the evening when he said he went to the cinema with Ralf. And then to a bar. Remember that?"

"Yes, I remember. How do you know about this?"

I ignored the question. " I can't believe he's playing around with us like this. And in cahoots with our own son at that. Well, can you think of any explanation for such behaviour?"

"What do you mean, explanation?" She looked at me, shaking her head. "You don't have to look far to find one."

"I'm sorry, but I can't think of anything in the least acceptable."

She turned back to the platter of cold meat. "He needs money. The pathetic amount of currency they gave him to bring must be running out by this time. And I expect Herr Schumann paid him a good fee. I'm afraid it's as simple as that."

"Simple? You call it simple?"

She shook her head. "No, of course it's not at all simple. It's all rather hole and corner, you're right." She looked at me. "But I hope you're not going to tell him so this evening."

"You expect me to let him go on believing he can fool us like that?"

"But you can't, Christian!" She was obviously upset. "Not this evening. The poor man's devastated."

I did not let Julia's glances during supper deter me from trying at least to get a little more out of Ninoshvili on how he saw the situation in Georgia. He gave only monosyllabic answers, ate little, and soon, after asking Julia's permission, moved to the TV set with his glass and sat there, switching from one news bulletin to the next, and staring absently at the screen in between times.

104

He doesn't seem to support Gamsakhurdia the nationalist. But maybe it only goes against the grain with him that the former president has made common cause with the recalcitrant Abkhazians. On the other hand, in his own way of course Shevardnadze is also a Georgian nationalist, despite his celebrated past as Moscow's Foreign Minister, and he heads the government on behalf of which Ninoshvili says he came here. However, before that Shevardnadze held office as head of the Georgian Communist Party, and in that capacity, as nationalists like Gamsakhurdia see it, was no less than a slave-owner appointed by Moscow. But then again, that could mean that a former KGB agent felt very much safer on Eduard Shevardnadze's side, and must now fear for himself. Unless Zviad Gamsakhurdia too is actually in league with the KGB.

Once I realized that my thoughts were going around in this back-and-forth kind of way, I gave up. I cleared the supper dishes and sat down with our guest and Julia in front of the box. Ninoshvili was drinking a good deal. After the ten-thirty news, which had nothing very recent to report, he rose to his feet and said, "Please forgive me. I'd like to get some rest." As he went out, walking rather unsteadily, his shoulder collided with the door frame.

We listened. Once the spare room door had closed behind him, Julia said, "Thank you."

"What for?"

"I know how hard it was for you not to ask him to explain himself at once." She smiled. "You're a good person." Then she stroked my hair and kissed me on the nose. "Don't worry. I'll speak to him about this whole silly story as soon as he's feeling a bit better."

28

I don't want to speak too soon, but it could be said that the first lesson in my four-part series was a success. Of course there was the usual silliness and some troublemakers, even before I asked what they would think if we spent four lessons studying a topical subject. When asked, "What subject?" I replied, "Georgia." Oliver Zacher instantly bleated, "Never heard of it. Where's that supposed to be?"

Manni Wallmeroth, who as far as I know takes no interest in either football or any other kind of physical exercise, cried, "Dinamo Tbilisi! Everyone knows Dinamo Tbilisi!" And Charlotte Keusch, who is bosom friends with Wenka Jovanovic, objected that Georgia wasn't so very important these days, and she thought it would be better if we studied Bosnia.

But what most of them made of the texts I handed out for them to read before the first lesson was very encouraging. I had not just duplicated a passage each from the absurdly similar speeches of those mortal enemies Gamsakhurdia and Shevardnadze, I had also chosen an extract from Naira Gelashvili's reports on the explosive complex of demonstrations and counter-demonstrations in Tbilisi before Zviad Gamsakhurdia was overthrown. I thought this text particularly suitable for them because of the gentle irony that the reporter preserves in spite of all the bitterness, for instance in the account of clashes in the Square of Heroes, so-called in popular parlance because it has traffic flowing in from five different directions, and those drivers who manage to cross it intact are considered heroic.

Particularly effective was Gelashvili's account of the distress of the animals in the zoo on the same square, and the panic into which the constant noise of gunfire, shells and detonating mines cast them. The cries of the owls, drowning out even the chanted slogans of the demonstrators; the plaintive roar of the tigers forced to go hungry because their keepers were taking home the meat supposed to feed them; the night when the wolves broke out of their enclosure and unexpectedly appeared among the demonstrators; and the pitiless hunt as the guards pursued the terrified animals down the streets and shot them.

A good half-dozen of the girls, together with Hasan Ileri and Christian Berkhan, began with the animals in the essays I set them to write: this, they said, was an example of the lack of restraint with which humanity abuses and destroys its environment; it is a familiar observation that in ideological struggles animals fall by the wayside, and those who don't feel for animals cannot be expected to respect other human beings.

But such reactions were not all. Only a few students failed to notice or mention the give-away similarity of the arguments proposed by Shevardnadze and Gamsakhurdia. Those few included Oliver Zacher, but I assumed that he had in fact understood what I wanted and acted stupid for that very reason. Also Helmut Freese – well, I'd expected nothing else of him. Helmut the recalcitrant dimwit said that in a case like that there was no solution but to let weapons decide the outcome, and then everyone could see who was right. I reprimanded Hasan Ileri because after this contribution he looked at the writer of the essay and tapped his forehead, muttering, "Talk about a silly sod!"

In the extract from Gelashvili's reports I had also included its quotation from John Steinbeck's Russian diary:

Wherever we had been in Russia, in Moscow, in the Ukraine or in Stalingrad, the magical name of Georgia came up constantly. People who had never been there, and who possibly could never go there, spoke of Georgia with a kind of longing and a great admiration. They spoke

of the country [...] as a kind of second heaven. Indeed, we began to
believe that most Russians hope that if they live very good and virtuous
lives, they will go not to heaven, but to Georgia when they die.

Then I told them the Georgian version of the Creation story, which I have found again and again in both the belles-lettres and the historical writings on Georgia: the Lord God, when he made the world and gave every nation its place there, forgot the Georgians. But they bore him no grudge, and instead invited him to visit them, served him wine and sang him their songs. The Lord God had such a good time that he decided to give these cheerful, dauntless people the place on earth that he had planned to keep for himself: the hills and valleys in the south of the great Caucasian mountain range.

I asked them whether they thought that was a special kind of national pride, or more like arrogant nationalism, or if they could see any points of comparison with other nations. One boy called out at once, "God's own country, the Yanks have the same idea." It wasn't long before Günsel Özcan said, "And *la grande nation* is pretty arrogant as well." Manni Wallmeroth, who had been intent on biting his nails until now, took his finger out of his mouth and said, "The Brits are just as crazy – 'my country right or wrong'!" The quotation I had been hoping for was provided by Christian Berkhan: "How about the saying that German virtues will put everything in the world right?"

I said perhaps that sounded a little more moderate in the words of Emanuel Geibel, who coined the phrase, and quoted the last verse of the original poem on *The German Vocation*:

Upright, free, strong in the fight,
Clear in mind and eye alike,

108

Let us banish from our sight,
All but lawful grounds to strike.
Then those German virtues may
Cure the whole world's ills some day.

There was laughter. Someone called out, "So what? Where's the difference?"

I was very pleased with them. I just wondered whether it hadn't been a mistake to send Ralf to a different school to avoid clashes between the two of us.

I wonder how he would have turned out in this class of mine, which often enough infuriates me, but also makes me hope for a certain amount of progress in humanity.

29

If it wasn't Matassi on the other end of Ninoshvili's phone call, then who was it? Maybe some KGB comrade in the Abkhazian region, and Ninoshvili was phoning the KGB man to find out for certain about the situation at the front.

The House of the Republic on Rustaveli Square in Otshamshira; night has already fallen, the square is deserted. From a side street comes a bus, tilting over and creaking, rattling as it spews diesel fumes, rounds the Stalin memorial and disappears down another side street. A dull rumbling is audible in the distance. Of the windows in the House of the Republic, only a few in the upper storeys show any light. Half the ground floor is burnt out, and the empty, smoke-blackened frames yawn in the pale light of the arc lamps.

Behind one of the lighted windows, a telephone rings. The comrade steps through the open doorway of the next room, glass in hand, a cigarette in the corner of his mouth. He lifts the receiver, pulls up a chair, when David Ninoshvili greets him.

"We'll have to wait, David. If I were you I'd stay put for the time being. Yes, that's right, the two regiments are going to join Zviad. I don't know where Eduard is. He's not in Otshamshira, anyway. Maybe he's gone to Tbilisi already to save what he still can. And it looks as if things are about to get uncomfortable here pretty soon. No, I don't think so. Zviad holds better cards, that's as good as certain. Me? I don't know yet. But yesterday I had a word with Merab Zereteli, you must know him. Yes, he's already carried out a mission for Zviad."

Another explosion, not far away, shakes the House of the Republic. The light flickers. The comrade says: "Good luck, David. And stay right where you are. The wall in here is beginning to wobble, I must get my arse out of the firing line." He hangs the receiver up, puts out the light, goes to the window and peers out. Two militiamen are running along the other side of the square, beyond the circle of light cast by the arc lamps. The comrade drains his glass and leaves the room.

If Ninoshvili was talking to some such comrade rather than his wife, and she would have been the first person to spring to any normal man's mind, why did he give me Matassi's regards? What could be behind such a ploy? Was it just to hide the fact that his life is in danger, and he can't go back to Georgia in a hurry?

And I can't shake off another idea. Maybe Matassi is dead, dead of an illness, in an accident. Or as a victim of the civil war. Or maybe she died even earlier, during the demonstrations when the Georgians who wanted a revolution were trying to wrest their independence from Moscow by force. On the night of 9 April 1989, Russian special troops violently broke

110

up the crowds who had gathered outside Tbilisi University. They beat the demonstrators with sharp-edged spades and fired poison gas at them. Nineteen women and one man were killed on the spot. Thousands are said to have died of the consequences of gas poisoning.

Matassi struck down by an army spade – oh, come on, that's just my imagination. I obviously feel tempted to turn the woman in Ninoshvili's life, whom I once took for a KGB agent, into a freedom fighter. Let's just drop that. Perhaps she's still alive, never had anything to do with the KGB, but instead she and Ninoshvili have separated, a perfectly ordinary rift. For instance, maybe when we were leaving Tbilisi Dautzenbacher really did make some insinuation about Matassi's visit to my hotel room, and it brought Ninoshvili's blood to boiling point.

So then he goes straight home, flings the little gate in the high wall open, strides across the yard, pushes the children aside and climbs the creaking steps. Matassi is sitting on the bed in the little bedroom, folding laundry. She looks up when Ninoshvili stops in the doorway, preserving an ominous silence, a dark shadow in front of the shafts of sunlight that fall from the balcony into the living room. "What is it?" she asks.

He wants to know what she was doing in my hotel room. She tells him he knows; she was bringing me the copy of that article. No, he says, that's exactly what he doesn't know, and she is well aware of it; he naturally assumed that she'd hand the copy, as agreed, in at the hotel reception desk. Or should he have entertained the possibility that she would evade the receptionist, like a tart, go straight up in the lift and knock at a foreigner's door in an unobserved corridor?

Matassi loses her temper. She says if he dares to call her a tart again she'll scratch his eyes out. She has nothing to hide, but she doesn't owe him any explanations either. And whatever she was doing in my hotel room, she tells him, it's nothing at all to do with him. David the Avenger takes a step into the room. He doesn't bring out his flick knife, but his sweeping gesture tells Matassi to leave. She sweeps the laundry off the woven bedspread, flings a suitcase down on the bed and starts to pack, while Ninoshvili goes into the kitchen and gulps down a glass of Armenian cognac.

The break was a lasting one, and they haven't had any kind of contact since.

So then how to explain the greetings sent by Matassi over the years, written on Ninoshvili's New Year cards, the present he brought me from her, and the card "in remembrance" that came with it? And always, from the first, in the same handwriting?

It wasn't Matassi's handwriting. I only thought it was. I never saw anything written by Matassi in Tbilisi. Ninoshvili has persuaded her successor, the woman who's been sharing that bed with him since Matassi moved out, to write messages on the cards in her name. He has told the woman – let's call her Nana or Nona – who I am, and that it might come in useful some time if he keeps me believing that he's still living with Matassi. Nona was slightly hurt, but then she laughed, and wrote the good wishes he dictated to her on the cards.

But why would he have been playing this game?

Because he wanted to hold on to a means of putting pressure on me. I was to "owe him" something, and the debt was still unpaid. Matassi's reaction when asked what she had been doing in his hotel room invited all kinds of suspicions, could be interpreted as an admission of the most brazen infidelity. The claims of the law on adultery might be satisfied by disowning the dissolute woman involved. But I too was subject to them, and there satisfaction still had to be and would be required.

He wanted to keep an option open for payment of what I owed him, so as to get compensation, for instance in cash, maybe in food and lodging too, and payment of enough pocket money to last until his application for asylum was decided. And if I should refuse, then he can always bring out his flick knife to avenge the insult to his honour with my blood.

That's enough. I've lost myself yet again in the hysterical fantasies that I thought I'd overcome. But hard as I try, I can't be easy in my mind.

Just now I got up, listened for a while to see whether, now that Ralf has taken his moped out of the garage and ridden away, roaring the engine, I was alone in the house. I climbed the stairs to the top floor and stole into the bedroom, opened the drawer of the bedside table. My hopes were not disappointed; he still keeps the photo there. Matassi, standing by the balustrade of the lookout point, smiled at me.

Her round cheeks, her dark, thick brows, the shadows around her eyes. Her full lips. Her pale-brown forefinger, the fragrance of her skin, the Orient and myrrh when we kissed on my hotel bed. I don't want to think that the present wasn't from her and that it wasn't a trace of her perfume that I detected on the pink card.

I wonder what has become of her. The actor in Otar Chiladze's novel moved from Tbilisi to Batumi when he no longer felt comfortable in the capital. But the railway no longer runs from Tbilisi to Batumi, the locomotives have fallen silent. Some sort of heavily armed band, probably of Abkhazian freedom fighters, has made incursions into the tracks and is occupying them.

In a report from Tbilisi, I read that the city presents a dismal picture. Refugees hang their washing on the hotel balconies. The smashed glass in the bus windows has been replaced by sheets of plywood. Shady security men lurk at every street junction in their blotched combat outfits, Kalashnikovs in front of them. Even during the hours of curfew at night, hungry people lay siege to the empty bakeries. They are not deterred by the bursts of fire from sub-machine guns that keep echoing through the streets.

Matassi and her coffee. The crisp croissants from the confectioner's, her white teeth biting into them. What has become of her?

After Julia and I spoke to him about his lecture in Herr Schumann's summer house, Ninoshvili apologized to me. He most genuinely asked my pardon, he said, but the fee that Herr Schumann had offered him had seemed like a small fortune, and he was afraid he couldn't resist the temptation. However, in his lecture he had confined himself to an outline of Georgian history, and where the civil war was concerned he gave an objective analysis of the present military situation; he had said nothing at all that could have been mistaken by the young people. He was well aware, he added, that a guest ought not to engage in political discussion with his hosts, and he had strictly observed that principle – "You must believe me there, my friend, I beg you in heartfelt terms!"

Julia is going to take him with her on a visit to Frankfurt. She has to see a client there, and as Ninoshvili was able to arrange personal interviews with the two publishing houses on the same day, she offered him a lift in her car.

30

A man! The strange potency of manhood upon her! Her hands strayed over him, still a little afraid... Such utter stillness of potency and delicate flesh! How beautiful! How beautiful! Her hands came timorously down his back, to the soft smallish globes of the buttocks... The life within life, the sheer warm, potent loveliness. And the strange weight of the balls between his legs! What a mystery! What a strange, heavy weight of mystery, that could lie soft and heavy in one's hand... the primeval root of all full beauty!

Perhaps we men ought to go around with our backsides bare, letting the balls dangle to give an idea of their weight. And we could get many a pleasant surprise if all women secretly felt like the well-brought-up Connie Chatterley. Yet I can't rid myself of the suspicion that Lady Chatterley could just as well be presented as a psychiatric case study illustrating masculine derangement, rather than as a fictional character of literary merit. However, of course I can't rule out the possibility that the strange potency of manhood, manifested in ways that I myself find repellent, may be irresistibly attractive to certain women. Yes, well, how beautiful, how beautiful!

The gamekeeper who brings Connie to such ecstasy doesn't even have to seduce her; he behaves badly throughout the novel, he's an arrogant brute, but she runs after him until he does as she wants. He spreads an old brown army blanket on the floor of his hut and lays Lady Constance – Her Ladyship, if you please – down on her back. A moment of remorseful horror – "*Stranger! Stranger!*" – does not last long, for the good reason that she *"felt again the slow momentous, surging rise of the phallus, that other power. And her heart melted out with a kind of awe."*

To be sure, we must take into consideration that Lady Constance's husband, the unfortunate baronet Sir Clifford Chatterley, who comes home from the front in Flanders "more or less in bits" and has nothing left to offer her below his waist, even expressly suggests that she should look for a lover, perhaps get pregnant by him, and thus provide the house of Chatterley with the heir it needs. Poor Sir Clifford, to crown all his bad luck, must have been an idiot. No wonder he later regretted his magnanimity.

I sympathize more with Shah Moabad, who dyed himself yellow when he found out that Princess Vis, who shone like the moon and was betrothed to him, was sharing her bed with another man. Moabad did not just speak bitter words, his warriors did not just grind their teeth, they set off instantly to avenge such infidelity.

Not that it did Moabad much good. He did succeed in bringing the lovely Vis home, but a little later the princess began a liaison with his younger brother. She let her lover into the palace by night while Moabad was out hunting, and the adulterer, mowing down the guards with his sword, seized the throne.

The outcome of this old Georgian version of a tale of the joys and sorrows of love was not at all satisfactory for the cuckolded husband: he sat over his wine through the night, planning a campaign of revenge, and a mighty wild boar broke out of the dark forest at first light of dawn. Moabad mounted his horse to enjoy the pleasures of the chase for a while before setting out. However, the javelin that he threw at the boar missed its mark, or perhaps the eye of the man who cast it was still clouded with drink, but at any rate the boar charged the Shah and knocked him and his horse down. Before Moabad could remount, the boar charged again, thrust its tusks into his chest and tore him apart.

"A prince as mighty as Moabad died that pitiful death," says the poet. But I won't blame the unreasoning animal. It seems to me that we can draw good lessons from the fate of both Shah Moabad and Sir Clifford Chatterley. A man who trusts women shouldn't be surprised if there are unpleasant consequences.

31

I've had a shock. As far as I can see it's going to take me some time to recover from it.

This morning Julia and Ninoshvili set off for Frankfurt at seven. Ralf was still asleep, so I ate breakfast on my own, but I didn't feel like reading the papers, I just glanced at the front pages and then put them aside. At midday today, when I had eaten my curd cheese and sat down at the desk, I picked up the local paper; I had found it difficult to get down to work, and thought I would pass a little time reading first.

On an inside page I found the report of a murder, illustrated by the picture of a blonde woman. I stared incredulously at the photograph. I felt a wave of heat running through me, and the sweat broke out on my forehead. The murder victim looked like the identical twin of the blonde whose picture I had found in Ninoshvili's suitcase, although a couple of years older.

Yesterday afternoon, the woman was found stabbed in a small hotel in the city centre. She had been dead for about six hours. The name she gave at the reception desk when she checked in a day before is presumably false; at least, the police have no record of her at the address in Hamburg that she gave as her place of residence. No ID papers or other personal documents were found in the hotel room.

The woman, according to her naturally doubtful account at the hotel reception, was thirty-seven years old and had been born in Dresden. She had also had one phone call from a man, but none of the hotel staff noticed her having a visitor. Only in the evening, when the card saying *Please Do Not Disturb* was still hanging over the door handle, did the chambermaid feel suspicious. She discovered the woman lying on the floor in her blood. No clues to a sexual motive for the murder were found.

I remembered that on the evening of the day before yesterday, a woman phoned asking for Ninoshvili. He'd told me later, volunteering the information, that she was an editor in a publishing house.

After sitting staring at the newspaper for a while, as if paralysed, I climbed the stairs and went into the spare room. The leather suitcase was locked. I searched the whole room, although I knew nothing would come of it, looking for the books in Georgian and the four photos, but I found neither them nor any other piece of evidence, and of course I didn't come across the flick knife. I couldn't find Matassi's photograph either.

I spent a good ten or fifteen minutes wondering if and how I could force the locks of the case without leaving any trace behind. I even bent a paperclip straight and cautiously poked about with it in the locks of the clasps. Then, realizing that my efforts were getting nowhere, I came to a sudden decision.

I took out the card that Herr Hochgeschurz had given me at our first meeting, and phoned the agent. He didn't seem surprised when I told him that if possible I would like a little more precise information about the talk given by my Georgian guest at Herr Schumann's summer house. That was perfectly possible, replied the agent, and when could we meet? I asked him if he might have time to fit me in this very afternoon. He'd be happy to see me, said Herr Hochgeschurz; he would just have to ask me to visit him at his office, because he was expecting several phone calls.

I set off at once, feeling as if I had been promised a miraculous cure for some painful illness. The agent has a small room on the sixth floor of an office building; apparently the local branch of his outfit contents itself with just this floor. The nameplate outside the door does not indicate that he works for Internal Security; the authority functions here under the name of a communications company, as Hochgeschurz had told me so that I would not go wrong. I rang the bell. A man in a leather jacket opened the door and, when I gave my name, asked me to come in.

Herr Hochgeschurz has a desk in his room, a swivel chair and a chair for visitors, two telephones, a computer terminal, a filing cabinet, beige curtains, a pot plant on the window sill, woodchip wallpaper, a fire extinguisher, and on the wall there is a framed, signed photograph of the former head of Internal Security, Günther Nollau. The window of the office has a view of higgledy-piggledy flat rooftops, two church towers and a jumbled forest of chimneys. The air shimmered slightly above them.

As soon as I was inside this office I wanted to leave it again. I had once sat in an oppressively sterile room like this on an autumn day on some other occasion, maybe it was in a doctor's waiting room. I took a deep breath and smelled the sweetish cleaner with which presumably the cleaning lady had mopped the plastic flooring.

Herr Hochgeschurz asked if I would like a coffee. I said yes, and he opened the door of the next room and spoke to someone inside. "Could you make us two coffees, please, Gabi?" Then he sat down in his swivel chair, smiled and nodded, and I heard him draw two heavy breaths. He immediately picked up a file folder, said, "Yes, well, let's see about this," opened the file and leafed through it.

Ninoshvili had not by any means confined himself, at least according to the agent's account, to giving his audience a crash course in Georgian history and telling them who was firing at whom just now, and where and why. Instead, he

119

spoke at length on the question of race, drawing parallels between the Republic of Georgia and the Federal Republic of Germany, both of which had to defend themselves against domination by foreign powers.

The extensive nature of his information suggested that Herr Hochgeschurz had successfully infiltrated a useful informer into the circles in which Gero Schumann moved. Herr Hochgeschurz had only just broached the topic of the Abkhazians when a red-haired young woman came in from the next room with a tray and, without a word, put two cups of coffee in front of us. The agent fell silent until the young woman had closed the door behind her. He interrupted himself a second time, when there was a knock at his door, and a grey-haired man in a suit of a muted hue with a waistcoat came in. "Oh, sorry," said this gentleman. "I only wanted to bring you these files. We can discuss them later."

He nodded to me with a smile, and handed Herr Hochgeschurz a folder. The agent half-rose and said, "May I introduce you to our departmental head, Dr Schmidt?" And indicating me, he added, "This is Herr Kestner, senior teacher." Dr Schmidt gave me his hand, and held mine firmly for a moment, nodding as if it were a long time since he had been so pleased to see someone. The agent sat back, smiling. "Herr Kestner is married to Dr Kestner the lawyer."

Herr Schmidt raised his eyebrows. "Indeed, indeed? My congratulations! A very able woman, one has to say, even if she does make a little trouble for us now and then." Then, as neither I nor Dr Schmidt could think of any way to continue this conversation other than with a friendly smile, he took his leave and went out. Herr Hochgeschurz continued his peroration.

I'd heard enough of it. I had certainly known already that Ninoshvili was a cunning liar, and the fact that Ralf was mixing with some very disreputable characters was no news to me either. I waited impatiently for Hochgeschurz to conclude his account, and as soon as he closed the file I made an attempt to come closer to the real subject of my interest. It was clear to me that I was treading on thin ice here, but I was bent on knowing more.

I rubbed my forehead as if I were thinking hard. "What do you think of Herr Ninoshvili?"

Hochgeschurz shrugged. "He comes across as an ardent nationalist. At least, that's what one would conclude from his lecture at Herr Schumann's place."

I nodded. Then I asked, "Do you know any more about him?"

"What do you mean?"

"Well… you did at least have him observed in that summer house, if I interpret your information correctly." Hochgeschurz nodded. I asked, "Are you keeping tabs on him for any other reason?"

The agent smiled. "Even if we were… well, I couldn't say anything to you about it, as I am sure you will understand." He immediately leaned forwards. "Would you care for a shot of spirits?"

I accepted. Herr Hochgeschurz leaned over to one side, took a bottle of gin and two small glasses out of his desk, and filled the glasses to the brim. After he had raised his glass to me and then tipped the gin down his throat, he leaned back.

He massaged his nose for a while, and then said, "Of course we are always on our guard. We have to be, considering the large numbers of people who come here from the former communist countries." He smiled. "The KGB hasn't gone into retirement yet. Even the Stasi hasn't, as you've presumably heard before now."

I don't know if what I felt was triumph or horror. After a pause, during which Hochgeschurz looked at me in silence, I said, "Do you think it possible that Herr Ninoshvili has some kind of connection... well, a connection with the KGB seems to me downright absurd. After all, he's obviously a staunch Georgian nationalist, and that would hardly go down well with the KGB. I mean... Tbilisi and Moscow, they've always been poles apart."

Herr Hochgeschurz laughed. "Ah, there you underestimate the Soviet secret service! They don't just stick false beards on. The comrades of the KGB can act like nationalists if need be. And the Georgians, moreover, haven't exactly been the Soviet Union's poor relations. Not only was Stalin himself a Georgian, his secret service chief Beria came from the same country. And so did Ordzhonikidze. As a historian, I'm sure you know more than I do about the methods that arch-Bolshevik used to bring his native land back home to the empire."

He paused briefly, and then added, "Not that I'd like you to think I said Herr Ninoshvili works for the KGB."

I nodded. "No." After a while, I said, "But you do give me plenty to think about."

"Why?"

I realized that my present venture could easily run out of control, but I couldn't bring myself to beat a retreat. I said, "I'm thinking of what you said about the KGB and the Stasi. And that those people haven't gone into retirement yet. Of course that's not entirely news to me, but... that murder just occurred to me, the one in today's paper. The woman found stabbed in her hotel. Did you read about it yourself?"

"Yes."

Apparently Hochgeschurz was going to confine himself to that answer. Perhaps he intended to provoke me, but in any case I went on. "Do you think it possible that there's something of the kind behind that story? How shall I put it? A background to do with the intelligence services? I mean… it obviously wasn't done by a sex murderer. And all the circumstances are rather mysterious, no ID, a false address…"

Herr Hochgeschurz did not say: you've been reading too many spy thrillers. He said, "At present the matter's in the hands of our colleagues of the police force. That's what the murder squad is for."

I nodded. After a pause, the agent remarked, "As for Herr Ninoshvili, I think you must certainly know him much better than I do. After all, he's a guest in your house. You see him every day."

"Of course."

"Is there anything in his conduct, then, that gives you cause for concern?"

Here we were. Now it came to the crunch. I thought feverishly. The evidence I had to bring against Ninoshvili was far from constituting proof. The photo of the blonde woman was hidden in his case, and I could hardly invite Herr Hochgeschurz to my house for him to open the locks with his pocket knife and convince himself that she was identical to the murder victim. And perhaps Ninoshvili had taken the photograph with him on today's outing, or even destroyed it. After all, the crime was committed now.

What I had to say would have been no more than simple denunciation, and I shrank from that after all. I shook my head. "No. No. Nothing worth mentioning." I stood up, shook the agent's hand and thanked him.

"You're welcome. My regards to your wife." He smiled. "That is, of course, only if you're telling her about our conversation. Otherwise of course it remains between us."

32

Julia and Ninoshvili didn't get back from Frankfurt until nine thirty yesterday evening. When Ralf asked, at around seven, what there was to eat, I improvised a meal for him and myself: rösti from the freezer, fried eggs and salad. He seemed pleasantly surprised, even said, "Great!" and ate with a hearty appetite. However, he didn't fulfil my hope that this rapprochement might lead to a conversation between us.

He remained monosyllabic during the meal, and seemed to be brooding over something. He did clear the dishes away, unasked, but then disappeared, announcing that he was going round to see Achim, one of his friends.

My wife and our guest had already eaten on the way back. The journey seems to have been worthwhile for Ninoshvili; he said that the two publishers, who had given him and his manuscripts a very friendly reception, were going to come to a decision within the week. To celebrate this success, and because the weather was so tempting – perhaps the last fine autumn day – Julia took her time over the journey back, and did not drive our guest along the motorway but took him, at their leisure, through the Rhine valley. Ninoshvili was enthusiastic about its beauty; he had read a lot about it, he said, but had not imagined it quite so beautiful, "so uplifting".

I felt no inclination at all to hear how they had seen the Niederwald Memorial, and had not failed to visit the picturesque Drosselgasse in Rüdesheim. All I needed was for the Georgian to praise "the delicious wine" and recite that patriotic anthem of the nineteenth century 'The Watch on the Rhine', "Dear country, hear these words of mine; Firmly stands the watch on the Rhine", and whatever other feeble-minded stuff he may have picked up about the great

German river. I interrupted him by quoting Karl Simrock's contrary sentiments of 1839: "Go not to the Rhine, go not to the Rhine, dear son of mine, go not to the Rhine!"

He looked at me in surprise. "What's that?" I said it was another German poem, and recited the last verse:

> *Bewitched by sound, bemused by show,*
> *Hymning the Rhine, the river Rhine,*
> *On to your doom I see you go,*
> *On to your death, dear son of mine.*

He laughed. I don't know if he didn't get the message or didn't want to, but anyway he was not to be deterred from telling me how they had passed the Loreley. "If you know Heine, and I do know him a little, you might think you saw the maiden sitting up there combing her golden hair and singing her song 'with its powerful, wondrous melody'. You know those lines, my friend, and that wonderful folk legend." I said it wasn't in fact a folk legend, but a work of literature, and Clemens Brentano very likely made up the Loreley.

Even that couldn't discourage him. He went on with his description of the reverent awe he had felt when they crossed the river Lahn. "Do you know that Goethe went along that river in a skiff from Wetzlar to far down the Rhine? But yes, of course you know that, my friend, you know it much better than I do!"

I said yes, I had heard of it, only as I was sure he also knew that was not so much a pleasure trip as a flight; things had become rather too hot in Wetzlar for the young poet, who was paying marked attention to his friend's wife the lovely Lotte. Still, I added, he had shown more sense than Werther, the hero of his novel. Goethe definitely did not kill himself at midnight by blowing out his brains, while wearing his boots and a blue tailcoat with a yellow waistcoat, but instead made for safety and new love affairs.

My guest seemed much struck for the first time, and shook his head. "Can one really be so down to earth about Goethe, even of his literary masterpiece *The Sorrows of Young Werther*?" I said well, yes, one could, and left it at that.

Julia asked me, as we were going to bed, whether I'd had a difficult day at school. I said no. After a while, she asked, "Surely you aren't jealous, are you?" I asked her what made her think that. She shrugged, and said no more.

I had taken Brentano's *Folk Tales of the Rhine* up with me for bedtime reading, leafed through them a little, and came on the place where Black Hans, the miller Radlof's pet starling, suddenly begins to speak, but from that time on will no longer eat and drink, so that Radlof, who loves the bird dearly, goes to the trouble of cheering him up with a quatrain. I laughed to myself, and then said, "And here's another pretty poem."

Julia turned to me. "And how does it go?" I recited, with much expression:

Eat and drink just as you please,
Whistle a tune, my honey.
You can't pay? Put your mind at ease,
I'll let you have the money.

Julia turned away and looked at her own book. After a while she said, "You're not being fair." I did not reply.

I feel wretched. If Hochgeschurz is having the Georgian watched, then he knows about Julia going around with our guest as well. It won't have stopped at that sighting of the two of them together at the courthouse, and then perhaps sharing lunch. It could be that my imagination is running away with me again, but the agent may also have gained information, one way or another, about their trip to Frankfurt. In fact that would actually be among his official duties if he really did have instructions to check up on Ninoshvili's contacts in the Federal Republic. Perhaps he's had my telephone tapped so that he can keep up to date with the Georgian's arrangements.

If so, he could have found out some connection between Ninoshvili and the woman in the hotel even before I visited him. Or no, that's not conclusive. If she was indeed the supposed editor who called Ninoshvili at my house, maybe she didn't give the name of her hotel. Their meeting could have been arranged in advance. And if Ninoshvili was really the man who called her at the hotel, he would not have conducted that conversation from my house. Say he called her from a phone kiosk. And before visiting the hotel to murder her, he shook off the observer sent by Hochgeschurz to shadow him.

He didn't necessarily have to take such precautions on the journey to Frankfurt. Perhaps he was even glad to be shadowed. After all, he was going about his business as a representative of the Georgian Ministry of Culture, all above board.

The man watching him, a lanky young fellow in jeans and parka, sits in the car provided by Internal Security, yawning, outside the building containing the publisher's office into which Ninoshvili has disappeared for his second appointment that morning. He sits up straight when he sees Julia's car stop outside the building. He sees the Georgian come out of the front entrance. Ninoshvili waves triumphantly to Julia, gets into the car with her and kisses her on the cheek. The two of them talk for a while; Ninoshvili describes his meeting with many gestures. Julia gives him a kiss on the cheek. She starts the engine and drives away with her cheerful companion.

The lanky observer follows them along the road into the valley of the Rhine.

He mingles with the Japanese, American and British tourists climbing the broad steps to the Niederwald Memorial, following Julia and Ninoshvili at a little distance. He wonders what the hell the two of them are doing up there. The monument means nothing to him. No one taught him at school what the figure of Germania means, that mighty, regal female twelve and a half metres high, with her majestic dignity and the magnificent curves of her proud breasts. He doesn't know that this amazing statue of 1871 was erected in memory of Germany's defeat of her old enemy France. Perhaps it would leave him cold to hear that the sly Frenchmen had wanted to get their hands on the free German river Rhine, but were forcefully repelled by the Germans, united at last.

The lanky observer knows nothing about that, but he does know his job. He follows Julia and Ninoshvili to the Drosselgasse and the restaurant. When they have ordered their meal, he sees Ninoshvili drink to his companion, take an appreciative sip, and then put his arm around her shoulders. He gazes deeply into her eyes and kisses her on the lips. The lanky observer has a chance to see a long kiss, nothing unusual in the Drosselgasse.

The idea of Hochgeschurz hearing a detailed account of what my wife and the Georgian got up to together on their trip makes me feel miserable. I can still hear the agent's tone of voice when he sent Julia his regards. I'm almost sure there was a touch of malice in it. He knew that I wouldn't tell Julia about my visit to him anyway.

What torments me most is the terrible feeling that I myself have opened a doorway into my private life, my marriage, my house to that snooper. Of course I would be happy to see Ninoshvili revealed as a KGB agent, possibly a murderer,

128

and thus removed from my house and my life. But after the hints I so freely supplied to Herr Hochgeschurz, he'll be all the keener to find out about the relationship between Dr Kestner from Halle and Herr Ninoshvili from Tbilisi. And I have done a great deal to lead my wife into this trap.

Herr Hochgeschurz won't let go. He noticed something at once when I asked him for more information about Ninoshvili, and he took his precautions. None of the phone calls which he'd said he was waiting to take in his office arrived while I was with him. But Dr Schmidt came in, as if by chance, and took a good look at me: Dr Kestner's husband who allegedly just wanted to know more about Ninoshvili's outpourings in the summer house, but who eagerly responds to mention of the KGB and suddenly begins talking about the hotel murder case.

33

Raphael Lohmüller, the five-year-old next door, kicked his football over the garden fence at noon today. I heard the ball bounce on the terrace, went to the window and looked out. Raphael was slowly approaching the fence, stopped when he reached it and looked anxiously for his ball. I went out, picked up the ball and took it over to Raphael. He said, "Thank you, Herr Kestner," like a good boy.

Ninoshvili, who had been sitting in front of the TV set, appeared in the doorway to the terrace and waved to Raphael, smiling. The boy looked at him in silence. Ninoshvili moved away. Raphael asked, "Is that man living with you now?"

I replied, "Why do you want to know?" Raphael picked his nose for a moment and then asked, "Is it true that he's Turkish?"

"No," I said. "He comes from Timbuktu."

Raphael thought about this for a while, and then said, "I don't know where that is."

"Never mind," I told him. "Even your parents don't know."

Frau Birgit Lohmüller, flaxen-haired and red-cheeked, opened a window on the first floor of her house and leaned out. "Raffy, what are you doing there?" she called. "Has he been making a nuisance of himself, Herr Kestner?"

No, he has not been making a nuisance of himself. But you'd do better to mind your own business, my dear neighbour. For instance, you could get that dandified husband of yours to mow the lawn again. Your garden does not look at all the way a German family's should.

Frau Lohmüller called, "That's enough football, Raffy! Come on in now."

"I wouldn't do that if I were you, Raffy," I said.

34

Something absolutely outrageous has happened at school, and in my drama group too. I thought I'd picked the best pupils this school has to offer for that group.

I had fixed a rehearsal for yesterday afternoon using the stage set designed by Christa Frowein and Dirk Papenhoff, a small work of art: two partitions, one showing the wall of Capulet's garden with luxuriant vegetation behind it, the other a part of his house, modelled on the Veronese style of architecture, and Juliet's window in it about two metres up. When Günsel Özcan got up on the bench behind the partition to appear at the window, the partition began to rock. "Wait a moment, Günsel!" I called. "Are you steady on that bench?"

I jumped up on stage to look at the scenery. Christa Frowein came out of the wings and took hold of my arm. "It won't be any problem, Herr Kestner, we'll fix it after the rehearsal!"

I said, "I believe you, but I'd like to take a look myself."

Christa barred my way, smiling at me and placing both hands on my chest. "Now, do be honest! You don't trust me, do you? Oh, I'm so disappointed." I thought this banter was one of the rather obvious advances she can't seem to help making from time to time. Once, when she was following me down the corridor, she even tickled the back of my neck.

"None of that nonsense, Christa," I said, removing her hands from my chest, and I put her aside and went round behind the partition.

Günsel was standing on the bench looking sheepish, her head bent. I wondered what that meant, but then I saw the slogan on the back of the partition. Someone had scrawled over the hessian, with bright red spray paint, *SHEVARDNADZE IS A TRAITOR LIKE BRANDT AND WEHNER. REVENGE!* And underneath it was a bright-red swastika.

President Eduard Shevardnadze humbled himself before the Russians on Friday. Finding that the Abkhazians and Zviadists were successfully maintaining their offensive, he boarded a plane to Moscow, asked for military support there, and said that his government was prepared to incorporate Georgia into the Commonwealth of Independent States. Ninoshvili's comment on this news was inscrutable; he confined himself in essentials to what I had hear him say before: "Bad situation, very bad situation." I don't doubt it for a moment.

But I would never have dreamed that this "bad situation" could provoke such a disgraceful reaction in my drama group. I interrupted the rehearsal at once, called everyone together on stage and took up my position in front of them.

I was moved to see them standing around me looking so downcast, Günsel and Jürgen Dahlmann already in costume, and Christian Berkhan had put Mercutio's cap on, just for fun. Now he had forgotten that he was still wearing it. They had been going to settle the problem by themselves; probably Christa and Dirk would have set about painting over the sprayed slogan that very evening.

But I was too worked up. I was determined to make an example. When I had let the deathly silence that was spreading take effect for a while, I said I assumed that the graffiti artist would own up of his own accord, here and now. And if he was so much of a coward that he couldn't even summon up enough decent feeling for that, then I trusted that none of the others would think of shielding him. They had been my pupils long enough to know what a swastika means: it is the emblem of terror and inhumanity. And if this matter was not cleared up, I would cancel the whole performance and resign from directing the drama group.

I stopped and let my gaze move around them. No one stepped forwards. After a long pause, Micky Rautenstrauch cleared his throat. He said, "Herr Kestner, I don't think it was any of us."

Christa nodded. "No one in the drama group would do a horrible thing like that. Everyone here knows how long Dirk and I have been working on the scenery."

Oh, indeed? So how had this unknown person gained access to the stage set, I asked, how had anyone got into the room where it was kept under lock and key?

Manni Wallmeroth, playing Benvolio, put up his hand. "Maybe he nicked the key. Or made a duplicate key. I mean, it's been known to happen."

I asked him to be good enough not to indulge in fantasy. Jürgen Dahlmann asked, "What do you mean, fantasy? Last year someone got the door to the chemistry labs open, and he was never found either."

I said I was not about to engage in this kind of discussion. I thought I had expressed myself clearly enough, I said, and I hoped everyone knew what to do now. If the perpetrator really couldn't summon up the courage to admit what he had done, I would give him one last chance: he could phone me at home or come to see me. And that was a course of action open to anyone who was now, perhaps, keeping silent from some mistaken idea of solidarity, without stopping to think that this meant all the work we had done together would come to nothing. I left them there, standing on stage and looking miserable, and went home.

In the evening the phone rang. When I answered it, no one spoke; all I could hear for a while was thudding music in the background. Then someone said, in a whisper, "It was Manni Wallmeroth," and hung up.

This morning I told Herr Trabert, the principal, about the incident and asked for a meeting of those of us on the staff who taught in the upper school. I told him I had already received anonymous information about the graffiti artist, but I wanted to test it out first. I had thought long and hard overnight whether to bring him into it, I said, but there was no keeping the scandal within bounds any more. Of course some member of the drama group or another was bound to spread the sensational news, hot off the press.

Brauckmann promptly approached me in the corridor when I was off to the staff room at break. He asked, grinning, "Well, on the trail of your little Nazi yet?" I said, "That was no little Nazi, it was some vandal of the kind we can't tolerate at this school."

Brauckmann raised his eyebrows. "Oh, come on, aren't you going a little too far? You're usually so understanding.

Your vandal didn't smash anyone's face in. Once upon a time, you'd just have entered something like this in the class register, and that would be it."

"Not for me. And you surely should know that entries in the class register are out of date these days."

"I know, I know. They were an offence against data protection, right? Indefensible, or what would things be coming to?"

Perhaps Brauckmann had irritated me too much; at least, in the discussion that developed in break I fell back on the argument that all the dams would be breached if this case wasn't cleared up and rigorously investigated. I found support, unfortunately, in my colleague Frau Schacht, who waxed indignant about the thoughtless damage to school property, claiming yet again that only last week a leg of her chair had been broken off by brute force and fitted back under the seat so loosely that she might well have suffered a heavy fall.

Most of the others reacted with some degree of surprise, either greater or lesser, when I said that I thought exclusion from the school an entirely appropriate punishment for the graffiti artist. It was not Philippovich but our colleague Frau Fasold, an amiable lady of fifty, who asked, smiling, "I wouldn't like to think you have trouble at home! Has your wife really infuriated you so much?"

After break, Elke Lampert walked a little way with me, accompanying me to the door of the room where I was taking my next lesson. When we were alone, she said, "Listen... don't you think you were overdoing it?"

I said I was sorry, but as the perpetrator was obviously pig-headed, and was also counting on remaining unidentified, I myself thought he should be punished, if only to discourage potential copycat offenders.

"I don't mean about exclusion," she said. "Anyway, I don't think you'll get anywhere with that idea. If the stupid idiot is found at all. It's the pressure you're putting on your drama group that surprises me. You're really fond of those young people. I can't understand how you came to threaten them with cancelling the play and walking out of the group. Do you really think you could... well, blackmail them like that? You practically ordered them to give up one of themselves to suffer for it. Or am I getting the wrong end of the stick?"

I said yes, she probably was. I'd already been given a name, admittedly by an anonymous informant, but it showed that the group knew what I meant.

She asked, "Anonymous? Do you approve of that?"

Not entirely, I said, but at least it was helpful.

In the last lesson I asked Manni Wallmeroth to come and have a quick word with me afterwards. Neither Günsel Özcan nor Jürgen Dahlmann raised a finger to say that if it was about the drama group they would like to come along too. They didn't so much as exchange glances, they looked down at the tabletop. Charlotte Keusch, the class delegate, kept quiet as well.

When everyone else had gone and the last student had closed the door, Manni Wallmeroth came up to me, carrying his backpack. I was getting my things together, and he watched me in silence. I closed my briefcase, looked up, and asked if he had sprayed those stupid graffiti on the stage set.

It was two or three seconds before he opened his mouth. "Me?" He went bright red. "You think I did it? What gives you that idea?"

I said his name had been given to me. He asked who said so. I said I couldn't tell him. He swallowed, nodded, and then said, "That was really mean. I didn't do it. Do you want to suspect me now?"

I said I didn't want to suspect anyone. I just wanted to ask him once more, clearly and distinctly, if he had sprayed that slogan and the swastika on the scenery.

"How often do I have to say it?" His voice was shaking. "I didn't do it. Someone's trying to make trouble for me," he said with difficulty.

I said all right, that was all, he could go. He muttered, "Goodbye," and left the room. I stayed sitting there for a while and then went to the window. He was walking over the school yard alone, on his way to the bus stop, shouldering his backpack. His arms were dangling, and he stooped slightly. I'll admit, I felt sorry for him. And not just that: I felt ashamed of myself.

35

The four of us were having supper when Julia suddenly said that Erika had called her at the office and announced that she was arriving on Saturday. I was rather annoyed about Julia's thoughtlessness in confronting me with the news in front of Ralf and Ninoshvili. However, I restrained myself. And in fact that wasn't too difficult, because I immediately realized that the advent of my wife's friend from Halle was more of a problem for her than for me.

There was no way that both Ninoshvili and Erika could occupy our spare room. One of them would have to be asked to go to a hotel, and I couldn't wait to see how Julia would decide between the Georgian and her friend. I for one had no intention of relieving her of the decision and making myself useful as a bouncer.

However, my enjoyable anticipation of a refreshing quarrel in my house, whether with friend David or friend Erika, was frustrated. A solution had already been found on the quiet, and yet again without bothering to ask for my opinion.

Ralf, I now discovered, was vacating his room for a week. He was going away on Sunday because he wanted to spend the autumn half-term holiday at a chess tournament for young people in a place called Schwitte-Minnenbüren. A tournament in seven rounds by the Swiss rules, with tutorial sessions by various grandmasters in the mornings. The Schwitte-Minnenbüren Chess Club, sponsored by a furniture factory in the town, is very active. Its first team got into the Second Federal League not long ago.

I also learned now that Ninoshvili holds the title of International Master, IM for short, and that this rank features only just below that of Grandmaster. IM Ninoshvili had encouraged Ralf to take part in the tournament, and has given him a little coaching in his free time by way of preparation.

I controlled myself with difficulty. I said, "How delightful to hear such news at exactly this moment." Ninoshvili cast me an enquiring glance. Ralf ate in silence. Julia said, "I'm sorry, but it all came up only today. I didn't know anything about it myself this morning."

I hadn't expected my son, of all people, to provide me with this small satisfaction. Julia obviously wanted to bridge the silence that now fell and went on talking, as if the solution were still under discussion. "I'll improvise sleeping arrangements for Saturday night. Erika can sleep on the sofa, I think, she's spoiled enough as it is. And after that she'll be happy, because David has offered to move out of the spare room for her on Sunday and sleep in Ralf's room while Ralf is away."

In the new silence that fell it was Ralf, surprisingly, who spoke up. He said, "No." Julia and Ninoshvili looked at him in some annoyance. He said, "That wasn't what we said. If

anyone's going to doss down in my room it can be Erika."
Then he went on eating in silence. Ninoshvili raised his
eyebrows and nodded. "Of course, of course. I didn't mean
to intrude. I only thought…"

Julia said, "That's no problem. Erika will just have to do
without the spare room. She'll get over it."

I didn't clear the dishes. I said I had to prepare for school
next day and went back to my study. When I heard Ralf
coming upstairs I felt tempted to haul him into the study and
ask if he had anything against Ninoshvili. But I didn't.

All I needed to do now was to find an ally in my own family,
if no one was going to offer spontaneously.

36

My great-aunt Laura died an untimely death. I don't mean
she was too young to die; on the morning when she failed to
open her eyes where she lay in her silk sheets she was seventy
or seventy-five years old, and she had lived life to the full: any
amount of travel, men, Egyptian cigarettes and champagne,
and right up to the last at that. But for that very reason no
one had expected her to die, including me, and she'd left me
30,000 marks. I cursed the irony of fate when the notary
told me.

Four weeks before, I had bought myself a used car because
I couldn't afford a new one. Well, I decided to stand up to
Fate; I wouldn't write off my inheritance, I'd use it and save
my legacy. I went on driving the used car, and immediately
turned it and myself over when a bolt in the steering broke
at high speed. The car was a write-off now anyway, I ended
up in hospital, spent seventeen days there, and missed three
exam papers which I sat at a later time.

Today Fate let only two hours pass before cocking a snook at me. I'd been wondering whether to apply for a postponement of the staff meeting that I had demanded, and now it had been fixed. After all, I had nothing to cite in evidence on the offence of introducing of a Nazi symbol into the drama group except for an anonymous accusation, and I couldn't properly bring that up. But I shrank from humbly retracting, and I promptly found myself offside.

Trabert, who had fixed the meeting and said that he personally would chair it, began by asking for the results of my investigations. As soon as I replied, "Nothing yet, I'm afraid, or nothing I can say with absolute certainty," there was a loud murmuring. Brauckmann, raising his voice, said, "So that's it, is it? Does anyone but Herr Kestner still think it necessary for us to waste our time here?"

Only Elke Lampert opposed him, saying we could at least think about the basic principles for evaluating such an offence.

Brauckmann asked, "What offence? Herr Kestner's, for drumming us up to come here for no good reason at all?"

Trabert flapped his hands. "Please, please! Let's be objective." I said I thought it necessary for the meeting to issue a statement condemning the graffiti and urging everyone who had any useful information to come forwards. That not only brought more loud murmuring, but also provoked Frau Jellonek to fall back on the stock-in-trade of her Religious Studies lessons. She put her head back, looked sternly at me, and said, "You really do surprise me, Herr Kestner! Do you realize what you are suggesting? That's nothing but an entirely immoral call for denunciation!"

Trabert raised his voice. "No, no, there's really no point in such accusations!" He shook his head and then looked at me. "But now, with the best will in the world, Herr Kestner, I don't see that this is getting us any further forwards. I suggest that you go on with your enquiries and we can meet again after the holiday week. Always supposing you have found out anything tangible by then."

Brauckmann pushed his chair back and said, "Excellent! I'm sure Herr Kestner will be very happy to spend his half-term on all this." Trabert's proposal, in short, was agreed. Everyone crowded out. But Elke waited at the door for me. When I joined her, she said, "What's the matter with you, Christian? Do you have a problem?" I said no, and that my only problem, if that was the right word, was the staff of this school.

Two hours later, when I was sitting at my desk at home trying to work, the doorbell rang. Ninoshvili, who had been sitting in the living room, called, "I'll go, Christian, I'll open the door." After a while he called, "Christian? There's a young man here who would like to speak to you."

I went out into the corridor, and up the stairs came Manni Wallmeroth. He cleared his throat when he saw me and swallowed hard. Then he said, "Can I have a word with you, Herr Kestner?"

I closed the door after him and indicated the chair at the desk in silence. He sat down slowly, put his hands on his knees and looked at his hands. Then he raised his eyes.

He said, "I did... okay, I did spray the slogan on the scenery. And the swastika. I don't even know why. I didn't mean it that way. I came into the room, and there was that can of spray paint. Lying with Christa and Dirk's things. And then I picked up the can and sprayed that... that graffiti stuff on the scenery. It all happened so fast. I just wasn't thinking." He swallowed. "I wanted to apologize to you. And for not saying so at once too." He hesitated, and then he said, "I was shit-scared."

140

I stared out of the window. He went on. "I saw something on TV at the weekend. About Shevardnadze visiting Moscow. I was interested because we'd been discussing that speech of his. And on Monday I saw a piece about it in the paper. Saying that Shevardnadze had gone right out of his mind, and now lots of Georgians think he's a traitor. I don't know... perhaps that's when the idea came to me."

"And how on earth did you come to think of Brandt and Wehner?" I asked.

"I heard about them once." He cleared his throat. "There's two old people live in the apartment above us, they come from East Prussia. Or anyway somewhere in the East. They were among the bunch exiled from their homes or something." He shrugged. "The old man is nuts, but he likes to tell everyone that Brandt and Wehner sold his native land to the Russians. I never took it seriously." He shook his head. "I really don't know why I wrote that stuff. And I'm truly very sorry."

I asked him whether one of the others had persuaded him to come and see me. He shook his head vigorously. "No, certainly not. I thought about it all on my own." He swallowed, and then said, "I mean, none of the others knows it was me."

I looked out of the window again. After a while he asked, "I suppose this can't be kept between us? You and me, I mean?"

"No, Manni. Put that idea out of your head. Unfortunately it's not so simple. And that ought to be clear to you too."

"Yes." I heard his loud swallowing. He asked, "Will they chuck me out of school now?"

I looked at him. He said, "I was nearly chucked out once before." Suddenly tears came into his eyes, and he passed the back of his hand over his nose. "But that was

141

quite different. That was still in middle school. I shut Kai Lehmann into the cupboard. He'd nicked my homework book and hidden it. And then I knocked the cupboard over, and it fell apart in pieces, and Kai didn't come out because he was pinned down under the back of it. But he wasn't much hurt otherwise."

I said, "I know that story. Did your parents get a letter at the time warning them that you might be excluded from school?"

He nodded. "Yeah. It said something like that." He looked at me intently and rubbed at the corners of his eyes. "Don't these things kind of go out of date?"

"No, Manni. They're kept on record. It doesn't look good for you."

He nodded. A tear squeezed its way out and rolled down his cheek. He dug a crumpled handkerchief out of his jeans pocket, blew his nose loudly and wiped his eyes.

I said, "Nothing will be done before half-term. And when the staff meet again I'll tell them you came to me of your own accord. But I can't tell you what the end result will be. It doesn't look good for you, Manni, and you can hardly be surprised."

"No." He put the handkerchief away.

I stood up. "Send a sick note along tomorrow. Maybe you'll cope better if you don't show your face before half-term is over. Unless you have something urgent to do?"

"No. No, nothing urgent." He stood up and gave me his hand. "Thank you, Herr Kestner." He suppressed an abrupt sob, turned and left.

142

37

Erika arrived just before five on Saturday afternoon on the InterRegio line from Halle. Julia and Ninoshvili met her at the station with her large suitcase and bulging travel bag. I had already set out for a long walk at four so as to avoid the hurly-burly of greetings that inevitably accompanied Erika's appearances. There was no danger that Ninoshvili might want to come with me. He had started preparations for a Georgian banquet to celebrate Erika's arrival and in farewell to Ralf, and he had already spent all morning on them. Julia had gone into the city centre with him to find the necessary specialities. Among other items, they had found some Kakheti wine, a case of six bottles. I didn't want to know what Julia had paid for it.

I walked through the woods in cold, drizzling rain, trudging over wet foliage as I climbed the narrow path leading to the Mäuseberg, a densely forested hill. There's a view of the distant rooftops and towers of the city from the top of the hill. But today the horizon was cloudy.

I was feeling chilly. I thought of the day when I first went to Halle with Julia. Erika had been waiting for us in the restaurant of the hotel that stood on a rise along the banks of the river Saale. She accompanied us to our sparsely furnished double room with shower, inspected the shower and the sheets, even ran her fingertips along the top of the wardrobe and found it dust-free. "I should hope so too, at that price!" I had gone out on the narrow balcony to get away from her chatter and her perfume.

Twilight was falling. A light rain veiled the opposite bank and the pallid apartment buildings of Halle-Neustadt, rising ahead like a mountain range. I smelled the acrid vapours of the coal-burning stoves which had told me we were in the

GDR, as it then was, when we stopped for a rest in Eisenach. I felt isolated, shut out of everything the two women had in common; I heard them talking on and on beyond the balcony door, whispering and laughing. I still felt isolated when we were in the spacious marketplace that evening – four of us, because we had been joined by a thin, taciturn man whom Erika introduced as her boyfriend and whom she never mentioned again – looking at the dark walls of the Red Tower, before going into a crowded, overheated wine bar.

When I came back from my walk a warm cloud met my nostrils: the smells of the banquet mingled with Erika's perfume. There were *khachapuri* cooking, warm flatbreads with a cheese filling, a soup called *chikhirtma*, made from lamb and seasoned with cinnamon and vinegar, and *satsivi*, which turned out to be grilled chicken with walnut sauce. I heard the sound of lively conversation in the kitchen. The two women were assisting the chef, who was hard at work in a red-and-blue checked apron. Erika kissed me on both cheeks, and Ninoshvili offered me a glass of Tsinandali, which they'd opened already to taste it.

I said it was still too early for me; I had to get a little more work done before supper. Erika clapped her hand to her mouth. "Oh God, oh God!" she cried, and ran out of the kitchen. As she hurried upstairs she cried, "My luggage is still in your room!" Julia said, "David left it there temporarily because we couldn't find anywhere to put it on the top floor."

I followed Erika. She met me in the doorway of the study, heavily laden with her case in one hand and her travelling bag in the other. "Where are you taking them?" I asked.

"I don't know. Maybe I'll find a spare corner up there."

I took the case and the bag from her and put them down beside my desk. "You really are a darling, Christian!" she

144

said. "I'll get them out of here tomorrow as soon as Ralf leaves." She kissed me on both cheeks and quickly went away, closing the door carefully behind her.

I spent the time until supper leafing through a book of pictures of Halle. The memories I'd conjured up during my walk on the Mäuseberg didn't do the city justice. The solid, spacious corner house where Handel was born three hundred years ago looked a comfortable place to me when I first saw it. A sign of life from a past that can't affect the present and is cherished with well-justified pride in that city. There's a picture of the parade of the Saltworkers' Fraternity, the men in their black hats and long red coats, the women in white dresses with frilled sleeves and blue bodices. There are the creaking wooden floorboards laden with precious books in the library of the Francke Foundations.

Little as I like to say so, Ninoshvili's banquet tasted better than anything I'd eaten in a long time. I had no hesitation in catching up on the wine that the three of them had opened earlier. And I offered no resistance worth mentioning when Ninoshvili, after the five of us had assembled round the table, rose to his feet and said that if we were going to do it all properly, we ought to choose a Tamada before beginning the meal. Erika asked, "What's that?" Julia explained it was the name for a master of ceremonies, whose job it was to see that the banquet went with a swing. Erika liked the idea, and Ninoshvili said, "Let me suggest Christian for the office of Tamada."

I said I wasn't qualified for that honour, but I thought Ralf would be good in the part. He'd make sure the dishes were brought in briskly. Ralf said, "David can do that himself," and emptied his second glass of the beer he had preferred to the Kakheti wine. Julia and Erika agreed that the post of Tamada called for a connoisseur, and also suggested

Ninoshvili. Finding that he had a majority of three votes, from Ralf, Julia and Erika, he accepted.

He proposed the first toast to the Federal Republic of Germany and the hospitality of the Germans, a nation that had always been particularly close to Georgia. "Let us empty our glasses to that!" I drained my own, and everyone else did the same. I was wondering how soon Ralf would be under the table.

After the Tamada, with Julia's help, had served up the cheese flatbreads, he asked me to open the banquet proper with a word of welcome. I rose and said that, as the Tamada had already rightly remarked, international friendship between Georgia and Germany could look back on a long tradition. Let us, I said, gratefully remember some of the founders of that friendship, such as Herr von Bodenstedt, who appreciated the beauty of the Georgian people; Herr Radde, the discoverer of *Iris caucasica*; and Herr Haeckel, who observed the fauna of Georgia very attentively, and even counted the population of the Caucasian *Cimex lectularius*. Let us empty our glasses to those pioneers of our joint culture, I said.

Erika, having drained her glass and held it out for a refill, asked, "What's *Cimex* thingummy?" I cut a piece off my flatbread and said, "The bedbug." Erika burst out laughing. Ninoshvili gave a thin smile.

When it came to Julia's turn, she proposed a toast to Georgian literature and to David, the writer who would also help it to make its breakthrough in Germany. After the soup, the Tamada asked our friend from East Germany, now reunited with the West at last, to speak next. Erika, giggling, stood up, collected her wits with some difficulty, and said, "Right. I'm afraid I can't speak as well as the rest of you, but I think this meal is really fantastic. So now let's drink to David Dzhugashvili, master chef. Long live David!"

Ralf was already on his third beer when his turn came to propose a toast. I hoped he'd say, "Kiss my arse," or at least just grunt something surly. But he got to his feet, began swaying slightly, reached for the edge of the table, and looked all around, smiling, his eyes swimming. Then he said abruptly, "Cheers!" and emptied his glass.

As the Kakheti wine was running out, I went down to the cellar and brought up a basketful of fresh supplies, choosing a Riesling from a winegrower in St Goarshausen from whom I had bought an inexpensive selection. This gave me a chance to bring the river visited by Julia and Ninoshvili on their way back from Frankfurt into the toasts.

When the Riesling had been poured, I asked the Tamada for permission to propose a toast, and he gave it. Rising to my feet, I said that Rhine wines were known to be the best Germany had to offer. However, since time immemorial every foreigner would have been well advised to tread with great care in the valley of Germany's great river and its vine-grown ravines, as mentioned in a classic German poem, which runs:

The ancient Romans in their day
Sampled the valley and its wine.
But when with girls they'd sport and play
They had to leave the river Rhine.
The German warriors threw them out.
It was an ancient Roman rout.

Erika laughed out loud, raised her glass and emptied it. Julia drank a sip and then asked, frowning, her voice slurred, "And who's supposed to have written that?" I replied, "Oh, some German poet or other. I've forgotten the name. Stupid of me." Ninoshvili smiled.

147

If I counted the bottles correctly, then we must have put back four more in the course of the banquet. Ralf left half his fifth bottle of beer. After he had eaten almost a whole chicken, gnawed the bones, and mopped up the very last of the walnut sauce, he got to his feet and said, "Night, all." On his way to the door he began staggering and had to brace his legs. Ninoshvili jumped up and took his arm. Ralf brushed the hand away.

I stood up and supported my son under the arms. He let me lead him out, and on the stairs I put his arm over my shoulder and hauled him up to the top floor, as heavy and clumsy to handle as a sack of flour. I got him over to his bed, he dropped onto it, and I took his trainers off. By the time I put out the light and closed the door, he was already asleep. Climbing down, I nearly missed a step myself.

Meanwhile Ninoshvili had opened another bottle. Julia said, "Ninoshvadze, if you're going to propose another toast I'll fall off my chair. Thump!" She began to giggle. Erika burst into shrill laughter. Ninoshvili, who as I noticed, with some resentment, seemed to be feeling no ill effects, raised his forefinger and wagged it at Julia. "Oh no, oh no! We can't part like this, my dear friend!" He refilled the glasses. "We haven't drunk our last toast yet. And with that last toast, as Georgian custom demands, we will honour the master of the house."

Julia said, "Oh, all right, but that will be the end of it. Who's going to make the speech? Shall I…" She tried to stand up, but Ninoshvili took her shoulder and pressed her gently back into her chair. "No, no! The Tamada himself has to do that." He rose and looked at the ceiling. Then he looked at me.

He said it was a pity that Ralf had already left, so that he couldn't see due honour paid to his father, Christian Kestner, the master of this hospitable house. Kestner was a great, a famous name, borne in the past by a friend of Goethe, Johann Georg Christian Kestner, secretary at the Imperial Supreme Court, who features under the name of Albert in *The Sorrows of Young Werther*. Who was Albert, who was Kestner? Why, the master of a household where hospitality reigned supreme; an upright man, who unhesitatingly asked his friend to stay with him and his wife Charlotte. Albert could not have known that his friend would fall in love with Charlotte, but he did all he could to prevent the terrible end of the novel – the death of young Werther by his own hand – although, alas, in vain. And so it was that they had to bury Werther.

The Tamada looked around. Erika was listening to him as if spellbound. Julia had propped her chin on her hand and half-closed her eyes. The Tamada said, "They buried him at night, around eleven o'clock. Tradesmen carried his coffin. No priest accompanied him to his grave." He raised his glass. "But let us not be sad. Let us empty our glasses to an immortal work of literature. To men like Albert and Christian Kestner. And at the same time let us empty them to the master of this house, my friend. Long may he live!"

"Cheers!" said my wife, and she reached for her glass.

38

Julia is already asleep. I got up once more, went into my study and found *Werther* on the bookshelf. Yes, of course, he was quoting the end word for word. *Tradesmen carried his coffin. No priest accompanied him to his grave.*

There was a bookmark in the middle of the book, and as far as I remembered it wasn't one of mine. I opened the novel at the marked page and found the passage in which Werther,

149

before Albert's eyes and as if playfully, puts the muzzle of his pistol to his forehead above his right eye and then, when the horrified Albert knocks the pistol away, defends suicide against Albert's stern condemnation of it as a sinful crime.

It is true that theft is a sin, but does the man who robs to preserve himself and those close to him from imminent death by starvation deserve pity or punishment? Who will cast the first stone at a husband who, in righteous anger, sacrifices his unfaithful wife and her worthless seducer?

He has been poking around in my books and taken *Werther* off the shelf. He has understood my message, oh yes, and he is striking back. He left the bookmark in place so that I would find his own riposte. And it certainly doesn't mean that he is afraid I might kill him. It means that *I* ought to be afraid.

39

I got up at around eight on Sunday morning. Julia was asleep, buried in her pillows. I showered and dressed, carefully went downstairs and into the kitchen, where the crockery from the banquet was still stacked. I heard Erika snoring in the living room. I poured some coffee and laid myself a place at the dining table. As I sat down, Ralf looked in at the door, still unkempt and in his pyjamas.

"What did you get up for?" I asked.

"I set my alarm. Where's Julia, then?"

"Still asleep."

"Didn't she say when she'd be getting up?"

"No."

He shook his head. "What do you want her for?" I asked.

"She and David were going to take me to Schwitte."

"What, so early in the day?"

"Yeah, of course. I mean, we're playing the first round this afternoon."

I drank a little coffee, put down my cup and looked at him. "I'll take you there if you like."

He scratched his chest and then said, "Yeah, okay. I'd rather that anyway. Goodness knows when those two will be up."

I felt better than I had in a long time. While Ralf was showering I laid him a place at the table, looked in the fridge for the chocolate spread – he still loves it as much as a five-year-old – and cut some bread. He didn't turn down the scrambled egg I offered him either, but tucked in as if he had had nothing to eat for days.

When he had finished, and went up to the top floor to fetch his backpack, I looked in on Julia. I shook her gently by the shoulder. She turned on her back, opened her eyes and clutched her forehead. "Oh God!" Her face twisted. "My head is splitting!"

I asked if she was happy for me to take Ralf to his chess tournament. She asked, "What's the time?"

"Nearly nine."

She thought for a moment and then smiled at me. "Oh, that would be really kind. I'm still knocked right out."

"I'm not surprised. You just rest."

"Where's David?"

"No idea. I expect he's still asleep."

Ralf didn't talk much on the drive, and I avoided coming too close to him by trying to strike up a conversation. When we came to the motorway he leaned back in the passenger seat, grunted contentedly, and closed his eyes.

At some point, without opening them, he asked, "Have you remembered who the poet was?"

151

"What poet?"

"The one with the verse about the ancient Roman rout."

"Er... no." After a while I told him, "Actually I made it up myself, thought of it when I was down in the cellar."

He laughed. I added, "I meant it ironically. And I was rather tipsy as well."

"Sure. Me too."

Schwitte-Minnenbüren lies among tree-grown hills in the valley of a winding little river, the Laaxe. As you drive in, you pass the extensive premises of the company that acts as patron of the chess club, Friedrich Hünten Furnishings Ltd. Herr Hünten also runs a direct-sales outlet adorned with coloured flags: a huge warehouse with a car park at one side of the street, and a board on its roof bearing the inscription *Buy Now, Pay Later, Big Savings!*

The town centre, as I thought it must be because there was a fountain in the middle of it, was deserted. Presumably the housewives served up Sunday lunch at twelve on the dot. I asked two characters of Mediterranean appearance who were standing outside an Italian ice-cream parlour whether they knew where the chess tournament for young people was being held. They looked at each other, then one said, "Youth hostel. You drive youth hostel." The other nodded. I asked where the youth hostel was. The second man said, "Go on along street. Then right by river."

Behind me, a man with two boys craning their necks on the back seat had stopped. He called out of the window, "Are you going to the Youth Open too?" I wasn't sure whether the Youth Open was the same as my own destination, but I didn't want to reveal my ignorance, and called back, "Just follow me."

I found the youth hostel, an immaculate whitewashed clinker-built wooden structure, on the banks of the Laaxe.

Ralf's application had been registered, the hostel warden, a sturdy woman in her forties wearing an overall, said, "Room Three, please lock the door after you again and hand in the key. To get to the tournament you want to go to the comprehensive school, that's back to Schwitte and take the second turning right."

There were four bunk beds in the bedroom. Ralf said, "Can't wait to see what kind of guys I'm hanging out with here." He put his backpack into a free locker. The two boys came storming in, one flung himself on a bed, the other climbed the ladder to the bed above it. The hostel warden appeared in the doorway and said, "Out of here. I told you, Room Two, can't you read numbers?" And the two boys stormed out again. "Well, there you are," I said.

The tournament tables were set up in the school's sports hall. A good two dozen chessboards stood at the long rows of tables, with the chessmen standing on them, the time clocks and notation forms beside them. There was an ear-splitting din in the hall; a good third of the participants were no older than fourteen and acted accordingly. Ralf made his way through the pushing, shoving crowd in front of the tournament manager's table. As he had shown no inclination to say goodbye, I waited.

When he came back with his starting number, I asked if it was all right with him for me to stay a little longer and take a look at one or two of the games. He said, "Sure. If you have time." Then he saw a boy who went to his school and was in the year above him. I left the two of them together and wandered out.

In the room outside the hall I found the Youth Open Tournament advertised on a board with other posters, as well as a Rapidplay Tournament to be held next weekend (first prize 5,000 marks), presentation to the winner of that

153

tournament and the Youth Open (first prize 400 marks) on the same occasion. The Youth Open poster also gave the names of two Russians (both described as GM, presumably "Grandmasters") whose coaching services for training promising young players could be won.

Over loudspeakers from the sports hall I heard the tournament manager delivering a speech on behalf of Herr Friedrich Hünten, who had generously made this tournament possible, but unfortunately was unable to come this afternoon, and so on and so forth. The speech ended with the words, "And now for a fair and sporting competition! The boards are open!" All was quiet in the hall. I went back and looked for Ralf. I found him at a corner table opposite a boy of ten or eleven, who could only just get a proper view of his pieces.

Ralf had chosen an opening that I didn't know. His opponent obviously did. He examined the board as soon as Ralf had made a move, never needing more than half a minute, made his own move, pressed the clock and, pressing his pencil hard entered Ralf's move and his own on the notation form in round letters. Then he put the pencil down and studied Ralf's face. He twice subjected me too to a thorough and silent examination, from my eyes down to my shoes. Another time he leaned back in his chair, put his head back and looked at the ceiling of the sports hall as if inspecting the framework of the roof structure for weak spots.

From the tenth move on I began to fear for Ralf. The child, his thin fingers moving fast, snapped up one of his pawns from the centre of the formation and set about moving into its position. I thought I sensed Ralf getting nervous; he rubbed his hands together under the table, took out his handkerchief and blew his nose. I strolled on. The child craned his neck and looked over his shoulder at me.

154

I lingered for a while beside a board where a well-developed girl of about sixteen was trying to defend her pieces against a boy with thin black down on his upper lip who was trying to checkmate her. The girl shielded her eyes and her flushed face with both hands, kept only her toes on the floor, and was constantly shifting back and forth on her thighs. The boy suffered from acne, and had a severe tic of his left eyelid that came over him now and then at very short intervals. He sometimes opened his mouth and moved his lower jaw as if to make certain that the bones were still properly jointed.

I liked Ralf's opponent better than this twitching youth, who very likely, however strong his game might be, did not have a better grasp of chess than the girl rocking back and forth. All the same, I didn't want to see my almost grown-up son humiliated by a provocatively self-possessed child. For all I cared the younger boy could win his games in all the following rounds, just not this first one.

When I steeled myself to return to Ralf's board after a good half an hour, he had one more chessman left than the child, and was in the process of driving the black king into the middle of the board. The child must have made a fatal mistake. I waited for him to start crying, which I wouldn't have wanted either, because he really was a nice kid. But after a couple more moves, in which his situation became even worse, he suddenly turned off the clock, offered Ralf his hand, and wrote on his notation form "resigned" in round letters. He stood up, put the form in his pocket, said, "So long," and walked away.

I congratulated Ralf. He nodded a little awkwardly and said, "That little kid really wasn't bad." I said I could see that, and asked if he'd like to have a cup of coffee with me. He hesitated, then said he'd have to let the tournament management know the result of the game, and after that he wanted to have a look around and see how the other boy from his school was doing. I said goodbye, wishing him luck. He gave me his hand and smiled. "Well, we'll see. I'm not knocked out of my first tournament just yet."

When I got home I found no one in. Julia had left me a note on the desk, saying that she and Erika and David had gone into town to see a film, and then they were going to get something for supper from Felipe's. I could follow them if I liked. I didn't like.

40

I wonder how Ralf is doing in Schwitte-Minnenbüren. He'll have the first coaching session from Mr Tretyakov or Molotov or Ustinov – or whatever those eminent experts are called – behind him by now. Perhaps he is still sitting in the dining room of the youth hostel at the moment, eating the vanilla pudding with raspberry sauce donated by Herr Friedrich Hünten as dessert after the first course of a casserole, cuffing a small chess genius who jostled him in passing and then got stuck at his table, and thinking a little nervously of the second round, which begins in an hour's time, and the opponent he may be facing in it.

I once felt very much at my ease in a place like Schwitte-Minnenbüren, admittedly when I was a child, and not staying in a youth hostel, nor was there any factory or even a comprehensive school around. I used to stay with my uncle and aunt in the holidays, sleeping in a huge bed with turned, highly polished bedposts which shone in the glow from the street lights by night, and gave me the comfortable feeling that I was resting in an impregnable fortress. I didn't notice it if the main street emptied at twelve sharp every morning, not just on Sundays, for at that time of day I was sitting down to the table myself and letting my aunt fill my plate.

In the morning I would go out to the woods in sunny weather with the friends I had easily made locally. We crossed the tracks of the branch railway that ran along the slope, and when a train was coming laboriously up from the valley we played chicken, seeing who would be the last to dare to jump over the sleepers in front of the engine. The engine driver would ring his bell furiously, the shrill steam whistle blew, he leaned out of his window and shook his clenched fist at us as he drove by – "You louts, you want a good hiding, you do!"

There was a little river much like the Laaxe there as well. We took our shoes and socks off and picked our way over the slippery stones, trying to catch the tiny fish that shot through the splashing water in our hands. We were more successful looking for blackberries. Sometimes we agreed that we would all bring a container from home, and my aunt gave me the enamel water scoop that hung over the sink. We used to climb up into the woods, intending to come home with our harvest. But once the containers were half full we stopped picking, sat down at the top of the slope, looked down at the church tower and the rooftops, and devoured all the berries we had gathered.

I never had such a sense of happiness again. When I have found myself in the Schwitte-Minnenbürens of this world now and then later, they have usually depressed me. I've seen to it that I get back home to the city as quickly as possible. I have felt lonely and abandoned in their quiet, empty streets, amidst the tree-grown slopes, under the wide sky: exposed in a strange, indeed a hostile world.

It is easy to explain the contradiction. It's nothing to do with the place itself, or the difference between staying somewhere abroad or in familiar surroundings. We can feel just as lonely

157

at home as abroad if there are no friends around, people with whom we feel a bond, and who let us see that they feel a bond with us in return. I hope Ralf will be spared this experience in Schwitte-Minnenbüren. I hope he'll find a friend as well as opponents there.

Julia is off on another trip with Ninoshvili tomorrow. She has a date with her client in Frankfurt in the afternoon, and at the same time Ninoshvili is going to see one of the publishing houses he visited last week again. They'll come home in the evening.

41

Dr Lawrenz has written me a letter. Dr Lawrenz, a medical doctor who runs a flourishing gynaecological practice and is much in demand for treating outpatients, is chairman of the section of the Parents' Association responsible for the welfare of my drama group.

It has come to his attention, the gynaecologist writes, that I have been making enquiries among the students in the group to discover which unknown person damaged a stage set for a play. He would have expected me, he says, at least to inform the Parents' Association before embarking on an investigation of this kind. However, as I obviously did not think that necessary, he finds himself obliged to insist on a meeting of the Association immediately after half-term.

Dr Lawrenz is a bastard, and I ought to have expected that he wouldn't let this opportunity to puff up his own importance pass. His own brainless son doesn't belong to the drama group, but even that lad's dull mind will have grasped what it was all about. I just hope that Trabert, whom I have informed about Manni Wallmeroth's visit to me – I told Elke Lampert as well – hasn't yet spread the story of his confession.

I wanted a reason to leave the house before Julia came home from the courthouse to pick up our guest and drive to Frankfurt, so I phoned Elke. I told her about the outrageous letter that that stuffed shirt had sent me – he once muscled in on her territory as well, making a complaint to the principal – and asked whether she felt like talking to me again about Manni and his swastika, if she had the time. She said I could come to her house; she'd just been idling around since early morning.

I looked in at our living room. Ninoshvili was sitting in a chair reading the paper. Erika had slept a little later than he had; I found her at the dining table eating her diet breakfast: low-fat curd cheese, crispbread and a hardboiled egg. I said I had to go and see a colleague. Ninoshvili called, "Are you off for the rest of this morning, Christian? I wanted to show you the publisher's catalogue." I said I was sorry, I didn't have time now, but I hoped he would have a good journey and do a successful deal. Erika glanced at me over the rim of her teacup.

My conversation with Elke signally failed to cheer me up. She came to the door in a baggy pullover, slippers trodden down at the heels on her bare feet, her hair untidy and her face only perfunctorily made up. She was obviously feeling depressed, and I immediately suspected that her husband had come home late yet again, claiming that one of the pill-rolling machines was out of order and urgently needed servicing. But I did not ask about her husband. I didn't feel up to having Elke unload her troubles on me in addition to the rest of it.

She got her own back, though certainly not with any malicious intent, poor thing, by saying she saw major problems ahead for me. She read the gynaecologist's letter, folded it up again carefully, nodded and said, "He'll have the whole Parents' Association up in arms against you. He did that with me. They'll blame you for being too hard on the poor children. And the stupid thing is that they'll be right."

"You said that before. Do you really think so?"

"Yes, I do, even if you don't like to hear it."

"Well, at least my methods persuaded Manni to come and see me."

"So they did. And now what?" She said that Dr Lawrenz, like Brauckmann and one or two other staff members whose names she didn't need to tell me, probably thought the slogan and the swastika no more than thoughtless, stupid conduct, a silly prank. They would certainly go on the warpath if I insisted on Manni Wallmeroth's exclusion from the school. Not because they particularly liked him, but they liked me and my principles even less. Yes, yes, my chances were certainly better than she would have expected because that silly boy Manni had already booked himself a place in the firing line. But how would I feel if he really was excluded this time?

I said nothing. She leaned forwards and poured me some coffee. "You don't really want that."

"Who says I'm going to insist on his exclusion?"

She laughed and threw her head back. "Well, that would be a new departure! A man admitting he's gone too far!" She looked at me. "Do you really think so? You'd have to take back everything you said at the staff meeting. A misdeed that must be sternly punished, because otherwise all the dams would be broken. Don't you remember? You'd have to climb off your high horse. You'd have to admit to minding more about a boy like Manni Wallmeroth than about your principles. Do you really think you could do it?"

160

I said, "So now you're trying to make it all into some kind of masculine failing? I don't think that's appropriate. In fact to be honest I think it's idiotic. Why couldn't a woman act in the same way? What's it got to do with sticking to one's principles? And why wouldn't a man be able to admit that he'd gone too far?"

All of a sudden she began to cry. She fished a handkerchief out of the baggy pullover, pressed it to her eyes and cried quietly. I said, "I'm sorry, I didn't mean to speak roughly." She didn't answer. After a while I moved closer to her on the sofa, put an arm around her shoulders and shook her gently. "What's the matter, Elke?"

It all came pouring out, just as I'd feared. She had caught her husband again, this time in the front seat of the car with his flies open, and with the same lady as before leaning over him. He explained to Elke that the woman wouldn't accept his letter dumping her, she had given him no peace, threatening to kill herself unless he agreed to meet and talk one last time in the car park, and once there she positively attacked him.

I tried to comfort Elke, but my efforts were even less wholehearted than the first time. I was tired of having to find psychological reasons for Herr Lampert's quirky sexual habits. So we fell into mutual silence. She kept sniffing, I gently shook her shoulders now and then. I stopped when she suddenly raised her head and looked at me with a sad smile. "Christian, you don't know how lucky you are."

I walked through the city for a time before going home. When I had closed the front door behind me I stood there for a moment, and called, "Hello?" Erika's voice answered, from the living room. "Hello, Christian! I'm in here!" She was in an armchair with an open book on her lap. It was the first time I'd ever seen her reading a book.

"Weren't you going to go with the other two?" I asked.

"No, what makes you think that?" She smiled, raised her fingertips to her head and patted her hairstyle into shape. "Why would I want to go to Frankfurt?" After a brief pause, she added, "And anyway, I'm not necessarily hell-bent on enjoying the company of Herr Dzhugashvili."

"Ninoshvili."

"What did I say, then?"

"Dzhugashvili." I sat down with her. "That was Stalin."

She laughed and shook her head. "You can see how much we learned at school! The good old German Democratic Republic doesn't take its claws out of you in a hurry!"

"How long have they been gone?" I asked.

She looked at the time. "About an hour."

I stood up. "Have you had any lunch yet?"

"For Heaven's sake, that's the last thing I need! I put on two kilos at the weekend, and one of them's still with me, isn't that obvious?"

"I don't see anything."

She stood up, looked down at herself, passed her hands over her hips and looked at me.

"You're fishing for compliments." I got up and went into the kitchen, found myself some curd cheese in the fridge. She appeared in the kitchen doorway, leaning against the doorpost. "Oh, and David Thingy had another phone call this morning, from Darmstadt. From a publisher there. Does that sound likely?"

"Yes, it does. And what did the publisher want?"

She put a hand to her hair and tidied a curl into place. "They wanted him to go and talk to them about something tomorrow morning, something or other important. A contract, could that be right? Anyway, they were very keen on speaking to him tomorrow morning."

She stopped, and I stared at her. She said, "Julia's going to take him on there from Frankfurt. She said she doesn't have to be in court tomorrow." After a moment she added, "They're planning to spend the night in Frankfurt or Darmstadt. Julia thinks they'll be back here around midday tomorrow."

I walked past her with my curd cheese, sat down in a comfortable chair in the living room and spooned it up. She followed me, picked up the book from her own chair, sat down beside me and looked at the book. "Julia's going to call as soon as she knows which hotel they're staying in."

After a while, during which time she leafed through the book, she looked at me and smiled. "Do you know what? I feel like a little cognac. Will you drink one with me?"

"No, thanks, not my time of day for it." I rose to my feet, poured a cognac and handed it to her. She raised the glass and smiled at me. "To your good health, Christian! To your very good health!"

42

I went to bed with Erika. I can at least say in my own defence that her perfume washes off in a bath, and once she'd had one she was no longer enveloped in a cloud of the stuff.

After she had given me Julia's message, I stayed sitting with her for some time in the living room, trying to make conversation. When she mentioned David Thingy again and began telling me why she doesn't particularly like him, I stood up and said please would she excuse me, I had some work to do. She nodded, said she hadn't wanted to hold me up, and opened her book. I went to my study, closed the door behind me, and covered a sheet of paper with matchstick men, carefully moving from line to line.

Some time later I heard her going upstairs to the top floor. I listened. Ten or fifteen minutes later she came downstairs again. I felt a sudden fear that she could be going out, leaving me on my own. I opened the door and smiled at her. She stopped in front of me.

I asked, before I could think better of it, "Why don't the two of us go out this evening? What do you say?"

"Well, my word!" She began to laugh. "That would be quite something! Oh yes, that would be fantastic!"

I asked what she felt like – a film, the theatre, maybe the opera if there were still tickets available. She said I knew she was an opera buff. I looked up the programme, and there was no opera this evening but a ballet performance instead, *The Firebird*. That would be even better, she cried, fantastic! I called the booking office and got two tickets, for the most expensive seats, as I correctly assumed from the price, but it was worth it to me. Erika kissed me firmly on both cheeks.

She said I must go on with my work, and went down to the living room. I drew the next row of matchstick men. Half an hour later there was a knock at the study door, and I hastily reached for the notes on my series of lessons about Georgia and covered up the matchstick men. Erika put her head round the door. She didn't want to disturb me, she said, but she'd like to know what time we would have to leave. I said the performance began at seven, but maybe we should get something light to eat in town before it, or my stomach might start grumbling too loudly. She laughed. I asked if five would be all right for her. Of course it was, she said, and closed the door.

A quarter of an hour later there was another knock. "Come in!" I called, and looked up from the book I had been reading without taking in two lines running. She came in, stood beside the desk and smiled rather uncertainly, as if she had an embarrassing little confession to make. She said, "Christian, could I ask you an outrageous question…?"

"Fire away."

"Could I maybe, just for once, use your bathroom?" She laughed and shook her head. "I don't know if you'll understand this, but I'd really love a bath. I'd like to wallow in the tub for a change and then have plenty of room to get ready."

"Not an outrageous question at all." I stood up, opened the bathroom door and looked in. I pointed to the wall cupboard. "You'll find towels and flannels in there, and there's a bottle of bath foam. If you need anything else, just let me know."

She kissed me on both cheeks. I asked. "Could you do me a great favour?"

"Of course. What is it?"

"If you don't mind too much… could you not put your perfume on again after you've had your bath?"

She looked at me, wide-eyed. Then she asked, "Don't you like it?"

"Not particularly."

"Oh, why did you never say so?"

"I've never spent a whole evening sitting next to you in the opera house either."

She laughed and lightly prodded my chest. "What a funny one you are! But you really don't have to be so shy!"

After her bath she knocked again and took a step inside the room. She was wearing a short pink dressing gown and white slippers. "The bathroom's empty."

"Thanks."

She looked down at her breasts, and pulled the dressing gown together slightly. "I was just thinking…" She looked at me. "How can we leave before Julia calls? I'm sure you'll want to know where she's staying."

"I'll hear that soon enough. She can leave a message on the answering machine."

She nodded, smiled, and went out.

In the foyer of the opera house we met Tassilo Huber, who was wearing anthracite-coloured jeans, a dark-green velvet jacket and a black velvet ribbon instead of a tie. He was accompanied by a small woman in an ankle-length grey dress. "How's your son doing?" he asked. I said he was fine, he was spending the holiday at a chess tournament.

"Really? Well, that's good to hear." Tassilo cast a glance at Erika and combed his beard with his fingers. Then he said, "If you can spare the time, I'd be glad if you could look in on me again some day. I have a lot of new material that would interest you."

I said I'd come as soon as I had time, and offered him my hand. He asked, "And what's all this business at your school? I happened to hear about it by chance."

I told him we had everything under control, it wasn't worth mentioning.

When we had gone to our seats, Erika asked who that character was. I said, "A spy. But undercover, you understand, a secret agent. On the surface he seems to be a local politician." Erika looked at me, her jaw dropping, and then she said, "Oh, come on, you're trying to pull my leg!" I laughed and patted her plump hand.

When Kashchei the enchanter leaped out of the wings to the sound of a sudden clash of cymbals, performing demonic contortions, her left hand suddenly reached for mine. She placed her right hand on her bare throat, smiled, and whispered, "Oh, I was so frightened!" She held my hand tight. I thought of the enchanter Klingsor and King Ibert castrating him with his sharp knife.

After a while, when Erika pressed my hand slightly now and then, I withdrew it and acted as if I needed it to mop my forehead with my handkerchief. But once it was back on the arm of my seat, Erika used the next clash of cymbals to close her plump fingers around it once more.

I got used to it. Contact with her warm skin was not unpleasant. I even liked it when Erika, eyes closed as she listened to the lullaby, moved two fingers in a caress.

When we were home she said she could do with a nightcap. I opened the bottle of champagne that Julia had brought back from her latest shopping trip with Ninoshvili and put in the fridge in case it was needed. Erika raised her glass to me. "Thank you, Christian! That was a fantastic evening."

After the first glass of champagne I went into the living room and turned the answering machine on. Ralf's voice, sounding aggrieved, came over the loudspeaker. "For Heaven's sake, where are you all? This is the second time I've tried, and the chit-chat machine was on then too. Listen, I want Julia to send me two pairs of socks. I forgot to pack any. Bye. Oh, and if you call back this evening there's no point. I'm going out into town now with a couple of guys, there's a disco, not up to much, but better than sitting around here. And I won in the second round, but I lost in the third to a player in the regional league. Bye again, then."

Meanwhile Erika had appeared in the living-room doorway, carrying her glass. She laughed. I smiled at her, shaking my head. "That's Ralf all over."

The answering machine beeped, and on came Julia's voice. "Hello, Christian, it's me. It's a bit late now because we drove on to Darmstadt this evening. Everywhere was fully booked in Frankfurt, a fair of some kind. We're staying in the Hotel Hessia." She gave me the phone number and her room number. Then she said, "I think we'll be home early in the afternoon. David's appointment is at ten, and we hope it won't take too long. My love to Erika." And then, after a

167

brief pause, she added, "I'll be glad to see you. Goodnight, Christian."

I turned off the answering machine. Erika said, "That was a nice phone call." I went up to her, and she stepped to one side, leaving the way to the door clear. I stayed where I was, smiling. "Yes, I think so too. And at least it'll be just us here until tomorrow afternoon."

She sipped from her glass and looked at me in silence. I took her in my arms and kissed her. Holding her hand with the glass out to one side, she responded to the kiss as if she were parched. Then she put her head back and laughed. "Just a moment! If that's how it is, I want some too!" She put her glass down on the table, came back and flung both arms around me, holding me close.

We took the rest of the bottle and the glasses up with us. We had some difficulty getting up the stairs, closely entwined and kissing. I missed her mouth and got her nose between my lips. We almost fell downstairs backwards. I slept with her in Ralf's bed.

43

I got up at seven thirty, picked up my clothes from the floor and went quietly out. As I was closing the door Erika made a slight sound. I looked back. She half-opened her eyes and smiled at me.

When I had showered and made breakfast I called the Hotel Hessia. A man answered. "I'll put you through." After a while he came back on the line and said there was no answer from Dr Kestner's room, and he would get someone to look for her in the breakfast room. It was a long time before he spoke again, saying he was afraid

Dr Kestner was not in the breakfast room either. I asked if she might already have left. The man replied, "No, no, she hasn't checked out yet." He asked if I had a message for Dr Kestner. I said no thank you, that wouldn't be necessary, and hung up.

I went up to the top floor. I could hear water splashing in the shower on the other side of the door, and knocked. Erika called, "Just coming!" She opened the door, naked and steaming, a shower cap on her hair, glittering rivulets of water running down over her breasts, stomach and legs. She smiled at me. I said, "Sorry, I just wanted to say I'm going into your room for a moment. I mean Ralf's room. I want to find his socks. I'll have to take them to the post straight after breakfast or they'll be no use to him."

"Nothing to be sorry for." She pursed her lips, craned her head forwards and gave me a wet kiss.

When I had packed up the little parcel, she came down to breakfast in her pink dressing gown. "You don't mind if I enjoy just being alone with you a little longer?" She ate her egg with obvious enjoyment. "I ought not to, but it's so nice to have you spoiling me. I'm not used to this kind of thing." Then she stopped short, put her egg spoon down and looked at me. "Do you have a guilty conscience?"

"Do *you*?"

She looked at her plate. "Well, you see… I've always had a soft spot for you. Maybe you never noticed. I always managed to control myself."

"So why not this time?"

She finished her egg and drank some tea. Then she said, "Maybe it's no excuse, but I don't approve of what Julia has done. It looked to me like something rigged up in advance. As if she wanted to throw you and me together."

"How do you mean?"

She looked at me. "Yesterday morning she's still saying she'll be out for only a few hours. Then she comes back and fetches that man, sees you're not at home, and what does she do? Takes him into her study and talks to him with the door closed. And then she comes to me and says they'll both be staying out overnight. Leaving me on my own to tell you, saying she knows I'd do it well, I'm good at that sort of thing."

"Is that how she put it?"

She nodded. "Roughly speaking. I thought, well, who'd have thought it! And before I could say anything she and that man had gone off."

I said, "But she didn't know, first thing yesterday, that Ninoshvili had to go to Darmstadt. The publisher didn't ring until later in the morning, you said. Or do I have that wrong?"

"No. At least, that's what he told me." She put her head slightly on one side, raised her eyebrows and looked meaningfully at me. "But do you think it was true?"

She reached for a slice of bread, examined the cold meats I'd put out. "Heaven knows who called. Why does he tell me about it anyway? I answered the phone and called him to the phone, but I didn't ask him who the caller was. I didn't catch the name, but it was none of my business. And I wasn't interested anyway."

She drank some tea, put the cup down sharply and shook her head. "No, no, I don't trust the man. I didn't trust him from the start."

"Why not?"

She carefully covered her bread with ham. "You know... we had experience of that sort of thing in the good old German Democratic Republic." And she began telling me about visitors from the friendly Soviet Union, painting them in dark colours. Friendly, she said, what a joke, none of those visitors, not a single one, had been straight, they'd all had some ulterior motive. "Otherwise do you think they'd have had permits to travel at all?" They had all been informers. And people had deliberately kept clear of the German comrades who were their drinking companions too. "They were all in league, the Stasi and the KGB, they fixed their crooked deals together, everyone knew that."

She cut up her bread and ham. I picked up my napkin and wiped my hands on it. "You don't seriously believe Ninoshvili is something to do with the KGB, do you? He comes from Georgia. The Georgians never had much time for the Russians."

She laughed. "You think not? My dear, Georgia belonged to the Soviet Union, you know it did. And you can bet the KGB made itself at home there just as it did in my own lousy country." She leaned over the table. "Who else would have paid for Herr Ninoshvili's trip? They have even less money in Georgia than in Russia!" She shook her head vigorously. "No, no, I probably have a better nose for these things than you. You want to be careful with that man, Christian."

I needed some time before I asked, "What do you mean?"

There was a long pause. Then she said, without looking at me, "Back at the time when Julia disappeared and went over to the West I was rather surprised. She was really doing very well in Halle. Never got into trouble, was allowed to study too. I mean, she had no real reason to clear out of the Republic. Not like many who didn't want to play along and were always being harassed for it. Including some people in our class."

I was feeling hot under the collar. "Never mind the hints. Can't you say what you mean straight out?"

She picked a couple of crumbs off her plate and then looked at me. "Do you remember that character we went out with in Halle, the tall, bony man?"

171

"Of course I do. Your boyfriend."

She shook her head. "I just said so to do Julia a favour. I didn't know him at all. Julia asked me whether I could bring him along that evening. She said she knew him from the old days and would like to see him again, but you were rather jealous. She gave me the phone number, so I called the man and then he picked me up, and we met you two."

She picked at some more crumbs. "He'd come to Halle from Leipzig specially. He was staying at a hotel in Halle."

I was sitting in my chair as if numbed. She stood up, came round the table and bent over me. "I'm not saying that Julia had anything to do with the Stasi. I'd never claim a thing like that. I'm just saying you want to keep an eye on her. And in particular on this Ninoshvili."

She drew my head towards her and pressed it to the warm curves at the neck of her dressing gown. I freed myself and stood up. "I have to go to the post, or Ralf will never get his package." She nodded and kissed me on the cheek.

"Don't be cross, Christian. But I had to say it, I think. It hurt me to think you were groping about in the dark. You've deserved better, you really have."

I went to the post office and sent Ralf his socks by express mail. I had put a note in with them. "Check, or whatever they say. Good luck, anyway." After I had left the post office I drove into the Katharinenforst. I walked in the woods for three hours, climbed the Mäuseberg, looked out over the city. The veil that had blurred the horizon last Sunday had disappeared. The distant roofs and towers were bathed in radiant sunlight.

Erika's taciturn boyfriend. The two of them had walked back to our hotel with us after we went to the wine bar. Julia had gone ahead with the boyfriend for a while, I followed with Erika. I found Erika heavy going, but Julia and the man were conducting a lively conversation, so far as I could tell from their gestures.

172

I came home from the Katharinenforst about one thirty. Julia and Ninoshvili had just arrived. Julia seemed a little breathless, she was about to go out again, wanted to go to her office, but Ninoshvili was in an excellent mood. He said the trip to Darmstadt had been really worthwhile. The conversation had gone very well, the publishing house would be sending him a contract soon, the managing director of the firm was already planning to publish one of the stories, 'The Woman with the Pomegranate', in an anthology. The book will be on the market in spring. He was deeply grateful to Julia, and of course to me as well, me above all, he knew Julia wouldn't take that the wrong way.

44

Four weeks ago a member of the City Council, a Social Democrat and by profession a business manager, was unmasked as a former agent of the GDR's Ministry of State Security. I looked at all the reports of the case in the old papers I store in the garage until it's worth driving to the recycling centre.

The man comes from Magdeburg. He left East Germany furtively twenty-six years ago, that is to say, he committed the crime of "flight from the Republic", as it was called. To the West German authorities, he made out that he was a victim of political persecution. In fact he told a credible-sounding story to the effect that flight was the only way he could escape arrest and condemnation for the criminal offence of running a seditious smear campaign.

Now it has emerged from the Gauck files, named after the head of the agency investigating the Stasi records after reunification, that his flight was all a hoax. The man had been recruited by the Stasi as a twenty-year-old student of the Socialist Business Management department at Rostock University, had taken a special training, and at a given moment in time was infiltrated through the Berlin Wall. He was what they call a sleeper agent: he was to work his way up to an influential position in the Federal Republic and be activated as a spy as soon as it was worthwhile.

Apparently that time never came. The man went on with his studies of business management at Göttingen University, and switching to the capitalist system gave him no problems; he took a good degree. Even as a student he joined the Social Democrats and rose in the party to deputy chairman of a sub-district, but that, apart from his election to the backbenches of the local parliament, was the peak of his career. Professionally, he rose no higher than the job of business manager of a retail and wholesale ironmongery supplier.

Whether he couldn't or didn't want to do better for himself does not emerge clearly from the newspaper reports. In any case, what he gave away, at least according to his own account of it, was unable to harm anyone, which doesn't surprise me, since the Stasi could hardly gain any very crucial insights from information about the activities of a sub-district in local government or the garden rollers sold in the Federal Republic. Nor was the man urged to produce results; his supervising officer got in touch with him now and then, but even these contacts gradually ceased. Maybe someone in the Ministry of State Security had filed his details in the wrong place.

When all this came out, the man had been peacefully settled in the West for many years, living in a terraced house with his wife and three children. He had, as he is said to have confirmed during his interrogation by the Deputy

Public Prosecutor, rejected the socialist system long before the reunification of Germany, and was convinced that the democratic system of our Federal Republic served mankind much better.

Among his colleagues in the wholesale ironmongery business, including the head of the firm, his brief arrest aroused incredulous astonishment. He was popular with everyone, down to the staff of the company's three retail shops, a hard-working but always open-minded manager who would lend an ear even to the troubles of trainees. His Social Democrat friends confirmed that he was not only industrious but also showed the kind of human solidarity seldom found in political life. Even his political opponents, as represented by Christian Democrat City Councillor Grünberg, respected him. As Grünberg explained on regional TV, this man had not transgressed the bounds of decent conduct even in an election, in which, said Grünberg, he was a shining exception among Social Democrats.

I saw the man on television myself; the camera team of a commercial broadcaster had been hunting him down, and trapped him when he left the Federal Prosecution Office building through a side entrance. His legal adviser put his hand in front of the camera lens, and was going to get the unfortunate sleeper agent out of the way, but the latter objected, saying, "No, no… I'd like to… I don't want to…" He straightened his shoulders and looked into the camera.

His face was flushed, his eyes lay deep in their sockets, his forehead was gleaming with sweat. He clutched the knot of his tie as the reporter, a woman in her mid-twenties with her hair cut extremely short, put her first question. The reporter, obviously unable to believe her luck, had to start it twice. She said, "Herr Reinhardt, have you…. How come

175

you're free, Herr Reinhardt?" She waved her canary-yellow microphone in front of her victim's lips.

The victim said, "The Federal Prosecutor has decided that in my case there is no danger that I'll run for it or suppress evidence."

"Does that mean you're innocent?"

"No." The victim cleared his throat and clutched the knot of his tie again. "As a young man I made a bad mistake, and I admit it freely. But I would also like to say that I have never harmed anyone. That was always my priority in all my actions. I have always taken care that everything I did was…"

The short-haired woman interrupted him. "But if someone is accused of such serious crimes as you are, isn't there a danger that he will evade the consequences by running for it after all?"

"No. Definitely not." The victim opened his mouth to say more on the subject, but the short-haired woman wasn't about to depart from the questions she had prepared in advance. She moved the microphone back to herself and babbled into it. "What did your wife say when you were unmasked? What do your children think?" and then pointed her weapon at her victim's lips again.

The victim said, "I would like to leave my wife out of…" His voice faltered and broke. The lawyer raised his hand. "That's enough!" Grabbing his client by the sleeve – and this time Reinhardt put up no resistance – he led him quickly to a black limousine waiting at the roadside. The camera, swaying, followed the two of them. The lawyer bundled his client into the back seat and climbed in after him. The limousine began moving. The merciless camera caught another glimpse of the spy. The victim's head was bent, and he was rubbing each eye with thumb and forefinger.

If someone hadn't come upon his dusty file, Herr Reinhardt could have grown old in peace and quiet and died a well-respected man. Perhaps not entirely in peace and quiet. The fear of being unmasked will have tormented him for years, will have woken him abruptly from sleep on many a night, while his wife slumbered beside him, his children on the floor above, and then I imagine Herr Reinhardt wiping the sweat from his brow and staring at the net curtain as it moves slightly in the light from the street lamps.

But if even this sleeper agent, in whom the Workers' and Peasants' Republic had invested a certain amount, was apparently forgotten by his employers, if even he could have survived the GDR but for someone nosing through the files and stumbling across him by chance – then why should a young woman, who certainly didn't go to the West in order to undermine capitalism, still be interesting to her employers and their ilk a quarter of a century later?

I don't know. But I for one would have done everything in my power to keep poor, amiable Herr Reinhardt, who was sweating with fear and whose voice broke when he was asked about his wife and children, from being unmasked. I would have tried to prevent him from being thrown to the vultures to be devoured, from having to let some brash, naive representative of the public interest hold a microphone in front of his lips.

And if I could summon up great understanding and heartfelt sympathy for Herr Reinhard, then how much more so for my wife. I don't know whether there is anything in Erika's suspicions, but if Julia really did make a foolish mistake in her youth, I shall do all I can to shield her from the repellent self-righteousness of this decent society of ours.

45

Herr Hochgeschurz called late in the afternoon. I was just wondering how I could question Julia without perhaps putting her under even more pressure, when the phone rang. The agent spoke in his slow voice. "Hochgeschurz here. Good day, Herr Kestner. How are you?"

My heart began hammering. The agent said he would have liked to speak to me again. Dr Schmidt was also interested in talking to me, he said, although of course he would suggest such a double appointment only if I agreed.

I asked what it was about. Herr Hochgeschurz said he didn't like to explain on the phone. The agent took a couple of breaths and then said it was nothing that should make me feel very uneasy, but the matter was rather urgent all the same. He also wanted to ask, on behalf of Dr Schmidt, if we might perhaps meet in the beer cellar of the Town Hall for a meal, or at a restaurant of my own choice. Of course I was also welcome to go to their office in the afternoon, if I preferred that to a meeting in public.

I said that unfortunately I was very short of time and didn't see any chance of such a meeting. "That's a great pity," said Herr Hochgeschurz. "But of course we don't want to inconvenience you." He breathed laboriously again, and then said, "Please reconsider it, Herr Kestner. What we wanted to discuss with you is something that you would find not uninteresting. If you do happen to change your mind, you can call me at any time. Did you keep my card? I think I wrote my private number on it, or I'd give it to you again for all contingencies."

I said that wasn't necessary, I had kept the card. Then I thanked him for calling and hung up.

I won't be able to allow myself much time for reflection any more. This agent is more active than his phlegmatic manner might suggest.

46

It wasn't the managing director of the publishing firm in Darmstadt, whatever one might imagine by that term, whom Ninoshvili saw, but the editor whose name Gerd Buttgereit had given me and to whom I had turned with the Georgian's literary offerings. At least, it turns out that he was the one who talked to Ninoshvili yesterday morning.

I called the editor, one Herr von Janowitz, on a pretext. I told him I wanted to tell Herr Ninoshvili I was offering to revise the German text of the story 'The Woman with the Pomegranate', and I'd like to know how much time I had to do it. Herr von Janowitz, who was suffering from either adenoids or a heavy cold, seemed rather surprised. He told me it was a very kind thought, but there was no particular hurry.

I said I hoped he would forgive my ignorance, presumably I'd had the wrong idea of a publishing firm's production deadlines. I'd assumed that the story had to be ready to go to press very soon if the anthology was being published in the spring. Herr von Janowitz said, "Yes, yes, but whether and when we put this volume together is still in the lap of the gods." I said I must have misunderstood then; I had thought that the contract he was going to send Herr Ninoshvili also mentioned a publication date.

Herr von Janowitz said, "We haven't yet reached the point of a contract. For now, we've only asked for an option to publish the story."

I wasn't particularly surprised. Ninoshvili is an accomplished liar, but then I knew that already.

Since it's impossible to say a word in our house these days without some guest barging in unexpectedly, I had to postpone any conversation with Julia until bedtime. Neither Ninoshvili nor Erika had let Julia's yawns disturb them, and they went to bed only when Julia nodded off on the sofa for the second time.

When we were in bed at last, luckily Julia picked up her book again. I opened my own book, so as to avoid any dramatic opening to this interrogation, but soon cut short the risk that she might fall asleep. After turning the first page, I said, still looking at the book, "You do realize that Ninoshvili is lying, don't you?"

She turned to me and looked at me in silence. I said if she was going to accuse me of spying on Ninoshvili again, very well, you could call it that, but unfortunately my suspicions had been confirmed. I told her what I had learned from Herr von Janowitz. "Empty words, that's all our friend David got out of those negotiations. Did you know?"

"No. He told me exactly what he told you." She lowered her book, lay on her back and closed her eyes. After a while she said, "It won't do much good for me to defend him. But at least I understand why he's lying." She sighed. "He's ashamed. He'd like to go straight home to his Matassi, but of course he has to bring results back to Tbilisi. And he thinks he needs them to keep his end up with us too. It hurts him badly to be treated like a beggar, just a nuisance. That's why he pretends to us."

I said, "I'm not sure whether that's the only reason why he's lying."

She turned her face towards me, a question in her eyes.

I did not reply for a while. Then I said some odd things had happened during my visit to Tbilisi, and they had only

180

just come back into my mind. Pointed questions about the activities of some of my travelling companions, and my own personal circumstances too. Obvious knowledge of a critical remark made by Herr Dautzenbacher, one of those on the trip, during a conversation between him and me in my hotel room, one that no one else could have heard unless I was being bugged. And not least, a kind of team performance put on by Ninoshvili and his wife, who even when I first saw her had looked to me like a decoy. Dautzenbacher had reacted strongly to their act as well.

At the time I hadn't taken it seriously when the organizers of our visit to Georgia warned us to assume that our Soviet hosts, even the high-ranking people who talked to us, might also be interested in us on behalf of the intelligence services. But I had now been thinking a lot about it. And if any other reason was needed to wonder why our guest had been provided with hard currency just to pursue some hopeless cultural project here, then we could have learned from the newspaper reports. The KGB still plays an important part in Georgia, as we read in the papers almost daily.

I paused for a moment. Then I said that was one thing the Soviet secret service obviously had in common with the Stasi, which as we also knew was still operating.

She lay without moving for a while. Suddenly she sat up. She passed her hand over her face, shook her head and looked at me. "Do you seriously believe that David is working for the KGB? That can't be true, Christian!"

"Why not? Doesn't the KGB exist any longer? Or the Stasi? Did they never exist?"

She lay down on her back again and closed her eyes.

I touched her shoulder. "Julia, if that man is causing you any trouble, then tell me. Please. You can always tell me if you have problems. I want to help you."

She said nothing for a while. Then, with her eyes still closed, she said, "What kind of problems would I have? I think you're the one with problems. You're jealous, Christian. And I can understand that. It wasn't very sensible of me to stay away overnight with David, without discussing it with you first. But I had no opportunity to – you'd already gone out."

She switched off her bedside lamp and moved closer to me. "I'm sorry, Christian." She kissed me on the cheek. "There's really no need for you to be jealous. You have nothing to worry about. Your love is quite enough for me." She took my book away from me, leaned over me, and put out my own bedside light. Then she laid her head on my chest and began caressing me.

After a while I said I was sorry, but I wasn't in the mood. Which was true. She stayed lying close, put her arm around me and said nothing. I could tell, from the sound of her breathing, that it took her a long time to fall asleep.

47

At breakfast, which I had made, Julia said very little. She smiled at me now and then, and once took my hand and squeezed it. I went to the door with her when she set out for the courthouse, and stood there until she had got her car out of the garage and driven past, waving to me.

The house was quiet. Erika and Ninoshvili were still asleep. I went into my study and sat down at the desk. But I didn't think for long. I had to do something, that was obvious. It remains to be seen whether I did the right thing.

I picked up the phone. Herr Hochgeschurz was already in his office. He said he could see me at once, although he suggested that I wait until about ten to arrive, because Dr Schmidt was still on his way. Or would I rather Dr Schmidt did not take part in the conversation? I said that would be fine. One secret agent more or less no longer mattered.

This time I was admitted to Dr Schmidt's office. The boss's room is a little more lavishly furnished than Herr Hochgeschurz's, and the interior designer has dispensed with the fire extinguisher, thus sparing visitors the uncomfortable feeling that a Molotov cocktail might be thrown in through the window at any moment. However, the view of flat roofs and chimneys is the same, and so is the smell of the cleaning fluid. The Internal Security people probably buy it by the barrel to impress the Federal Audit Office with their economic management of their budget.

Herr Hochgeschurz in person opened the door of the communications company to me, and led me to the boss's office. Dr Schmidt rose from his swivel chair, shook hands with me, said, "Very good to see you; I'm glad you found the time after all," and pointed to the visitor's chair in front of his desk. Hochgeschurz drew up another chair and sat down beside me. He opened the conversation by asking, "How is your wife?" I thanked him and said she was very well.

There was a little pause, during which Dr Schmidt kept smiling and nodding. He left his subordinate to conduct the rest of this conversation as well. Herr Hochgeschurz leaned back, said, "Well..." crossed his powerful thighs, dusted off a trouser leg, "now for the reason why we have asked you to come and talk to us." He folded his arms and looked at me. "I am sure you know that Herr Ninoshvili is playing in a chess tournament this weekend?"

I cleared my throat. "No. No, this is the first I've heard of it. But it's very likely. Herr Ninoshvili is an enthusiastic chess player."

183

Hochgeschurz smiled. "He's even an International Master."

"Yes, I know."

Herr Hochgeschurz nodded. "Well, to inform you of the details, which I am sure he will be telling you himself: he has enrolled for a Rapidplay chess tournament to be held in Schwitte-Minnenbüren. A tournament at a high level of proficiency, prizes well worth winning. A couple of Grandmasters are going to be there. You are probably surprised to find us taking an interest in such things, but we want to be straightforward with you."

He glanced at Dr Schmidt, and his boss nodded. Hochgeschurz said, "We know that you are a trustworthy man." He massaged his nose thoroughly before going on. "On your first visit, I told you a little about the KGB. And the Stasi. And I mentioned that those old comrades have by no means gone into retirement."

I was wondering more and more what Hochgeschurz was getting at. He confided, once again, that Internal Security was of course always on its guard, had to be on its guard, particularly with visitors from the former Soviet Union. For instance, the chess experts cultivated in large numbers by that state, the Grandmasters who have been coming to the West in droves for a few years now and winning prizes at tournaments. All these star players, not even excluding the youngest, have been drilled by the Soviet sports system since childhood, and as I could imagine they have been trained not only in playing chess but also in politically correct principles.

Well then, he said, of the masters hoping to win the prizes at Schwitte-Minnenbüren, several were already well known to Internal Security: a Russian, also an Armenian whom they had already had to reprimand because, outrageously, he had tried to question a German MP who was patron of a chess tournament

184

in his electoral district. But of course Internal Security was also interested in the contacts these gentlemen made in Schwitte. New contacts, yes, but also those they'd known in the good old days and whom they might try cultivating there.

Herr Hochgeschurz rubbed his nose. Then he said, "For instance, we would be interested to know whether Herr Ninoshvili has dealings with them. Close dealings."

Dr Schmidt spoke up here. "Do you understand our meaning?"

I said, "No." Turning to Herr Hochgeschurz, I asked, "Didn't you tell me, when we talked in your office, that you couldn't say whether Herr Ninoshvili had anything to do with the KGB?"

Hochgeschurz smiled. "Quite right. And I still can't. But for that very reason we'd like to know what he does in Schwitte when he isn't sitting at the chessboard."

"Yes, I can understand that. But what business of mine is it? Do you think he's going to tell me about it?"

"No, of course not." Herr Hochgeschurz exchanged a glance with Dr Schmidt before going on. "Well, you see… your son is playing in the Youth Open in Schwitte." He raised his hand in a placatory gesture before I could open my mouth. "Don't worry, your son is not under observation. But along with the list of participants in the Masters' Tournament, the list for the Youth Open landed on my desk. And naturally I noticed your son's name."

Herr Hochgeschurz breathed heavily again. I stared at him. He said, "We're being absolutely open with you, Herr Kestner, because we trust you. For one thing, your son is in very close contact with Herr Ninoshvili. And for another, he would at least agree with us that if foreign agents are at work in our country, we ought not just to fold our hands and do nothing."

He leaned forwards, placing his hands on his knees. "So we wanted to ask you if you would agree to our asking your son to keep an eye on Herr Ninoshvili. And on the contacts he has in Schwitte. Your son would be able to go around with Herr Ninoshvili perfectly naturally. The last round of the Youth Open is being played on Saturday, as I am sure you know."

I said, "No."

Dr Schmidt asked, "Meaning what?"

I said, "You can't be seriously asking me this! Surely you don't imagine you can recruit my son into your service?"

Dr Schmidt shook his head, smiling. "No, no, you mustn't look at it like that!" He adjusted his glasses. "We would be asking him a favour. And a favour that he might perhaps do us of his own accord if he knew that Herr Ninoshvili... well, that he may be working for the KGB."

Dr Schmidt leaned back in his chair. He said, "Then again, there's the tit-for-tat principle, something that quite often pays off in life."

For a moment words failed me. I stared at Dr Schmidt. "What do you mean by that?"

He smiled. "Only what I said."

I rose to my feet and nodded to Dr Schmidt. "Thank you for this conversation. I have certainly learned a few things from it."

Herr Hochgeschurz rose and gave me his hand. "You shouldn't draw any false conclusions, Herr Kestner. It was only a question, after all, and of course it's your decision."

He went to the door with me. In the corridor, he said, "And by the way, you were right in your supposition. The murder in the hotel does indeed have a background in Intelligence. The woman used to work for the Stasi. She even held the rank of captain."

48

In the 1930s the agents of the Soviet secret service must have been easy to recognize at first sight. Although perhaps Grigol Robakidze was exaggerating the reality slightly in order to make it easier for his readers to tell the difference between good and evil. At least, in one of his novels he describes a tavern in Tbilisi, the dimly lit haunt of the Bohemian set, where unwanted guests turn up one evening: Bolsheviks. One of them is a Georgian, but is an agent of the GPU, and that is obvious to all present. He does not, like a pure-bred Georgian, carry a noble head on his shoulders, but "a viper's head, with sparse hair and almost no eyebrows".

Ninoshvili looked up when I said casually at supper that I was going to drive to Schwitte-Minnenbüren on Friday evening, to take a look at the chess tournament, cross my fingers for Ralf, and bring him home on Sunday, hopefully with a cup in his backpack. The viper didn't comment, but left it to Julia to reveal his own plans.

She said, "Oh, now that's what I call a lucky coincidence." I asked what she meant. She glanced at Ninoshvili and then smiled at me. "David was thinking of going there on Friday too. He's interested in a tournament taking place there, not for young people this time. Rapidplay or something like that." She looked enquiringly at Ninoshvili, and the viper nodded.

Julia hesitated for a moment, and then said, "I was already wondering whether I could drive him there on Friday afternoon; it's quite difficult getting to the little place. And I was going to ask if then you could perhaps fetch them both on Sunday."

"No problem. He can drive there and back with me."

Erika asked, "So you can bring yourself to leave Julia and me on our own all weekend, can you? What are we going to do without a man in the house?"

Julia drank a sip from her glass. "Don't complain… we can have a really good gossip at last." She patted my hand. "Thank you, Christian, that's really very nice of you."

The viper said, "Yes, very nice. Really." He mashed a potato on his plate, and then asked, "Will you be able to find somewhere to stay there?"

"I already have."

You're going to be surprised, I thought.

It may be that what I have now set in motion is exactly what Dr Schmidt and Herr Hochgeschurz wanted. They cannot seriously have meant to rope in Ralf; they wanted to mobilize me, not him. Very well. I'm not going to Schwitte-Minnenbüren to help Internal Security. I'm going there to defend my family. And if that happens to do Internal Security some good – well, why not, just so long as my family benefits. But I'm going to decide on that, not Internal Security.

49

Ninoshvili is staying on the second floor of the River Laaxe Sports Hotel, along with other players in the tournament. I am on the fourth floor. After unpacking my case and washing my hands, I went down and knocked at the door of his room. How about a drink in the bar before dinner? I called. He had left his room already, or at least, no one answered. I didn't see him in the bar either.

I walked over to the youth hostel and found Ralf just going out. He was standing outside the entrance to the hostel with six or seven lads of his own age. They were amusing themselves by handing around the headgear of the smallest, a red baseball cap, and trying it on. The smallest boy, whose hair was cut very short, reached in vain for his property, shouting, "Stop that crap, my brain will freeze!" Ralf replied, "You don't have one!" A couple of other youthful chess players, hanging out of a window in the hostel, were killing themselves laughing.

Ralf didn't seem to be unpleasantly surprised to see me. I said I had come with Ninoshvili, who was going to take part in the Rapidplay tournament. Ralf nodded. "Yup, I saw him on the list. But he'll be wiped out here." I asked how he himself was doing. He said that if he wins again tomorrow he could be among the top ten.

The boys had already set off along the path. One of them stopped and called, "Hey, Ralf, what about it? Coming?" I told him he mustn't let me keep him. He nodded, raised his hand, and said, "See you tomorrow, then."

I walked along the Laaxe for a little way, turned when I began to feel chilly in the cool mist now rising from the river, and ate dinner in the hotel restaurant that evening. Ninoshvili was nowhere to be seen. I found him only when I looked in at the bar after my meal. He was sitting in a niche with a brown-skinned, black-haired man of about thirty-five. Ninoshvili waved to me, but the gesture wasn't to be taken as an invitation to join them.

I went over to them. The man inspected me. Ninoshvili introduced me, then indicated his friend. "This is Herr Ohannissian; you'll probably know his name." I said, "Yes, of course!" and nodded to him with a smile. He showed no reaction, and Ninoshvili said no more either. It was a question of nerves, and mine proved the weaker. I wished them a good evening and sat down at the bar.

About five minutes later a slender man of around forty with a pale face and very fair hair appeared in the entrance of the bar, looked around, and went over to the two of them in their niche. They exchanged a few words, then Ninoshvili beckoned to the waitress, a chubby-cheeked girl in a red blouse and black velvet waistcoat. The two of them paid separately, and then they went out with the fair-haired man. Ninoshvili smiled at me.

This is the Russian who is already well known to Herr Hochgeschurz, presumably, who else? He's only just arrived. The three of them go to the Armenian's room. In broken English, the Armenian orders a bottle of vodka and a sliced cucumber from room service. He asks what it will cost. Ninoshvili and the Russian give him one third each, counting out cash on the table.

The Russian lifts the net curtain and glances out of the window. A taxi is coming up the drive, passes the yellow globes of the mushroom-shaped lights, and disappears under the awning over the hotel entrance. The Armenian, who has counted and pocketed the money, takes off his shoes, sits down on the bed and massages his feet in their black socks. Ninoshvili drops into an armchair, puts his hand in his jacket pocket, and brings out the papers that, as soon as the Stasi captain was lying on the floor in her blood, he looked for in her hotel room, found and took away. He gets the papers out of sight again when the room waiter knocks.

Around ten-thirty, after three whiskies at the price of ten marks each, I left the bar. Ninoshvili had not reappeared. I went to bed.

On Saturday I moved back and forth between the comprehensive school's Sports Hall and the Banqueting Room of the hotel, where the Rapidplay tournament was being held. Ninoshvili won in the first two rounds, in the

190

second because he had his opponent in such difficulties that the latter overstepped the thirty minutes allowed for considering his next move. Ralf lost in the last round of the Youth Open, and told me he could have taken a piece in the fifteenth move but can't have been concentrating. "Shit." I tried to cheer him up.

I didn't see Ninoshvili outside the tournament hall either during the lunch break or on Saturday evening. He suddenly disappeared around midday. I knocked on the door of his room, meaning to ask if he'd like to eat lunch with me, but no one answered. On the way back to the lift I met the Armenian, who didn't seem to recognize me, and passed me with an absent look when I greeted him.

On Saturday evening the top chess players disappeared into a side wing of the restaurant that had been partitioned off by a folding wooden screen. Herr Friedrich Hünten had invited them to dinner. I ate something light at a table not far from the screen; I didn't have much of an appetite.

Now and then the voices of people making speeches reached my ears. Presumably both Herr Hünten and the chairman of his chess club, as well as the mayor of Schwitte-Minnenbüren or the local MP or all of them, were paying tribute to the guests. A lady who was sitting with another woman over a half-litre of wine got up whenever one of the gentlemen came out of the side wing on his way to the men's room and asked for his autograph, while the other lady turned her head aside, covered her mouth with her hand and giggled.

After a while I tired of the giggling. I abandoned my observation post and walked along the banks of the Laaxe for a good half an hour. I didn't meet a human soul on the footpath to which the asphalt road led. A thin veil of white hovered over the meadows, and the woods stood like a black

191

wall beyond it. I looked at the lighted windows of the youth hostel. Ralf was probably still enjoying the disco, where the lads sat side by side, cracking jokes about the local beauties and their dancing partners, trying to see how far they could get away with behaving badly on foreign territory.

I went back to the hotel and into the bar. The chess masters' festivities seemed to be over. Some of the gentlemen I had seen at the chessboards were sitting in the niches in the bar. Ninoshvili was not among them, nor were the Armenian and the Russian. There were no women present except for the little waitress. I sat at the bar. A pale man with a moustache, two stools further away, smiled at me, raised his beer glass and drank to me. I remembered seeing him too in the tournament hall, and returned his smile. He drank some more beer, then changed to the stool next to mine and asked what had brought me to this dump. I said I'd been watching the chess. He raised his glass again and drained it.

I asked him if he'd have another beer with me. "Well, why not?" he said. The man was a Czech or a Slovak with an unpronounceable name. I don't know what kind of master he was, a Grandmaster or International Master or whatever, I didn't want to ask because I assumed the fact that I didn't know might hurt his feelings. I tried questioning him about his colleagues, and even asked what he thought of David Ninoshvili. "Well, I don't know," he said. "Must be Georgian. I've never played him. Maybe tomorrow."

After he had asked, "Let's have another beer, shall we?" causing me to order for the third time, I gave up. Ninoshvili hadn't shown his face. I paid. My companion didn't seem to worry about the state he would be in on Sunday morning, and said he was going to have another beer.

As I waited for the lift, I wondered whether to get out at the second floor again. Go down the corridor, only dimly lit for the night hours, and stand at Ninoshvili's door. Glance around and then put my ear to the door.

Hochgeschurz would probably do that. But no, much too primitive. Herr Hochgeschurz would put his hand in his pocket as he passed, bring out a mini-transmitter and, with a quick movement of his fingers, fit it in the angle of the doorway, where it was barely visible. Then he would go to his room and switch on his mini-receiver, his plump red ear bent over it.

No again, of course not. The Armenian and the Russian might only now be going to join Ninoshvili, waiting for the corridors to be deserted. They would see the mini-transmitter at a glance, remove it and show it, in silence, to their Georgian partner. Still too primitive.

Hochgeschurz probably wouldn't take the risk of operating on the floor of the hotel where the KGB agents were by night, when most people were in bed. Perhaps he would be standing, warmly wrapped up, on the balcony of his room in the darkness. He has put out the lights in his room, he is holding a directional microphone, he carefully lets it down on a rope until it's dangling over the top of Ninoshvili's window frame. Hochgeschurz fixes the cord of the microphone in place, goes back into the room and switches his receiver on. After a while the loudspeaker crackles, and then the furtive discussion in Ninoshvili's room is audible.

The Russian, the Armenian and the Georgian are speaking Russian. Never mind, Hochgeschurz knows Russian. He learned the language on an intensive course run by the Federal Office for the Protection of the Constitution.

I don't know Russian. And I'm not Herr Hochgeschurz, in either this or any other connection.

I press the lift button for the fourth floor, go into my room, and get into bed without indulging in any more nonsense.

50

Ninoshvili has won third prize in the Rapidplay tournament, 2,000 marks in a sealed envelope and an occasional table (we left it behind after Ninoshvili had failed to get its value in cash), plus a certificate and a cup engraved *Friedrich Hünten Furnishings Ltd.* Ralf came nineteenth in the Youth Open. He too received a certificate and one of the two dozen bedside lamps donated by Herr Hünten as consolation prizes.

On the drive back, Ninoshvili asked to see the notation of Ralf's last game, which cost my son a place in the top ten and a modern yet attractive table lamp. He analysed the match from the notation, did not agree with Ralf's claim that he could have taken a piece in the fifteenth move, but assured him that he hadn't played badly, and might even have achieved a draw. Ralf listened with interest, asked a couple of questions, but then he didn't go on talking to the IM. Instead, he leaned back and closed his eyes.

When we got back Julia was alone. Erika had left. Julia was not particularly informative; she just said Erika hadn't wanted to keep David out of the spare room any longer, so she thought it better to cut her visit short and go home. Ninoshvili didn't seem to have any views on the matter, and moreover he found another subject which no one could have expected to interest him less than the occupation of our spare room.

The Georgian government troops, Shevardnadze's fighting force, have put the Abkhazians and Zviad Gamsakhurdia to flight, they have retaken the harbour town of Poti and are now marching on Zugdidi, Gamsakhurdia's strongest base, his home town. The people of Poti, over which there has been fighting for days, have shown no enthusiasm about their liberation. "I wouldn't be too happy in their place either," admitted Kako Chogoshvili, a brigade commander of the liberating forces, speaking on television.

The government troops wreaked no less havoc in Poti than Gamsakhurdia's ill-disciplined men. The freedom fighters on both sides got drunk, committed rape, stole and looted, four civilians were murdered, including a young woman who wouldn't stand by and see her apartment cleared. An old Georgian woman told the reporter, weeping, "I'm so ashamed. Our country is a disgrace to the whole world."

After we had watched this news on three different TV channels, we sat down to supper at the dining table. Only Ralf ate heartily. Ninoshvili looked at his plate, deep in thought, and ate in silence. He was obviously lost for words. I thought there was only one conclusion to be drawn from this behaviour. He belongs to the party of the paranoid nationalist Gamsakhurdia, and very likely to the associates of the KGB whom the victorious president has accused in Tbilisi of being a fifth column of the rebellion. Now he sees the moment when he is unmasked approaching, and he fears for his neck.

This idea left me no peace. Oh no, my friend, not again!

After Julia had made an unsuccessful attempt to ask Ralf about his experiences in Schwitte and thus get some kind of conversation going, I cleared my throat and said, "David, if I understand all this correctly, at least now there's a chance of the war coming to an end sooner or later. Isn't that something to be glad of?"

He raised his eyes, looked at me, and went on munching in silence for a long time. Julia cast him a concerned glance. Suddenly I saw tears come to his eyes. He said, in a stifled voice, "You're wrong, Christian. Don't you see the suffering? The destruction? Many more are going to be affected. Think of all that human suffering!" He pressed his napkin to his

195

eyes and suddenly sobbed into it. Julia took his arm. Ralf looked down, staring at his plate.

Ninoshvili spoke into the napkin, which made it hard to hear what he was saying. "I have friends, many friends living in Poti. Good friends! I haven't seen them for a long time. Oh, what suffering!"

He let the napkin drop and went out. It looked as if he had difficulty in finding his way to the door, where he stopped and looked back. "Please forgive me. I feel very bad about this."

Julia got up and followed him. After a while Ralf put his fork down and left the room as well.

51

A number of years ago the American government invested a lot of money in investigating a technological military procedure developed by the Russians. I compiled a piece of reportage about this top-secret venture at the time, but I can't lay hands on it now. At any rate, the point on which the story depended was that after the CIA had tried and were still trying to solve the riddle, government officials found the miraculous procedure described in minute detail in an outdated Soviet journal.

The journal was stored in a cellar of the US State Department, which subscribed to it. Its issues were supposed to be regularly evaluated by capable linguists, and so they were, but the translators were behind with their work. Only a year or so after the publication of the article did they stumble upon the goldmine it contained.

This grotesque story, which I found in an American magazine, seemed to me to prove what I had long suspected.

The gigantic expenditure devoted both here and on the other side to investigating what the enemy was up to was largely wasted. The apparatus of espionage led a life of its own, circling deliberately around itself, devouring the millions necessary to keep it going, and coming up only with piffling bits of information of no use to anyone.

Of course the personnel involved developed ingenious techniques for this apparatus to maintain itself. A considerable part of their energy went on checking up on their counterparts on the other side. They knew a great deal about each other, prepared reports on one another, and thus mutually supplied evidence of their right to exist.

I also read, with grim satisfaction, the story of the resident placed by the Federal Intelligence Service in Hong Kong, whose well-paid job consisted in essence of reading the local newspapers, cutting out articles and sending them on to his control centre, with the occasional knowledgeable comment added. I don't know if the man charged with cutting out the articles also ever fell one or two years behind with his work, but it wouldn't surprise me, since the newspapers often had large advertising sections in very tiny print where all kinds of significant information could be hidden.

Of course I had also read spy stories which enthralled me because they dealt with vital characters like the unfortunate Margaretha Geertruida Zelle from Leeuwarden, who danced on stage under the name of Mata Hari before she was condemned to death and shot at Vincennes in 1917. But it's a long time since we've heard of such exotic women and demonic men. The fact that a self-satisfied idiot like James Bond had to be kitted out with futuristic equipment to engender suspense seemed to me just one more proof that the activity of real-life spies couldn't interest anyone but themselves – apart, that is, from the taxpayer financing their useless lives.

Even the top spy Günter Guillaume, a stout man with a crew cut and a pallid wife called Christel, did not convince me that the profession of secret agent is very effective. I don't want to snipe unnecessarily, but what harm did it do anyone, except Frau Brandt, if Chancellor Willy Brandt had an affair now and then? If the relevant information passed on by Guillaume to the East German Ministry of State Security had been assessed at its true worth, over here it would have been enough to cancel the informer's entitlement to state benefits, on the grounds that he had thrown a spanner into the works of the Chancellery, and then they could have sent him back to the German Democratic Republic to return to the honest profession of photography for which he was trained. And Herr Brandt could have stayed on as Chancellor, unless he'd lost the taste for it anyway.

That was how I thought. But now I'm not sure whether this way of looking at it does justice to the influence that spies can have.

They're interfering with our lives. Herr Hochgeschurz is gathering information about my wife and my son and using it shamelessly to make trouble. Herr Ninoshvili is driving a wedge into my family. What Hochgeschurz knows, or thinks he knows, is being countersigned by Dr Schmidt and stored in the data files of Internal Security, and my son will also probably figure in the Office's annual report as a digit in the total figures of members and supporters of far-right organizations. Meanwhile Herr Ninoshvili is using my house as a base of operations for his business, however criminal that may be.

They are well equipped financially. Herr Ninoshvili has funds for his trip abroad, money which would probably be enough to feed a family of four for a month in Georgia, and any extra sums that this culturally active character may need he gets by making a killing through guest appearances at Herr Schumann's summer house and the River Laaxe Sports Hotel. Herr Hochgeschurz lives off his authority's 220 million marks a year, and presumably from certain slush funds hidden away by the Federal Finance Minister in his own budget.

It's not enough for these vipers to live at our expense, they try to use us for their own ends. Hochgeschurz and Ninoshvili and their like have tempted me to try playing a part which is completely alien to me, a part that repels me. Christian Kestner, a respectable senior teacher, takes up an observation post on the pretext of wanting to eat a little light supper. He steals furtively along hotel corridors, he makes approaches to an unsuspecting beer-drinker who is feeling lonely and tries to sound him out. He pesters his wife with hypocritical questions to discover whether, after all, she is in league with a liar like David Ninoshvili.

I don't know anything. The agents are playing their own game with me, and I have no idea what they're after. I don't know whether Hochgeschurz already has a file showing that my wife left Halle and came to the Federal Republic on instructions from the Stasi. I don't know whether Ninoshvili really stabbed that woman in the hotel and what other missions he may be here to carry out. Hochgeschurz puts now one kind of bait and now another in front of me, he has me dancing to his tune, and so does my guest Ninoshvili, with whom this whole miserable business began.

It can't go on like this. Something has to happen.

52

Manni Wallmeroth's mother and father, who both turned up for the Parents' Association meeting, have confronted me with a severe crisis of conscience. Wallmeroth *mère*, who entered the room where the meeting was held wearing a pale blue winter coat now too tight for her and red knitted gloves, said not a word throughout the whole performance, but held her head slightly lowered most of the time and looked at her hands, which she kept clasped in her lap.

Wallmeroth *père*, a short man of forty in a black leather jacket, spoke only once, and that was when – as discussed with the principal – I had told the meeting at the start that the student Manfred Wallmeroth had admitted to spraying the graffiti. Herr Wallmeroth cleared his throat several times as he managed to say that Manfred had told him he didn't know why he'd sprayed that swastika on the stage set, the boy was very sorry, and he was terribly upset. Frau Wallmeroth didn't look up while her husband was speaking.

Dr Lawrenz made sure that I didn't capitulate. After peeling off his dark-blue trench coat and stowing his silk scarf in its sleeve, he had greeted me with a handshake and a silent nod, and didn't deign to look at me again after that. Instead he talked, while I was sitting on his left, to the deputy chair of the Parents' Association on his right, quiet Frau Dahlmann, straightening his white cuffs in his dark-blue sleeves and checking the knot of his tie.

In his opening statement – "I'll come straight to the point, but first allow me a few reflections that I believe to be relevant" – he held forth first on the general condition of youth as depicted every other day in the press and on television. It is far from being his way, he said, to play down anything. Much of what young people get up to these days definitely calls for stern retribution. However, we must also ask ourselves whether this subject is not deliberately exaggerated by the press in order to boost circulation.

He smiled, and adjusted his cuffs again. "Sex and crime – let's not delude ourselves, the public likes to read about such things."

In this gathering, said Dr Lawrenz, no one would need to ask whether racist excesses like those seen in Mölln and Solingen could or could not be tolerated. "Murder is murder, even if it is committed by young people who have been led astray. However, ladies and gentlemen," continued Dr Lawrenz, propping his elbows on the table and letting his gaze wander over the faces present. After a significant pause, he said that only if you were serious about tackling such abuses could you understand what the point at issue in this assembly was.

Here, a lad of eighteen had not thrown an incendiary bomb, he had not endangered human life, let alone killed anyone. He had sprayed a political slogan and a swastika on a piece of theatrical scenery, full stop. But now – "Forgive me, ladies and gentlemen, but I do have to make this point clearly" – now some people were acting as if the boy had committed a serious and violent crime, almost as if he were on a par with the murderers of Mölln and Solingen.

Here I blew my top. I said, "Forgive me, Dr Lawrenz, but no one present has made that ridiculous comparison. You are the first to have thought it up."

The gynaecologist ignored me, and directed his answer at our audience. "Perhaps you would be kind enough to let me finish what I have to say." I said that if he was going to continue in the same vein I couldn't promise that.

Dr Lawrenz let the air out through his nose and smiled. Then he said that if we were to make comparisons, he would recommend a comparison with the violent brawl that had taken place in the school yard not long ago. Everyone knew that some younger children had been brutally manhandled by older students on that occasion. But obviously no one had come up with the idea that those violent criminals should be excluded from school, not even the same members of the teaching staff who were now anxious to inflict the severest punishment possible in the circumstances on Manfred Wallmeroth, leaving him with a stain on his character for life.

Here Herr Ileri, Hasan's father, raised his hand and called out, "Hang on a minute! Those younger children were seventeen themselves! And they did their own kicking and hair-pulling, not to mention throwing hefty punches!"

Dr Lawrenz, after addressing short but sturdy Herr Ileri as "My dear sir", said that he had not been saying the participants in that fight ought to be excluded from school, although the matter could certainly have been discussed. He had merely suggested that a double standard was obviously in operation at this school.

Before I could cut Dr Lawrenz short again, which he urgently needed, I received unexpected support from Herr Meier-Bosbach, a district court judge. He rose and said, "Dr Lawrenz, are you aware that the use and dissemination of Nazi emblems is an offence as defined by Paragraph 86a of the Penal Code, and in some circumstances can bring with it a custodial sentence of up to three years? And that the graffiti artist in this case is undoubtedly of the age of criminal responsibility?"

There was loud murmuring. Dr Lawrenz asked indignantly, "Do you want to put the boy in prison too?" A discussion ensued between the two gentlemen, not that it contributed anything to the matter at hand, since the district judge and the gynaecologist were chiefly concerned to prove which of them was cleverer than the other.

The meeting of the Parents' Association was proceeding swiftly towards its final phase when Herr Steinbrecher, an insurance manager, stood up and called out, "This may all be very interesting, but I'd like to know exactly what's going to happen. Does the boy get excluded from school or does he not?"

I said the staff meeting called for the day after tomorrow would decide on that. With the best will in the world, however, I added, I couldn't foretell what the decision would be, as I hoped they would understand.

Dr Lawrenz was not happy with that. He said that at this point he would like to discuss a question that he had been asked to raise by some members of the Parents' Association. Certain parents were obviously wondering about the purpose of the series of lessons about the Georgian civil war that I had included in my history curriculum.

I said the purpose was quickly explained, if indeed it wasn't obvious anyway. The Georgian civil war, I continued, was a perfect example of the disasters and suffering that blind nationalism had brought down on mankind at all times and in all parts of the world.

Dr Lawrenz smiled and asked not me, but his audience, whether it wouldn't be more desirable for the young people to concentrate on German history instead. I said, "Please don't worry about that. German history, unfortunately, can't be left out of any discussion of the subject."

The cause of the agitation that arose at this point in the meeting was clear to me when Heuberger raised his hand, Lawrenz greeted this request to speak with a couple of nods, and said, "Yes, go ahead, Herr Heuberger!"

Heinz-Karl Heuberger is deputy editor of the local newspaper, and with his occasional comment pieces he ensures the preservation of a balanced attitude by dwelling, in forthright terms, on the old values that obviously mean nothing to some of the editorial staff. Herr Heuberger is in his mid-sixties and a grandfather several times over, but he has also had a daughter by his second wife, who is twenty years his junior. This girl attends my history classes, and I have not yet formed any opinion of her, either positive or negative.

The journalist, who knows a great deal about the Third Reich – and I suspect rose at least to the leadership of a small troop of men under that very regime – but whom I have never known to write a knowledgeable column about Georgia, said that there could be other opinions about the Georgian civil war besides the one that I had so simplistically put forward. I said, "Please go on. I should be interested to hear them."

Herr Heuberger propped both hands on the back of the chair in front of him, and rocked his torso slightly back and forth as he spoke. He said that so far as he knew, the trouble in Georgia was a matter of conflict between the old Communists and the free forces of the country. It was generally known, he added, that Shevardnadze had led the Georgian Communist Party, while Professor Gamsakhurdia was the country's rightful and freely elected president. Shevardnadze had overthrown him with the help of the army.

He was also sure, he said, that I knew Gamsakhurdia was the son of a great writer whom the Georgians honoured as a national hero, and that he had been part of the Georgian Helsinki group, for which he had been persecuted and thrown into prison by the Shevardnadze regime.

The insurance manager stood up, told the woman sitting next to him in loud, clear tones, "I've had enough of this!" and left the room where the meeting was being held. He started a general inclination to make a move, watched by Dr

Lawrenz with a disapproving shake of his head. I raised my voice above the sound of feet and the scraping of chairs, and told Herr Heuberger that his own views might perhaps be a little simplistic, but I would be very happy to discuss them with him some time. Herr Heuberger himself did not seem to welcome that idea this evening. He let go of the chair he was holding, waved my offer away with a smile, indicated to his neighbours, by shaking his head, that discussing anything with me would be a waste of time, and walked out.

When I was home I rang Trabert, who had been going to attend the Parents' Association meeting but then obviously preferred to stay at home, relaxing with his stamp collection and his three cats. I gave him as much of a brief account as I felt able to present. He grunted a couple of times, and when I said that was about the gist of it, he did not reply for a moment. Then he asked, "What do you think the atmosphere was like?"

"How do you mean?"

"Well… Dr Lawrenz was certainly representing a rather extreme view. But how do you think the parents would take an exclusion – the majority of the parents, I mean?"

I said that I suspected the majority didn't want to be bothered with such things. Herr Trabert muttered something, thanked me, and wished me goodnight.

53

This afternoon my son confided in me for the first time in a long while. Unfortunately that is not a reason for undiluted joy, more of a cause for concern.

He wasn't at home when I got back from school, and Ninoshvili was out as well. Around four I heard Ralf come upstairs. He went up to the top floor and slammed the door of his room behind him, as he sometimes does when he's in a bad temper, but also just to let off steam. I thought nothing much of this piece of bad behaviour, and went on working.

A quarter of an hour later I heard him coming down the stairs, and thought that yet again, after making a start, he'd lost interest in his homework and was going out to take his mind off it. But he opened the door of my room, came in, and asked, "Can I have a word with you?"

"Of course."

He closed the door, sat down on the chair beside the desk, and cast a glance out of the window. Then he looked at me and asked, "How long are you just going to sit and watch all this going on?"

"All what going on?"

He folded his arms. "Julia and David."

I stared at him. He said, "I saw the pair of them just now in Kaiserallee. They were in Möhlmann's shop, looking at watches. I waited on the other side of the street until they came out. They were in there quite a long time. And then I followed them for a bit, as far as the Café Wertmüller. They went in there."

He stopped, but he didn't take his eyes off me. I cleared my throat. It felt dry. I asked, "So? Why shouldn't they look at watches and go to the café?"

He gave a derisive grunt. "You should have seen the pair of them. People must have thought they were newly-weds. Walking down the street arm in arm, enjoying themselves. David gives Julia a kiss on the cheek, and she lets him. Even seems to have liked it."

I turned to the book on my desk, pushed it a little way off, then drew it towards me again. "Ralf, your mother is an adult human being. She knows what she's doing." I looked at him. "Why shouldn't she go for a walk with Ninoshvili? And show that she's in a good mood?"

He smiled grimly and nodded. "Are you taking the piss? You're not blind, are you? Right from the start David fancied her. And she's almost falling over herself – it's David this and David that the whole time. Don't you think it's obvious?"

I pushed the book away. "Ralf, please!"

He said no more for a while. Then he asked, "Did you know she's getting his visa extended?" I looked at him. He went on, "Anyway, that's what David told me. His visa will run out some time or other. But Julia has told him not to worry. That's what he said to me."

"And you believe him?"

"Yes, I believe him. And you think it's possible yourself. She wants the man to stay on here."

He was silent for a while, before saying, "You don't have to pretend to me. How did you like it when she stayed overnight in Darmstadt with him? David told me about that too. Probably wanted to show off. Tells me he's sold his stuff, the masterpiece that nobody wants, and it was possible only because Julia drove him to Darmstadt that evening."

I said, "She likes him, that's all – she wants to help him."

He snorted derisively again. "Too right she likes him!" After taking a deep breath, he looked hard at me. "David's turned her head! And I wouldn't be surprised if she's slept with him. You think he may have done too, you can't tell me you don't!"

I raised my voice. "Ralf, don't talk about your mother in that tone!"

He did not reply, but lowered his eyes and began biting one fingernail.

I asked, "And even if it was true... have you stopped to think what I could have against it? I told you before: she's a grown-up human being."

He looked at his finger and went on biting the nail. Then he said, "I'd know what to do."

"And what might that be?"

Another silence, and then he stood up. "Just leave it to me." He nodded to me and went out. I heard him running downstairs. I jumped up, went out into the corridor and called, "Ralf? Come back, please!"

The front door latched behind him.

54

A Dr Christensen at the Foreign Ministry, with whom I spoke after going through assorted hoops on the phone, has given very friendly and full answers to my question: what would be the necessary formalities for a Georgian wanting to visit me in Germany? Dr Christensen said that as he saw the matter, the gentleman could apply at any time to the German diplomatic mission in Tbilisi for a thirty-day visa. He would have to show proof that he had been invited to the Federal Republic. However, if I sent a telex from my firm to the diplomatic mission in Tbilisi, that would probably be enough. Or was the visit not for business purposes?

I said it was half on business, half private, but I didn't myself represent any firm. Dr Christensen said that was no obstacle either, I could always invite the Georgian in my capacity as a private person. He could still get a thirty-day visa then, but I'd have to send my invitation in the terms prescribed to the Tbilisi diplomatic mission. I could probably get a form for that purpose from my local Foreign Citizens

Office, he told me, and the staff there would authenticate the application.

I asked whether, if necessary, the visa could be extended. Yes, that would be possible, said Dr Christensen. If it turned out that my Georgian friend wanted or needed to stay longer than thirty days, he could apply to the Foreign Ministry for an extension of another thirty. It was even possible to get an annual visa, valid for a year, although it permitted a foreigner to be in the country for only ninety days of that year in all. In both cases it would be a good idea for me to go to the authority with the Georgian gentleman and speak to them myself, so that I could give the requisite explanation.

I asked what the requisite explanation consisted of. Well, said Dr Christensen, in the present case, making an application for any kind of visa, including one for business purposes, I would have to pledge myself, as the person inviting the Georgian, to meet without reservation any financial expenses that he might incur during his stay in the Federal Republic. That included the cost of any possible medical treatment of my guest in hospital. However, I could cover myself against that risk by taking out an insurance policy. The premium wasn't astronomically high; he rather thought it came to about three marks per day of the foreign guest's stay in this country.

I thanked Dr Christensen, hung up, and calculated the days since Ninoshvili's arrival. If he knew about the terms for the extension of his visa, and it was to be assumed that he did, then he must have applied for it already, unless he was prepared to risk peremptory deportation.

I had hoped that in that point at least I could disprove Ralf's suspicions. Knowing that I had been taken in yet again, and not I but Ralf was probably right, of course wasn't enough to make me go along with everything else he had confided to me. I was still looking for a good reason to tell him off and disabuse him of a few of his confused ideas.

Once again Ninoshvili thwarted me, preventing me from straightening my family out. He had come home half an hour before Julia, passed my study door and disappeared into the spare room. As soon as Julia came in she started making supper, and she didn't look in on me but called up the stairs, "Hello, Christian! I'm home, supper won't be long!" and disappeared into the kitchen. Five minutes later Ralf came in as well.

I intercepted him in the corridor, silently beckoned him into my study and closed the door. He looked at me in silence. I asked, "Why did you run off like that? I called after you to come back."

"Didn't hear you."

I sat down at the desk. "Ralf, I'd like to know exactly what you were insinuating before you left the house. You said you'd know what to do about Ninoshvili. And you said I was to leave it to you." I looked at him. "What did you mean?"

He shrugged. "Nothing special."

"Ralf, don't pretend to be stupid. I want to know what you're planning."

He snorted, and then said, "Why don't you wait and see?"

"Because I don't want you doing something stupid."

"I won't. You can rely on me."

"In this case I'd rather not. Ralf, you mustn't think that a man like Ninoshvili will let you drive him away as easily as that. I don't want you to do anything rash that might just make the situation worse. And that might injure you yourself."

He was looking out of the window. I said, "Come on, out with it. What have you been thinking up?"

210

He looked at me. After a while he lowered his eyes and scratched his cheek.

There was a knock. Ninoshvili opened the door, asked, "Am I disturbing you?" but before I could answer he came in, turned back the sleeve of his jacket, and with a happy smile showed me the timepiece on his wrist. "I just wanted to show you this watch I've bought myself. Isn't it great? I never owned anything like this before!"

I said yes indeed, he had really bought an excellent watch. Ralf left the room without a word. "What's the matter with him?" asked Ninoshvili, surprised. I said I didn't know, but he was probably hungry and wanted to ask Julia when there'd be something to eat.

55

It's getting harder and harder for me to start a conversation with my wife. And when I bring myself to do it, I feel that she understands me less and less. I can't believe she doesn't *want* to understand me. And I won't believe that she sometimes *seems* to understand me just to avoid further questions.

Not so long ago we understood each other almost without needing any words. A glance, a smile was enough to reassure us that we were in harmony. Perhaps it was being so certain I didn't have to make lengthy explanations to communicate with her that bound me to her most of all. I remember that randy provincial court judge, hopefully for the last time. At the time it was enough to describe my trick with the red wine to Julia as an unintentional accident, and she knew at once what I'd been feeling and how I had coped. No discussion was necessary; she ended the chapter with a laugh and a kiss.

Of course our very different professions mean that we mix with slightly different circles of people. But we've always been able to bridge the distance easily. She and I both even felt a need to tell each other about our separate experiences. She always told me what was going on at her law practice and in court, and in the same way I told her about the school. Even when we have had arguments recently about our son and his disturbing tendencies, we've discussed them in the certainty that we both wanted the same thing, if in our own different ways.

I've wondered whether, perhaps, I've missed noticing an estrangement that's been coming on gradually for some time. But I'm perfectly sure that only since Ninoshvili made himself at home here has the understanding between my wife and me stopped working.

When his letter announcing his visit came we did quarrel, yes, but even then neither of us hid anything from the other. She told me straight out that this guest was very unwelcome to her. However, it's only from her behaviour that I've been able to tell how much her opinion of Ninoshvili has changed since he arrived. She hasn't said anything about it to me.

And equally, I've kept what has been troubling my mind since then to myself. I haven't said a word to her about my Georgian studies. I haven't even confided in her about my latest crisis at school, the worst I've ever known. And the more my doubts about Julia, her relationship to me and our family haunt me, the more I shrink from breaking this oppressive silence. I only hinted at my fear that she may be carrying a heavy burden dating back to her youth in Halle, and she wouldn't give me a clear answer. It can't have escaped her that Ralf's relationship to both Ninoshvili and to her, his own mother, has changed radically, yet she hasn't said a word about that any more than I have.

Is our marriage, is our life together inexorably breaking up? I can't reconcile myself to that idea. But I'm finding it harder and harder to hope that I'm deceiving myself.

As soon as we were finally alone and in bed this evening, I asked Julia what she thought about Ninoshvili's purchase. She smiled, and then said he'd obviously dreamed of a watch like that for a long time.

I raised my eyebrows. After a moment's hesitation, she said perhaps I'd be surprised, but she had even advised him when he was buying it – he'd asked her to. I wondered aloud if she shouldn't have suggested a more sensible way to lay out his foreign currency. No, she said, far from it. He had explained that he could get this watch through into Georgia without much difficulty, and back at home there it would be worth many times its value here. So he had invested almost all his winnings from the chess tournament in the watch.

I felt tempted to put down my book, switch off my light, and thus demonstrate what I thought of this revelation. But I stopped myself. I certainly didn't want to drive her into a corner, but nor could I just stand by in silence as she was drawn further and further into the toils of a deceiver, blindly approving of anything he did.

After a pause, I said that if Ninoshvili had been in such a hurry to invest his money, then he was obviously thinking about going home. Some time or other his visa would run out; I wasn't sure how long it would be valid. She said nothing. Looking at my book, I asked, "Do you know?"

She said, "His visa's been extended by four weeks."

I looked at her. "Doesn't he need an invitation for that?"

"Yes, that's right."

"Then who did he get it from?"

She hesitated for a moment, and then met my eyes. "Me."

213

She said of course she ought to have told me before. But she shrank from the argument that would probably have been inevitable, and there she could understand me very well. However, she had hoped, and still did, that in a week or so Ninoshvili would be able to sign a contract for a reasonably good sum, and then set straight off for home. He was already almost ill with longing for his Matassi, she said. So she had hoped that we wouldn't have to discuss this point.

I said nothing. Once again she became talkative, swamping me with details that I hadn't asked for and that didn't matter at all now, since she had already taken her decision without asking my opinion.

David had got the invitation for the first thirty days of his stay from Dr B. Unger, head of the Lyra publishing house. But Dr Unger had held out false hopes; he hadn't wanted to take on one of David's manuscripts at a good price, and after David gave him a piece of his mind about that, Dr Unger obviously lost interest in the idea. Anyway, he declined to extend the visa.

David was desperate, because of course he couldn't ask one of the other publishing firms with which he was negotiating to see to that formality without exposing his own inadequacy, and then he would feel even worse. So she said she'd go to the local Foreign Citizens Office and Foreign Office branches with him, and provide the necessary signatures. It was only a formality. As long as he could stay with us, the Georgian Cultural Ministry's travel fund would be enough to keep him going, and if he were to fall ill she had sensibly taken out insurance, no problems there, and it had cost only a few pfennigs.

I said nothing for a long time. She took my upper arm and shook it slightly. "Christian. Don't you understand? Ought I to have said no, go away, clear off home, you're a nuisance to us?"

I said perhaps I understood more than she thought. I wouldn't even be surprised if it turned out next that our guest had asked for asylum and was planning to spend the winter with us waiting for the decision to come through.

"Are you crazy?" she said. "I told you he wants to get home as soon as he can. He's tired of this country and the humiliations he's had to put up with here. He's sick with longing for home and his Matassi."

I put my book down and switched off my lamp. She lay where she was, glancing sideways at me, then looking at the quilt. After a while she put her arm over her eyes.

56

Manni Wallmeroth is being excluded from the school. The staff meeting held today took an unexpected turn. I hadn't seen it coming.

I gave my account of the incident, emphasizing that Manni had come to me of his own accord, and there he had shown sense that did him credit, but I had stuck to my original line, arguing for Manni's exclusion. The fact that if I didn't I'd have had to eat my own words and come off my high horse, as Elke put it, had nothing at all to do with this judgement of mine.

Indeed, if I'd shown myself flexible here, I'd have been sadly short of evidence. I'd have had to give reasons why I wanted to allow an exception from the rule in the case of a certain student, and why this one in particular, and such a volte-face would have impressed no one, nor would it have done Manni any good.

However, the really crucial reason why I stood firm was that I thought I could afford it without doing much damage.

I was certain that the meeting would vote against Manni's exclusion from the school, and I was ready to swallow my defeat.

But against my expectations, the discussion became more and more heated, it acquired a fateful dynamic that I couldn't influence any more, even if I had retreated from my position in short order. I don't know if it was because of the article that appeared in the local paper, which must have drawn its facts from a well-informed source – don't ask me which source. The article – and Herr Heuberger had obviously been unable to stop its publication – cited Manni's slogan word for word, and raised the question of whether the right-wing radicalism that has not yet made any appearance worth mentioning at our school was now gaining a foothold there too.

It didn't surprise me that Frau Schacht, still resenting her broken chair leg, said at once that she entirely agreed with me: Manfred Wallmeroth must be excluded. But Frau Jellonek, who ought to know that a Christian is supposed to show mercy at all times, was also on Frau Schacht's side, and even Philippovich wanted to see Manni Wallmeroth excluded.

I could have understood him if we'd been talking about a girl, since in his view we had too many girls at the school anyway. But Philippovich even brought up, as an argument against Manni, the boy's strong enthusiasm for masculinity, the brute force he had shown when he tipped over the classroom cupboard, with his fellow student Lehmann inside it, in a manner liable to endanger life.

I was placing my hopes on Elke Lampert and motherly Frau Fasold, who both fought valiantly for Manni. But my optimism was in vain. The meeting closed with a majority of only three above the quorum necessary for the exclusion of Manni Wallmeroth, but it was three all the same. Elke left the staff room without looking at me.

I felt wretched for the rest of the day. Everything sickened me, most of all supper with my family and our long-term guest. I listened to the conversation going on around the table as silently as Ralf. I wasn't interested when Julia announced that tomorrow evening, Friday, she would be late home because, after a long absence from the lawyers' regular evening get-togethers, she thought she would go again. And it left me entirely cold to hear that on the same evening Ninoshvili had an appointment at the Lyra publishing house with the head of the firm, Dr Unger, with whom, according to Julia's account, he had fallen out.

When Julia sat down in front of the TV set with Ninoshvili after supper, I said I had a headache. I went back to my study for while and then went to bed. I was still lying awake, but pretending to be asleep, when Julia, stepping cautiously, came into the bedroom late, undressed in the dark and got into bed.

57

As soon as I was home from school this afternoon, I immersed myself in essays by my class of students who aspire to study German at university. It was a kind of escape strategy. I was looking for some peaceful area which I still ruled, and where no one would venture to cast doubt on my authority.

The class had taken the news that Manni Wallmeroth was being excluded from the school with curious stillness. I had feared they would involve me in discussion, and I'd tried to prepare for that. But no one asked if it was really necessary to throw him out, no one wanted to know if I was the person responsible.

They even kept quiet when I asked André Grothe there and then if he was prepared to take Manni's place in the part of Benvolio. Even André, who so far had not been particularly interested in the drama group, didn't fool around but just said okay.

Perhaps they were still too upset by the news. I don't know what they may come up with over the weekend. The question was still on my mind for some time after I got home. But after an hour I managed to concentrate on the essays. My work was getting somewhere.

I heard Ralf come in and felt an urge to ask him into my study at once and impress it upon him, yet again, that he mustn't try pitting his strength against Ninoshvili, whatever plan he may have thought up for that purpose. But I postponed the conversation, although it still seemed to me urgent. I didn't want to abandon my occupation with something I understood, something that required meaningful activity on my part, instead of just having people pull the wool over my eyes.

I stopped when, in Günsel Özcan's paper, I came upon the remark: "Although Herr von Briest may seem to us unjust and harsh, he is still a good father." I was just wondering what she meant by this sympathetic judgement of Effi Briest's father in Fontane's novel, when there was a knock. Ralf opened the door. He stood there holding the handle, jerked his head in the direction of the top floor, and asked, "Can you come up with me? Quickly, please." I got to my feet and followed him.

He opened the spare-room door, went in, stopped in front of Ninoshvili's leather suitcase and looked at me. Then he lifted the lid of the case and folded it back. He reached in and pushed aside the shabby knitted waistcoat. Underneath it lay the folder with the stamp of Julia's law firm on it. He

218

opened the folder and picked up the copies of Ninoshvili's manuscripts. An application form for political asylum came into view, and with it a leaflet entitled *Regulation of Rights to Asylum in the Federal Republic of Germany*. The form hadn't been filled in yet.

"Wasn't the case locked?" I asked.

"Yes, but I got the locks open."

"Are you out of your mind, Ralf?"

He shook his head. "Don't worry, he won't notice." He put his hand in his trouser pocket, brought out a small skeleton key and showed it to me.

The phone rang. I said, "Lock that case again at once! And get out of this room!"

I went down to my study and picked up the receiver. It was Erika. "Hello, Christian dear!" she said. "It's me, Erika. I hope I'm not disturbing you, but I thought you might be alone at home at this time of day."

Before I could stop her, she was telling me she'd been going to ring me ever since Monday, but something had always got in the way of it. And for the first few days she'd been too angry as well, although of course that hadn't been my fault. Anyway, she wanted to tell me she had been very sorry to have to leave without saying goodbye to me.

I didn't need to ask why she'd been so angry, she went on. She was sure I'd believe her when she said she'd have liked to hold me lovingly in her arms again, but on the Saturday Julia had simply thrown her out of the house, she'd said to her face that she couldn't move back into the spare room because David would be needing it for some time to come, and if she wanted to stay any longer Julia was afraid she'd have to find a hotel room.

Julia had even said, according to Erika, that I had promised David he could occupy the spare room as long as he liked.

219

"Is that true?" I said no. She was triumphant. "There, I was sure of that anyway. I'd have been surprised if it was!" She asked how things were going between those two, and if Julia was still acting in such a crazy way. I said there was no news.

She sighed. "Oh, Christian! I wish I were with you now, I'd so much like to hold you in my arms and comfort you a little. Do you sometimes think of me?" I said I did. She whispered, "I often think of you. That was a wonderful day alone with you." She laughed. "And a wonderful night, in case you were thinking I'd forgotten that!" She said I mustn't let things get me down. Before hanging up, she sent me a kiss down the phone, "a very heartfelt kiss – I hope you can really feel it!"

I hung up and went back to the top floor. Ralf wasn't there any more. I tried the clasps of the case, and they were locked. I couldn't see any sign that they'd been picked. I called Ralf, looked in every room for him, but he'd obviously left the house.

I sat down at my desk, stared at Günsel's round, sprawling handwriting, but I couldn't take in her train of thought, not a word of it. After a few minutes I phoned Elke Lampert. I was afraid she wouldn't be at home, but to my relief she picked up the phone. She sounded very cool when I said it was me. I asked if she had a little time to spare for me; I'd very much like to talk to her. The answer was no, she was sorry, but she was deep in her work.

I said, "So am I." And then, "Elke, I'm going out of my mind here within my own four walls. I have to talk to someone. You're the only human soul I can really talk to."

We agreed to meet in the bar that Brauckmann had chosen for the skittles evenings designed to promote contact between staff members. She asked if that would be all right; her husband might be home on the dot for once, and she wouldn't want him disturbing us. I said anywhere was all right just so long as I could talk to her.

220

58

The landlady of the bar, who knew our faces from the skittles evenings, seemed to be wondering what we had to do with each other. She came over to the table in the back room where we had sat down, smiled – "Here without the skittles club today, then?"– and acted as if we were a pair of lovers who could count on her discretion. Elke obviously didn't mind, and nor did I.

I didn't mind the atmosphere in the bar either, although I wouldn't have lingered there on any other day. At this time in the afternoon we had the back room to ourselves, the eight tables with their blue-check tablecloths, the creaking wicker chairs. There had been only two early drinkers standing at the counter in the bar itself, and a man at the corner table who kept his coat on as he consumed a plate of knackwurst and curly kale. Now and then we could hear the voices of the men in the bar involved in a ponderous argument. There was a sour smell of beer, and the sun was pale beyond the windows looking out on the yard.

I don't remember ever having begged another human being to listen to me before. As a child I once beat up a smaller boy who always had a runny nose, and whose pushiness infuriated me, doing him so much damage that I was afraid the police would come to our house and arrest me at the supper table. But I didn't confide my fears even to my best friend, an out-and-out young hooligan who would have understood and approved. I suffered in silence without telling anyone.

When my aunt Laura died four weeks too late, and I ended up in hospital because I hadn't made sensible use of her legacy, I had also felt I couldn't bear to stay within the four pale green walls surrounding me. I thought I'd go crazy, I seemed to be at the mercy of a malicious Fate playing cat-and-mouse with me. But when my mother came to see me on the evening after my accident, and tried to comfort me, I smiled and said oh, it wasn't too bad. When she had gone, and night was falling, I broke out in a sweat and ground my teeth. But I didn't call for help. I kept quiet.

I must be in a bad way. I don't know why I felt almost as if Elke were my last hope. Perhaps I was relying on her sense that she owed me something. And perhaps I thought I could safely bare my soul to her, since she herself had unashamedly told me her own troubles. I don't know whether I was expecting her to give me advice that would instantly dispel my misery, but I must have had some such vague idea.

After the landlady had taken our order, nodding and smiling in a confidential manner, as if she were ready to give us the key to an upstairs room if we wanted, I asked Elke how she was.

"I'm all right, thank you. But you don't seem to be, not at all."

I nodded. She said, "I'm sorry, Christian. But I did tell you what would happen. And if you're expecting sympathy or consolation from me now, I'll have to disillusion you. I can't feel any sympathy for you. And I have no intention of consoling you either. You failed to take the bend in the road and now you've driven into the wall. But it was your own fault."

I ought to have buried my hopes as soon as I heard her say that. I should have looked for a reasonably dignified reason to leave this depressing bar. But I was beside myself. All I feared now was that Elke would cut this conversation short and walk out.

"Won't you at least listen to me?"

"Yes, of course, or I wouldn't have come."

I said that there was probably no point in discussing the way I'd acted at the staff meeting. I only wanted to tell her that I had stuck to my point not because I was self-opinionated, but for the opposite reason: I'd been hoping that my obstinacy would annoy some of those who hadn't yet made up their minds and influence them in Manni's favour. I'd expected to lose, I had been sure that the vote would go against excluding the boy.

"Do you really believe that? Are you trying to cobble together excuses for yourself in retrospect?"

"Please, Elke! Let me at least finish."

She picked up her handbag and lit a cigarette.

I said I wasn't trying to excuse myself. The outcome of the meeting was a disaster, and I couldn't and wouldn't deny my own part in it. But I also wanted her to know that I'd probably have behaved differently all along if I hadn't been in a situation that was preying badly on my mind. It was a situation that shamed me just as much as Manni's exclusion, but I wouldn't conceal it from her. I wanted her to understand me.

She blew smoke into the air and looked at me in silence.

I told her about the guest in my house, the man whose cultural mission I had once mentioned to her already in passing. I said this Georgian, whom I had taken into my home in good faith, turned out to be a nationalist and a racist. He had made contact behind my back with sinister figures of the extreme political right, he'd even intoxicated my son with his ideas and turned him against me. This man had aroused my instinctive dislike of nationalism so much that I had simply freaked out when I saw Manni's graffiti. I'd been so obsessed that I overreacted and couldn't find a way out.

She asked, "Why haven't you told this man to leave?"

I did not reply for a while. Then I said, "Because he's cast a spell over my wife as well. She's developed a fondness for him. And I can't open her eyes because I'm afraid such a disappointment would hurt her very much."

The landlady brought our coffee and schnapps. "Here you are, something to cheer you up. Just call if you need anything else!"

Elke drank her schnapps without raising her glass to me. Then she asked, "What do you mean, a fondness?"

I had already opened the way into my house for Herr Hochgeschurz. One more observer made no difference. Why not let Elke look into my bedroom as well?

I shrugged my shoulders and looked at her in silence.

She asked, "Are you saying that your wife is being unfaithful to you with this man?"

"I don't know. I haven't caught them at it yet. But there are some indications." I drained my schnapps. "For instance, she went on a trip out of the city with him, and then they made an excuse to stay away overnight."

"That's not evidence."

"No. I'm groping in the dark. But maybe now you can understand why I sometimes feel I'm going mad."

She rose to her feet. "Would you like another schnapps too?"

"Yes, one more."

She went to the door of the bar and placed the order. After sitting down again she was silent, playing with her lighter.

I don't know why I still wouldn't give up hope that she, the only human being I could talk to, would at least say an understanding word. But perhaps I was also driven by a perverse pleasure in stripping myself to the bone, an irresistible impulse to reveal everything that weighed on my mind and put me to shame. Perhaps I expected that I could break down her reserve in this way after all, at whatever cost.

I said, "That's not all. The man has turned my life upside down so badly that I didn't just go to pieces at school." I cleared my throat, and then I said, "He brought me to the point where I was unfaithful to my wife. With her best friend."

She looked at me incredulously. I said I could see exactly why I'd committed this indiscretion. Really I'd always rather disliked the friend, and I had always avoided her on her earlier visits to us. But this time we'd got involved. "It was a cheap act of revenge, can you understand that?" Julia, I said, had been away with our guest, she had deceived me, not letting me know until after they left that they were going to stay away overnight. I'd been alone in the house with her friend. She had made advances to me, perhaps to console me. And I had used the opportunity to avenge myself on Julia.

The landlady brought our schnapps. "You don't need to get up and come out – I'll hear if you call me, I'm just next door." She smiled understandingly. "I'll make sure no one disturbs you."

I sipped my schnapps. Elke didn't touch her own glass. "Or maybe it simply happened because I felt lonely. Abandoned. Deceived. Anyway, it would never have gone so far if I hadn't taken that man into my house. Do you understand how I feel? It's as if he is intentionally undermining my life. Not just trying to take my wife away from me, but driving me to throw all my principles overboard. Making me behave like a total idiot. Like a berserker who won't shrink from anything."

She reached for her cigarettes, lit one, drew on it twice and stubbed it out again. "Why would he be interested in undermining your life?"

"I don't know." I shrugged my shoulders. "There's no good reason why he should."

"But it's his fault that you had that boy thrown out of the school? And it's his fault that you betrayed your wife with her best friend?"

I shook my head. "Yes, I know it may sound as if I'm trying to make excuses for myself again. I'm sorry, but I can't see it any other way. I would never, never have done what I did if the man hadn't plagued me like that. In a subtle, single-minded way. I could give you dozens of examples, but I don't want to unload all this on you. I think you can understand me anyway. You know what I'm like."

She shook her head. "No, my dear. Obviously I don't know what you're like, or at least I didn't. I think I do understand you now. But not in the way you want me to."

She said I was trying to pretend to both of us, her and myself. So I said I didn't want Manni excluded from school? Then why on earth hadn't I said so and defended the boy? And I'd always disliked my wife's friend, had I? Then why didn't I keep my hands off her? No, no, my dear, she said. I hadn't wanted to withdraw my demands at school because I couldn't have reconciled that with my masculine arrogance. And I'd gone to bed with my wife's friend because she happened to be available, and spending the night with her was presumably more fun than lying in bed alone, wondering if there could really be a man more attractive than me somewhere.

None of this, she queried, would have happened but for that man? Was I really going to tell her and myself something so ridiculous? I had made my guest into a phantom figure who could be held responsible for my mistakes. There was no good reason, I'd said so myself, for him to do me any harm. Couldn't I see how grotesque it was to claim that he was trying to destroy my life?

"No, my dear, it won't do." She drained her schnapps and put the glass down with a sharp little sound. "Do you want to know the truth? You're disgustingly self-obsessed, Christian. You're a classic example of macho man."

226

She rose to her feet. "If you go on like this you'll soon be grieving for the loss of your wife, the way you're sorry now about sacrificing that boy to your lousy principles. Well, take care, Christian."

She nodded to me and went out.

59

I didn't get home until nearly eight. I had driven from the bar to the Katharinenforst and spent almost three hours walking there, exploring small paths, clambering over wet, slippery leaves. The pale sun showed through the bare branches of the trees. There didn't seem to be anyone but me walking in these woods.

Only when twilight began to fall did I drive back into the city, but I still didn't go home. I went to the suburb where Lyra has its office. I left my car at the tram stop and walked to the apartment building where Dr Unger probably not only works but also lives and sleeps on the first floor. The way to the building leads past a kiosk in need of new paint, and some allotment gardens, and on the other side of the street there is a factory wall of dark-red bricks, many of them crumbling. It's not far from the building to the city boundary, the first patches of meadowland and some sparse bushes.

It was clear to me that Ninoshvili could have seen me if, in order to keep his supposed appointment, he was already on the floor of Dr Unger's office and happened to look through the window. Or he could meet me on my way back to the tram stop. But that didn't bother me. I would even have welcomed it. However, I very much doubted whether Ninoshvili was going to Dr Unger's office this evening at all.

I also doubted whether Julia was at the lawyers' regular evening get-together at this hour. When she last went to one of those occasions she came home in a temper, because some loquacious character had been getting on everyone's nerves all evening, and she hadn't been to any of them at all since Ninoshvili's arrival. As I got into my car at the tram stop I wondered whether to drive into the city, go to her alleged destination, and look in at the restaurant, which was called The Last Resort. If I had been misjudging Julia, I wouldn't have minded her surprise and displeasure. But I didn't want to embarrass her in front of her legal colleagues.

When I got home the house was empty. I sat down at my desk, with Günsel's essay still lying on it, and switched on the reading lamp. After a while I got up, went to the window and looked out. It was dark now, the night sky had clouded over and there wasn't a star to be seen. I sat down again and read Günsel's essay to the end. She had taken great trouble to show why Herr von Briest, however stern he might be, was a good father. I gave her a high mark.

After reading two more essays, which gave me less satisfaction, I went to the window again. I wondered where Ralf might be. There was no one out in the dark street. The light over the Lohmüller family's front door was off. Probably that dandified fellow and his flaxen-haired wife were sitting in front of the TV, and inquisitive Raffy was fast asleep in his bed.

I closed my eyes. After a while, the image that had been building up in my mind for the last few hours, although I had kept making grim efforts to suppress it, irresistibly forced itself upon me.

Dr Unger's building, the way from there to the tram stop. Ninoshvili leaves the building, he stands in the doorway for a moment, as if unsure which way to turn, glances at the city boundary, now lying in darkness. Then he sets off towards the tram. He does not walk very fast, his shoulders are stooped, his head is bent. He passes the wire netting of the allotments. The pavement is only dimly lit by two street lamps outside the factory wall.

Ninoshvili approaches the kiosk; its counter is closed off by a large sheet of wood. Three or four dark figures emerge from the darkness behind the kiosk. Their faces can't be made out; they wear knitted caps pulled right down over their eyebrows, and woollen scarves are wrapped around their mouths and noses. Ninoshvili casts them a sideways glance and quickens his pace slightly. He hasn't passed the kiosk when he suddenly collapses and falls forwards. One of the figures has struck him a murderous blow on the back of the neck with a baseball bat.

Ninoshvili lands on his knees and is trying to get up when the next blow fells him to the ground. He buries his head in his arms, but they pull his arms apart and turn him on his back. The next blow hits him in the face, blood shoots from his nose. They haul him to his feet, one of them kicks him in the stomach and then again between the legs. The man with the baseball bat strikes at his thigh, the blow makes contact, the bone cracks. They drop Ninoshvili, swing back their heavily booted feet and kick him in the temples and the sides. One of them jumps on him and tramples on his ribcage.

Ninoshvili has stopped moving, he's lost consciousness. The figures run away. They tear the caps off their heads, pull the scarves down and jump into a car waiting for them with its engine running. They have disappeared into the darkness when the tram with its yellow-lit windows drives up.

A fantasy. The spawn of an over-heated imagination. A nightmare not sent to haunt me by a malevolent Fate, but conjured up by me, all on my own.

I sat down at the desk again and tried to concentrate on the next essay. After five minutes I rose to my feet, went up to the top floor and into Ralf's room. I glanced around and then began systematically searching his drawers.

In his desk drawer I found a street map of the city. The site of Dr Unger's office was marked with a cross.

I put the street map in my pocket, ran downstairs, and was already on my way to the front door when I stopped. I thought hard, hearing my own heart beating. Then I turned back. I went into my study, took the telephone book off the shelf, searched for Herr Schumann's number with flying fingers, standing up, and dialled it. The line was engaged.

I tore my coat off the hook, got my car out of the garage, and drove to Herr Schumann's summer house.

60

It's midnight. Silence has fallen in my house. Ralf is in bed, Julia too has gone into the bedroom after taking a sleeping pill. Whether either of them is asleep I don't know.

There was still light at the windows of the industrial-consultancy offices when I rang the bell at Herr Schumann's garden gate. I looked at my watch, glanced up into the bare, black branches of the elms as I waited. I didn't wait very long, but rang a second time, keeping my finger on the bell push. The intercom crackled. "Yes?"

"This is Christian Kestner. I'm looking for my son Ralf."

"Ralf? Sorry, Ralf's not here."

I said, "Then I'd like to speak to you. Would you open the door, please?"

"Speak to me? Do you know how late it is?"

"Yes, I do, it's twenty-one minutes past nine. Please open the door."

There was a short pause. Then the intercom was switched off and the garden gate buzzed open. In the dim light I walked along the crunching gravel to Herr Schumann's summer house. Narrow strips of light fell through the Venetian blinds at the French windows.

Herr Schumann came a little way to meet me, led me down the paved path to the back of the house, and invited me in with a silent gesture. Then he went ahead of me. I followed him into the spacious living room where several standard lamps and table lamps were switched on. A pretty black-haired girl in jeans and pullover was sitting on a broad sofa, leaning back in a relaxed pose in the corner. Herr Schumann said, "This is Frau Kiwitt. This is Herr Kestner, a senior teacher." He pointed to an armchair and sat down on the sofa next to Frau Kiwitt.

Herr Schumann was wearing a dark-brown casual shirt, a yellow cashmere pullover, dark-brown jeans – designer jeans, I suspect – socks with a brown-and-yellow pattern and well-polished brown slip-on shoes. I glanced around. The flag of the Third Reich hung on the back wall of the room between two bookshelves. On one of the shelves stood a black portrait bust of Adolf Hitler, perhaps a replica of the heroic statues made in Arno Breker's studio in the Nazi era.

I sat down, looked at Herr Schumann and asked, "Where's my son?"

Herr Schumann raised his eyebrows, smiled, straightened his gold-rimmed glasses. "Your son? How should I know?"

"I'm asking you again where my son is. And I mean that seriously."

Herr Schumann cast a glance at Frau Kiwitt and shook his head, smiling. "Listen, Herr Kestner, you seem to have the wrong idea of my connections with your son." He stroked his sleek blond head. "Your son is a nice boy, but I'm not a second father to him. We see each other now and then, but he doesn't tell me what he gets up to when we aren't together."

Frau Kiwitt picked up her wine glass, sipped from it, and looked at me over the rim. Herr Schumann raised his hand. Frau Kiwitt handed him his own glass, he raised it to her with a smile and drank.

I realized that I wasn't going to be able to nail this gangster down. I got to my feet. "If you have been lying to me you'll be very sorry for it, I assure you. You've turned my son's head. And if you happen to have dragged him into some kind of venture with consequences that he can't judge, then I promise you will pay for it."

Herr Schumann asked, "Forgive me, but are you feeling all right?"

I turned away and left. When I was in the car I wondered again whether to go to Dr Unger's office and search the dismal street. But I was afraid that it was too late for that, quite apart from the risk I'd be running – for my son, for me, for my family – if I showed my face there. I drove home.

I found a note from Julia on my desk, obviously scribbled in great haste. I could barely decipher it. It said: *David's been mugged. He's in the Marienhospital. Am going there now, Julia.*

I felt for the chair at my desk, lowered myself into it and put the note down. After a while I looked at the time. Five to ten. I got to my feet, slowly climbed the stairs to the top floor and opened the door of Ralf's room. I looked in. In the dim light from the street lamps, I saw that his desk drawer was closed. I thought I remembered leaving it open.

I switched on the light and went into the room. Ralf was lying in bed facing the wall, curled up under the quilt. He raised his head and looked at me, frowning, his eyes narrowed. "What's the matter?"

"Where have you been?" I asked.

"To the cinema. What's up?"

"Do you really not know?"

"No! I'd only just dropped off to sleep."

I said, "Ninoshvili's been mugged. He's in hospital."

"Oh, shit!" He scratched his cheek. "Who did it?"

"That's what I'm asking you."

"How would I know? I told you, I've been to the cinema." He let his head drop back.

"Who did you go with?"

"I went on my own." He scratched again. "I went to the seven o'clock screening, and I was back at nine fifteen. Julia came in after me, but I'd gone to bed by then."

I stared at him. "Then no one can prove that you were at the cinema?"

"No. What's this interrogation all about?"

I said, "Ralf, this chapter isn't closed yet!"

I switched off the light and closed the door, went to my desk and wrote a note. *Dear Julia, in case we miss each other, I've gone to the Marienhospital. Love and kisses. Christian.* I tacked the note to the front door.

I met Julia on the front steps of the hospital. Her eyes were red with crying. She let me hug her, but she didn't return the hug.

Ninoshvili is in intensive care. He's unconscious. The doctor on duty told Julia everything possible will be done for him, but he's in a critical condition.

The police found our phone number in Ninoshvili's wallet. The police officer who called when Julia had just got home said they had found no trace of his attacker or attackers.

233

61

The sun was shining too warmly for the last day but one of October when I set off for the hospital today, Saturday morning. Julia had been going to drive there herself, but when she had phoned the intensive care ward and found out that there was no great change in Ninoshvili's condition, she asked me to do the hospital visiting. Meanwhile, she said, she'd try to reach Matassi in Tbilisi.

The city was sparkling as if it had polished itself up for the weekend and was getting ready to enjoy these hours of recreation. The hospital looked polished up too, an old brick building full of nooks and crannies, corridors with high cross-vaulting, lancet windows and stone flags on the floors. The corridors were empty. There was a smell of citrus fruit – probably from something in the cleaning fluid – coffee and only a hint of carbolic. As I passed an open door I saw a nun sitting at a desk; she raised a coffee cup and sipped from it.

Such peace as this, the silence of a solemn holiday, had both shocked and soothed me once before, when I was visiting my dying father on a hot Sunday morning in July. I hadn't been able to understand that most of the medical staff weren't around, only the two or three people on duty, and that even they preserved an attitude of relaxed calm while the patient breathed stertorously, as if death itself knew and respected the fact that it was a Sunday. But at the same time I had felt comforted. Death, coming into the midst of such peace, would walk quietly, without pain and terror.

After I had put on a green coat, a face mask and white galoshes, they let me take a look at Ninoshvili. He was in a large ward where the beds were separated from each other by screens, lying on his back with his chest bare and his swollen, discoloured eyes closed as if he were in a deep sleep. He was flanked by apparatus, connected up to it by tubes and cables. His head and nose were bandaged, his right leg splinted. He was breathing lightly but regularly. I saw his chest rising and falling.

I insisted on speaking to the doctor, as Julia had told me to do. After half an hour he came to the corridor outside the intensive-care ward to see me; he was still a young man, but obviously very self-confident. He questioned me closely to check my right to ask questions about the patient before giving me any information.

Ninoshvili has suffered fractures of the nasal bone, the lower right leg and several ribs. He has severe lacerated wounds over both eyes, bruising all over the body and a blunt abdominal trauma. X-rays have shown that a fracture of the base of the skull, suspected because of the ocular haematoma, can be ruled out. However, his unconsciousness and vomiting indicate severe traumatic brain injury. The possibility of delayed intracranial bleeding occurring is therefore not to be excluded. The patient is still in a critical condition. If he did not have a very robust constitution in general, he might well have died of his injuries already.

I asked the doctor if these injuries could be the result of a road accident. He shook his head. "Oh no! He'd have had to be run over from behind and in front at the same time. No, no. It looks to me as if he was systematically battered. The signs are of heavy blows and kicking. He's been struck with a blunt instrument, something like a baseball bat." He scrutinized me. "Can it be that Herr Ninoshvili got into a fight with skinheads or similar thugs?"

I said I could hardly imagine it, though of course I couldn't definitely rule it out either. I thanked the doctor and left. I called Julia from a telephone kiosk near the entrance, as she had asked, and reported back to her.

As I was leaving the hospital, Herr Hochgeschurz came towards me in the sunshine on the steps. He nodded, offered me his hand, and said, "Well, Herr Kestner, this is a bad business."

I asked him how he knew about it. "We read the police reports," he replied. After some of his heavy breathing, he asked, "How is he?"

I said Herr Ninoshvili was in a bad way, hovering between life and death. I was going to shake hands with Hochgeschurz and turn away, but he asked, "Did he tell you what he was doing in that part of town?"

I said that as far as I knew he had been going to visit Dr Unger, director of the publishing firm Lyra. Herr Hochgeschurz nodded and sighed. "Ah, yes. Another of those outfits."

I asked what he meant. Herr Hochgeschurz said, "Nothing concrete." He massaged his nose. "But as you may know, the mother house of that firm was founded under the German Democratic Republic and is in Leipzig. And you may even know that the profits of the books that Herr Unger publishes probably couldn't even pay the rent of that place in the suburbs."

I said no, I knew nothing about that, and gave Herr Hochgeschurz my hand. He asked, "How was the chess tournament in Schwitte?" I said, "Very interesting."

Herr Hochgeschurz nodded. As I was turning away he said, "I don't want to pester you, Herr Kestner, but what Dr Schmidt and I said to you still stands. We'd be grateful for any information, you may be sure of that. You have my word for it."

I said, "Thank you very much," and walked away.

62

The hawk and the wood grouse both drowned. The wood grouse had been trying to escape the bird of prey that King Vakhtang Gorgasal had taken out hunting, but it flew in vain. The hawk pursued it high above the trees of the Georgian forest and was not to be shaken off, however far the wood grouse flew in its time of need. They flew far over the land, from Mtskheta where the King's palace stood to the fortress of Narikala, built by the Persians a century earlier.

There at last, in the blue sky above the Kura Valley, the hawk seized upon the wood grouse. But it was not to return home in triumph. The long flight had exhausted the predator's own strength; it fell to the depths like a stone, with its prey in its talons. Hawk and wood grouse, indissolubly linked, fell into the sulphur-yellow bubbling water, and both died there.

King Vakhtang, who had long been looking for his hawk's return, did not want to lose his favourite bird of prey, and set out in search of it. The king was greatly distressed when he found the magnificent bird after many days, its claws still clutching its victim. But he also saw the incomparable beauty of the place to which his hawk, even in death, had led him. So King Vakhtang built a new city by the bubbling spring in the valley of the Kura, Tbilisi, and from then on he ruled Georgia from there, enjoying the healing powers of the bubbling sulphurous water.

I am not sure if the hawk doomed to die in a strange place deserves our sympathy, but I pity it. It must have been a pathetic sight: the beautiful, proud bird floating in the clouded, stinking water with its victim, its talons now still, its plumage shredded by the impact when it fell, and steeped in the sulphurous brew. A murderer may have deserved death, but even a murderer doesn't deserve a death that humiliates him and ends his life in the shame of defeat.

Julia has tried unsuccessfully to reach Matassi in Tbilisi. She got through to Ninoshvili's apartment three times, but no one answered the phone. It can't be because of the civil war. There's still some shooting in Tbilisi now and then, but Shevardnadze seems to have the situation under control.

He watched unmoved when, in one of his assemblies, a young man who had criticized Georgia's membership of the Commonwealth of Independent States was thrown out of the hall with violence. In an interview, the president referred to King Herakleios II of Georgia who two hundred years ago, in the struggle against the Persians, saw no alternative to calling on the protective power of Russia. "Perhaps our country would have ceased to exist long ago otherwise."

Zviad Gamsakhurdia's supporters must, however, prepare themselves for pitiless judicial retribution. They are being pursued in West Georgia by Dzhaba Ioseliani, former professor of drama and long-term inmate of penal institutions, who went over from Gamsakhurdia to Shevardnadze and formed a kind of volunteer corps against the Zviadists. Ioseliani, clad in baseball cap, T-shirt, windcheater and trainers, Kalashnikov slung over his shoulder and a gold chain around his bare neck, told the *Spiegel* reporter, "We are the defenders of the sole legitimate power."

Perhaps I was right to assume that Matassi separated from Ninoshvili long ago. Perhaps the Nana or Nona who took her place, who signed Ninoshvili's New Year cards in Matassi's name, who chose and packed up the present to me, has moved out again. She felt sorry for her self-confident partner but shrank from a showdown with him, and as soon as he set off for the Federal Republic of Germany she took her chance to carry her suitcase down the creaking stairs from the apartment that same day. Her new boyfriend was waiting for her outside the little door into the yard.

The blinds are down over the window looking out on the balcony; a striped pattern of sunlight falls into the living room. The door to the bedroom is open, the abandoned bed can be seen in its twilit cavern, the woven bedspread neatly adjusted, the pillows plumped up and tidily arranged. The telephone rings. After a minute the ringing stops. The voices of children rise from the yard.

Perhaps Matassi comes down the street now and then, glances at the little door in the high wall, and goes on her way. Perhaps she's come to terms with the Shevardnadze party. Her position at the University Library, for which she feared, is still to be hers, or so she's been told anyway, so long as she cooperates. Matassi has cooperated, she has not kept back information about Ninoshvili's past.

Maybe there's no one left in Tbilisi to weep for David Ninoshvili. David is dead? Better for him, perhaps, than if he had come back. He has acted a little too wildly. There are too many people here who would like to settle accounts with him. He's been battered to death? Well, who knows what he was up to over there in Germany? If he'd been clever he would have taken his chance to keep quiet and tried to stay there. He could always have said he was a political refugee. And in a way that would have been true.

Maybe no one in Tbilisi would demand to see David again. Not that there was anything to see that a sensitive person could bear without horror, without a tormenting pity. That swollen, battered face, no trace of its former handsome regularity left, just a distorted mask. The muscular leg, the powerful knee now out of action, needing a splint at least to give it some rest. The tubes and cables, emergency lines keeping him from succumbing to death. The bared breast,

239

rising and falling faintly. The bandaged brow. What can be going on behind it? What nightmares may be hunting him down, tormenting him, his companions on the way to death?

That's enough of that. I must think about my family if I want to keep David Ninoshvili from dragging them down into the whirlpool with him.

This afternoon, when Julia was at the hospital, I questioned Ralf closely again. He insists that he was at the cinema at the time of the attack. I've asked him if he knew about it, if he might perhaps even have staged it. He answered with another question. "What for? What's this third-degree stuff all about?"

I told him that if he was going around with any information about the attack not already known to me, he had better tell me as soon as possible, because otherwise I had good grounds to fear that he would be in serious trouble.

He said, "Don't go worrying about nothing. How stupid do you think I am?"

63

According to a story in the local paper, the city CID have been working overtime for the first nine months of this year. The number of criminal offences committed was over 90,000 to the end of September, which means that last year's alarming record is going to be exceeded yet again by about ten per cent.

Some forty per cent of those suspected of committing such offences are foreigners. The number of violations by foreign nationals and asylum-seekers of the Foreign Citizens Act and the Asylum Procedure Act has almost doubled since the

240

regulations governing those laws were tightened up. On the other hand, there has also been an above-average increase in offences motivated by xenophobia. Among other abuses of the law, the police place in this category anonymous threats made to foreigners on the telephone and graffiti featuring the swastika.

To be sure, the police are alarmed not just by such political criminality, as you might call it. They are also concerned by the spread of "unmotivated violence". Young people intent on snatching handbags are more and more inclined to beat up their victims, usually elderly women, injuring them badly, even though there was no need to do so to get possession of their loot. In fact it even happens now and then that someone is beaten almost to death just for fun.

The police describe the case of an elderly man who was assaulted out of the blue by two boys and a girl two years ago on his way home at night. The girl said, "Hey, Gramps, we don't like the way you slobber!" Then they knocked him to the ground, breaking his arm in the process. They didn't take the cash he was carrying, just over twenty marks, but went away at a leisurely pace, laughing.

Not that if I were looking for a straightforward explanation of the attack on Ninoshvili I'd even have to fall back on such unmotivated violence. The watch was no longer on Ninoshvili's wrist when he was found. He was still in possession of his wallet and purse, containing eighty-six marks twenty pfennigs; Julia counted it. But as the watch was missing, it could have been a simple case of mugging. Perhaps the perpetrators were disturbed and had been going to search his pockets, but they heard a car coming, took fright, and fled.

If my vision of Ninoshvili being attacked on his way back from an interview with Herr Unger had been fact, then one would have to ask why the perpetrators were out and about on that deserted street at the time. The question would be, had they planned the attack? But in fact Ninoshvili was found just after eight – half an hour after I had visited the scene. He was attacked on his way there.

Perhaps he looked at his watch with pride again in the tram, and his attackers, who happened to be lounging about in the same vehicle, latched on to him, got out when he did and then followed him. He was lost in thought and not paying attention. They caught up with him in between the two faint circles of light from the street lamps, beat him up and stole his watch.

Perhaps the doctor is right in thinking they may have been skinheads. But clearer evidence than just the nature of Ninoshvili's injuries would be necessary to prove his suspicion correct. And even if they were skinheads, judging by all one can read and learn from Tassilo Huber's collection of articles and other sources, thugs like that don't need any reason to beat a man to within an inch of his life. They sometimes wield a baseball bat just for the pleasure of it. And a watch like Ninoshvili's would certainly add to their pleasure.

Herr Hochgeschurz, if he is really supposed to be solving this case, would have to pursue another and quite different suspicion. Suppose he's still looking, as at least it appears, for some connection between Ninoshvili and the woman in the hotel, then it would also be his duty to consider whether it wasn't former Stasi comrades who executed the man from Tbilisi to avenge their captain's murder. And why might not those old comrades disguise themselves as skinheads and use baseball bats?

No, the explanation has to be, or at least I can't rule it out, that Ralf has met a number of dubious characters in Herr Schumann's circle of acquaintances. But in spite of all the

242

trouble my son gives me, it seems to me just about impossible
that he would go around with brutal thugs and skinheads
and even plot with them.

64

A quarter of an hour before the long break period, there was
a knock at my classroom door. The door half opened, and
Frau Kintgen, Trabert's secretary, looked round it. She kept
out of sight of my students and beckoned to me in silence.
I went out into the corridor to join her. Frau Kintgen told
me she had an urgent phone call for me. She didn't say who
the caller was, and I suppressed any urge to ask. I was afraid
of the answer. I followed Frau Kintgen into the secretary's
office and she handed me the receiver, which was lying on
her desk.

It was Julia, calling from the courthouse. When she went
into the corridor outside the courtroom during a break in
the current trial, Herr Hochgeschurz and a plainclothes
CID man had been waiting for her. She told me that they
wanted to know where Ralf had been on the evening of the
attack on Ninoshvili. She said she herself hadn't come in
until about nine thirty, but she assumed that Ralf had spent
the evening at home.

Julia was in a state of great agitation. She was also in a
hurry, because she had to get back to the trial. I told her to
calm down and I would see about it.

I didn't go back to my class. I hurried to my car and drove
to Ralf's school. On the way there I tried to work out what
to do as fast as I could. Once I overtook in the wrong lane,
another time I jumped the lights on red, and both times
angry hooting broke out in concert behind me.

The long break wasn't over yet at Ralf's school. I made my way through the milling throng in the school yard, pushing aside a stubble-haired boy who was in hot pursuit of another and trod on my feet. The boy fell to the ground yelling, "Hey, are you crazy or what?" I found Ralf in the middle of a group of boys and girls sitting on the low wall around the school yard, smoking.

When he saw me he stood up, looked at me and let his arms dangle by his sides. I waved him over to one side. He put out his cigarette and came towards me, holding the cigarette end.

I asked him, "Have the police been here?"

"The police? No." He looked back at his friends, who were watching us curiously. Then he looked at me again. "What do they want?"

"They want to know where you were on Friday evening. The evening Ninoshvili was attacked."

He looked at the cigarette end, scratched his cheek, looked back at me. "I was at the cinema. You know that already."

"Ralf, we don't have much time left. If you have anything to tell me, do it now. The police have already been with your mother. Julia is beside herself. You must tell me what you know about that attack before the police question you – can't you understand that, for God's sake?"

"But what am I supposed to be telling you?" He looked at the cigarette end. "I was in the cinema like I said, isn't that enough?"

"No, it damn well is not enough!"

He turned away, took a step in the direction of the litter bin standing in a corner of the wall. I grabbed his arm. "You stay here!" His friends on the wall were watching with interest. I let go of Ralf's arm.

He looked at me, his mouth twisting. "Why won't you stop going on at me?" He lowered his eyes. "What am I supposed to do?"

Three strokes of the gong echoed over the school yard. I saw a teacher already beginning to herd the smaller children back to their classrooms.

I said, "So you're sticking to your story that you were at the cinema?"

"Yes, what else?"

"And you still say no one saw you? This is very important, Ralf, so don't pretend to me."

"Damn it all, no one did!" He dropped the cigarette end, took out his handkerchief and rubbed it over his hands. "I can't help it if I didn't meet anyone I knew. Not in the cinema, not before and not afterwards either."

"All right." The teacher was approaching. Ralf's friends got off the wall, not in any hurry, and strolled off along the path to the school entrance.

"Listen, Ralf. If the police ask you, don't say a word about going to the cinema. If you can't name any witnesses, they'll be even more suspicious. Say you spent the evening with me. And tell your mother the same. We were at home together, understand?"

He looked at me doubtfully. "But that's no good. That'll just land us both in the shit."

"Why?"

He glanced at the teacher. "If we say that, how are you going to explain that you went to see Gero Schumann? Maybe they'll ask him questions too."

"Listen to me, will you?" I gave the teacher a friendly nod, took Ralf's arm and moved slowly towards the entrance with him. The teacher turned away.

I said, "I didn't go to see Herr Schumann until nine. By that time Ninoshvili was already in hospital. I'll tell the police, and your mother too, that you and I were at home at the time of the attack. We were talking and then we quarrelled. You were spouting some kind of Nazi nonsense – no, not just *some* kind of nonsense." I thought for a moment, then I said, "You told me the story of Mount Elbrus and the mountain troops, and you said the German flag would still be planted on Elbrus if Army Group A hadn't run out of supplies through sabotage and treachery. And we quarrelled violently over that. You went out of the house at nine and I went to see Herr Schumann. I thought you might have gone off to his place. I was very worked up about that Nazi nonsense, and I wanted to get him to explain himself in front of you. But you just walked around the block once, then you came home and went to bed."

I took his arm. "Do you understand that, Ralf?" He nodded. "Remember every word I've just said." After a brief pause, I added, "And don't think that's all there'll be to it. We still have a few things to discuss."

All of a sudden he grinned. "About Mount Elbrus?"

For a moment it took my breath away. Then I said, "Ralf, if you think you can be impertinent you've got a nasty shock coming."

"All right. Sorry." He nodded. "Thanks." Then he turned away from me and went into the school building.

65

This afternoon Raphael Lohmüller kicked his football over the garden fence, I suspect on purpose. I was sitting at my desk, doing nothing and staring into space, when I heard the ball bounce on our terrace.

I was still shaken to the core by the last few hours. After agreeing on our story with Ralf, I had just about managed to

246

get through three trying periods of lessons. I had wondered whether it wouldn't be better to cancel the drama group's rehearsal I'd fixed for the early afternoon, the first rehearsal without Manni Wallmeroth. Why shouldn't I suddenly feel ill for once? But I pulled myself together.

I had to defend my position not only at home but in my school as well. In any event, I wasn't about to hoist the white flag because of David Ninoshvili, either there or here, not even to give myself a little breathing space.

I received consolation that I would rather have done without at the drama group. I just felt even worse afterwards.

When I entered the hall they were all there already. I'd expected they would trail in gradually, as they did on the afternoon when I turned Micky Rautenstrauch out. Their wealth of invention is considerable when they don't want to come, and even more so when they're at odds with me.

As if at a secret signal they began running through their parts – Günsel Özcan has an excellent command of hers – involved me in discussions that Jürgen Dahlmann kept going with inexhaustible new arguments, getting on my nerves with more and more suggestions. (Wouldn't it be much better, Herr Kestner, if I went over to her at this line? Herr Kestner, can you tell me why I'm supposed to clap my hand to my forehead at this point? It feels silly, honest.) Whereas when they're in a bad mood they just stand around with their arms folded, giving me dark looks.

Nothing like that happened today. They got through their work without the commitment they show on good days, but without being bolshie either. No one interrupted when I was taking André Grothe through Manni's part. André took a lot of trouble, he'd at least learned Benvolio's lines over the weekend, and he even had some ideas, although the wrong ideas, about the way to perform the part.

But none of the others laughed when at the line *Blind is his love, and best befits the dark!* he suddenly planted one foot in front of him and stretched out both arms, as if requesting Juliet to jump off her balcony and let him catch her in the darkness. They listened in silence as I suggested a different gesture to André, and then went on rehearsing without making any comments. I was beginning to fear I'd lost touch with them.

During a break, in which I was looking at the text, Christa Frowein came over to me. "I think it's going quite well," she said, and smiled. I nodded. She moved a little closer, looking over my shoulder. I said, "Christa, don't bother me, please!" She said, "I was just going anyway. I only wanted to tell you I've spoken to Manni."

I looked at her.

"I met him in the street. He doesn't know yet if he's going to another school. They still have to accept him there. But he did tell me how kind you were to him when he came to see you at your home. He said if all the teachers were like you he'd never have done that stupid thing." She smiled. "Just wanted to tell you."

I was still trying to digest this revelation when I heard Raphael Lohmüller's ball bouncing. I stayed where I was, fiddling with my pen. After a while I noticed the suspicious silence in the garden. Was Raffy trying to climb the fence to get his football back? I got to my feet and went to the window.

He had hauled himself up and was hanging over the fence by both arms, swaying slightly and keeping his gaze fixed on our terrace. Then he turned his head, and looked back at the windows of his own house. Apparently he didn't dare come right over and fetch the ball; he was afraid his stern mother might catch him doing it. I felt sorry for him.

I went out on the terrace and brought the ball back to him. He said, "Thank you, Herr Kestner," let the ball drop in the

248

Lohmüllers' garden, but didn't move from his lookout post on the fence. I asked, "Are you comfortable hanging over the fence like that?"

He swayed again and nodded. Then he asked, "Isn't that man staying with you any more?"

"What man?"

"The man from Timbuktu."

"Good Heavens! Can you remember a difficult word like that?"

He nodded. After a while he said, "There's only black people in Timbuktu."

"Your father is wrong there. Has he ever been to Timbuktu?"

He shook his head.

"There, you see?"

He asked, "Where's that man now, then?"

I said, "He's in hospital. You can tell your parents I'll give them the address if they would like to visit him. And they should take him something nice. His favourite food is worms."

Raffy stopped swaying and looked hard at me. Suddenly he jumped down from the fence, picked up his football and ran indoors.

66

Our front doorbell rang at six fifteen. Ralf had gone to his room, Julia was making supper in the kitchen. I was sitting in front of the TV set, trying in vain to find fresh news from Georgia. I got up and opened the door. A man with a moustache in his mid-thirties stood there, and introduced himself as CID Chief Superintendent Steguweit, showed me his police ID, and apologized for disturbing me. He had a

249

few questions to ask me and my son about the attack on Herr Ninoshvili, he said, and he had been hoping to find us both at home at this time of day.

I asked Superintendent Steguweit in, told Julia, whom I had already tried to reassure in the middle of the day by telling her about my alibi for Ralf, and called Ralf down. The superintendent rose when Julia came into the living room, said, "We've met already," and shook hands with her. He offered Ralf his hand too. Ralf nodded rather awkwardly and sat down on the edge of a chair.

I asked Herr Steguweit if I could offer him any refreshment. He thanked me but declined. There was a brief silence during which he took out a notebook. I asked him whether Herr Hochgeschurz wasn't taking part in the investigation any more. "Yes, yes, he is," said Steguweit, leafing through his notebook, Hochgeschurz just happened to have to keep another appointment. But it was very likely that he might want to come and see us again.

Julia asked, "Why?"

Well, said Steguweit, looking up from his notebook, it couldn't be ruled out that the attack on Herr Ninoshvili had its background somewhere in far-right politics. She knew, of course, he said, and so did I, that Herr Hochgeschurz works for Internal Security.

Julia said, "Yes, we know. But that doesn't answer my question."

Herr Steguweit raised his eyebrows and smiled. Before he could open his mouth, I said my wife had told me that he and Hochgeschurz had wanted her to tell them where our son had been at the time of the attack. I was not, I said, going to conceal my surprise at this question. Our son did have contacts which I didn't entirely approve of, but surely the authorities were not seriously thinking of linking him with that brutal act of violence.

250

Herr Steguweit shook his head, smiling. "Herr Kestner, in a case like this we have to ask all kinds of routine questions. Your wife knows that, in fact she knows all about it. Herr Ninoshvili was staying here, after all. I can't spare you and your family this procedure, but there's no need for you to agitate yourself."

I said I didn't see it like that. The superintendent turned away from me, looked at Ralf, and asked, "Where were you on Friday evening, Herr Kestner?"

Ralf swallowed, and then replied, "Here. I was at home."

Steguweit nodded and made a note in his book. Julia looked askance at Ralf.

I said he knew where my wife had been. I also assumed that that could be proved without much trouble. As for Ralf and me, I could tell him that we had both spent the hours in question at home together.

Herr Steguweit looked up. "From when to when, roughly?" I explained that we had eaten supper together at about six thirty or a little later, and then we talked.

"And neither of you left the house?"

I replied I hadn't said that, but to make his researches easier for him I was even prepared to give him more information about our private life. Herr Steguweit looked at me in silence. I said I had not only talked to my son, I had quarrelled with him, and in the course of the quarrel we parted company. Ralf left the house, and a little later I drove to Gero Schumann the lawyer's house because I assumed that my son had gone there.

"When was this?" Steguweit asked.

I said we had parted at about nine. "I can even tell you just when I arrived at Herr Schumann's. I looked at my watch because Herr Schumann asked if I knew how late it was. Not only can Herr Schumann confirm that time, so can a certain Frau Kiwitt.

She was sitting on Herr Schumann's sofa when I arrived, and she stayed there until I left again and drove home."

Steguweit made some notes. While he was still writing he asked, "What were you quarrelling about?"

Julia said, "You don't either of you have to answer that question."

"Why shouldn't we?" I nodded at my son. "Ralf, perhaps you'll tell Herr Steguweit what we were quarrelling about."

Ralf cleared his throat. "About Mount Elbrus."

Steguweit looked up. "About what?"

I said, "It's the highest mountain in the Caucasus. On 21 August 1942 an advance party of the first German Mountain Division planted the Nazi flag on it. And it's my son's opinion that it would still be flying there if further supplies had arrived from Army Group A, but they didn't. Because of treachery, you understand."

Herr Steguweit stroked his chin. Then he looked at Ralf. "And did you go to Herr Schumann?"

Ralf said, "No." He cleared his throat again. Julia glanced sideways at him. He said. "I just… I just walked round the block, and then I came home and went to bed."

Julia stood up. "I really think that will do. At the time of the attack, my husband and my son were together at home. That ought to be clear by now."

I don't know if she just wanted to act the lawyer at this point or put an end to this interrogation for some entirely different reason. I'm not sure if she had accepted my alibi for Ralf. Maybe she was afraid that our son could lose his nerve and get muddled.

Herr Steguweit said, "Forgive me, Dr Kestner, but I have another question for your husband." Julia folded her arms. Steguweit leafed through his notebook and then looked at me. "You said that shortly after your son walked out of the house you drove to Herr Schumann's because you thought your son was there."

"That's right."

"But he couldn't have reached Herr Schumann before you, could he?"

I smiled. "My son has a moped. And sometimes he goes faster on it than I do in my car."

"I see." Steguweit nodded. Then he asked, "So you heard your son ride away on the moped?"

The man was no fool. I almost said, "That's right." But I smiled at Herr Steguweit and said, "No, he told you just now that he only walked round the block. Walked, you understand? I thought he had ridden off to Herr Schumann's place on his moped, but I was wrong. I was very upset, as I'm sure you will understand."

Steguweit nodded. Julia said, "I'm sorry, but that really ought to be enough. We would like to eat our evening meal, if you don't mind."

Herr Steguweit put his notebook away and rose to his feet. "Thank you for being so helpful. If there should be any more questions I'll let you know." He smiled. "And I ask for your understanding. But in all probability this is a case of attempted murder, and if Herr Ninoshvili is unlucky, it will in fact be a murder case."

67

Delayed intracranial bleeding can sometimes be quite late in occurring. You think the patient is over the worst, and then it suddenly happens. A damaged blood vessel tears, the cranial cavity fills with blood, increasing pressure puts a strain on the brain and can do incurable damage.

I've talked to Wolfgang Zahn, who works as a surgeon at the University Hospital. He told me about a case in his own experience there. A woman whose head had struck the windscreen in a car accident had recovered relatively well from the aftermath, and was no longer showing symptoms that gave any particular cause for concern. But a full three weeks after the accident, she suffered life-threatening intracranial bleeding.

I didn't ask Wolfgang Zahn what they were able to do for the woman, and what happened to her. They probably wheeled the patient straight into the operating theatre, late in the evening or in the middle of the night, opened her skull, got the blood out by suction, and closed up the leaking vessel. Perhaps she survived. Or perhaps she's in a wheelchair, paralysed down one side, able to communicate only by babbling.

Ninoshvili is improving. He's improved so much that they've been able to move him to an ordinary ward, a room with three beds and a shower cubicle. The walls of the ward are painted pale green. The insurance Julia took out for him pays only for basic care. Julia wanted him moved to a private room, but he refused. Perhaps he's still slightly confused. He said he didn't want to be a burden on her.

I visited him this afternoon. They've given him the bed under the two tall, narrow windows, the bed with a view of the garden. In the first bed by the door there's a young man who had to have one of his legs amputated below the knee after a motorbike accident, and who seldom opens his eyes; in the middle bed there's an old man with a fracture of the neck of the femur. He keeps muttering to himself. Ninoshvili opened his eyes when I went up to the bed, raised his hand, smiled, and said in a clear voice, "My friend!"

His head is still swathed in bandages, his right leg is in plaster, with his long toes sticking out. The swellings on his face have gone down, but the skin is still bruised green and yellow; his eyes are bloodshot. They have also bandaged his right wrist now; perhaps it took a blow when he was trying to protect his head.

I asked how he was feeling. He said, "Fine." He's being very well looked after, he said, all sorts of medicine, various doctors, and the nurses take good care of him too. He smiled, pointed to the crucifix above the door. The senior nursing nun had even asked him if he'd like a priest to visit. As a guest whose own country was at war, he knew how lucky he was. "A wonderful country, your fatherland, my friend! Even in terrible trouble you feel life is worth living here."

I asked if talking didn't tire him too much, and said we could easily sit together in silence. No, no, he was glad he could talk to me. Indeed, he couldn't find words enough to say how close he felt to both me and Julia. He didn't have to tell me what he owed me, I knew that very well myself. As for Julia, she had shown such devotion... well, she had cared for him like a sister caring for her only brother.

I nodded. He said he would never forget this. Oh, and a Georgian diplomat had visited him too, a gentleman with the rank of embassy counsellor who came specially here from the embassy bringing him good wishes from the Ministry of Culture. The diplomatic mission had also given Matassi the news, so we didn't need to worry about that any more.

I asked him how Matassi was. He said very well, considering. Of course she had the same difficulties as everyone in Tbilisi, various kinds of trouble, supplies of food and fuel for heating were very unreliable.

The door opened, and a small, round nun pushed a trolley of instruments into the room and went quickly from bed to bed. She tapped the young man on the cheek, he opened his eyes and she handed him a thermometer. The old man's muttering grew louder. The nun said, "Now, now, no grumbling!" She put her hand inside the old man's shirt and stuck a thermometer under his armpit, raised a finger. "Hold it nice and tight!" Smiling, Ninoshvili put out his hand; the nun said, "Under the arm will do today," and gave him a thermometer too. She took hold of the handle of her trolley, wheeled it out, and closed the door behind her.

Ninoshvili said, "Sister Bonifatia – very capable." He pushed the thermometer under his armpit, and closed his eyes. His chest was rising and falling only very slightly. He said nothing. After a while his eyelids began to twitch, and now and then I could see the bloodshot rim of his eyeballs through the crack. I asked, "David?" He didn't reply.

I felt hot. The intracranial bleeding – perhaps he had lost consciousness. I was about to stand up and call for Sister Bonifatia when he suddenly murmured. "A Herr Hochgeschurz was here too." He opened his eyes and smiled. "You know him."

He said Hochgeschurz had asked him a number of questions. Did he have any idea who might have attacked him? Or could he think of any reason why he had been attacked? He smiled. "Stupid questions."

After a short pause, I said that it was important for whoever did it to be arrested. He surely felt a great interest in that himself.

He asked, "But what was I supposed to tell Herr Hochgeschurz? What can I tell him, my friend?"

He closed his eyes and said no more. I was afraid his eyelids would start fluttering again, but he lay there as peacefully as if he had fallen into a gentle sleep. After a while he began talking in Georgian. He declaimed two or three resounding, rhythmic sentences, then fell silent again. A shiver ran through me.

Suddenly he spoke in a clear voice. "A hero shows his greatest courage not in killing his defeated enemy, but in showing him mercy at the right moment."

I cleared my throat. "David?"

He opened his eyes and smiled. "'The Man in the Panther's Skin'. You know, Shota Rustaveli's immortal poem. I was quoting from it."

He kept his dark, bloodshot eyes fixed on me. I said, "Yes, I understand. But I don't know what you meant by quoting those lines."

He smiled. "Those people didn't kill me after all. They injured me badly, but they left me alive. They showed mercy at the right moment. Or don't you think one can put it like that?"

I shook my head. "No, I don't. Those were no heroes who defeated you." I hesitated, then I said, "I'd call them criminals."

"Yes, of course. You're right again. I didn't use the quotation properly. My head's a little confused. But it's a fine quotation. Very wise."

I took the opportunity of saying goodbye when Sister Bonifatia wheeled her trolley in again. He held my hand firmly and looked at me. "I will not forget what I owe you, my friend. I will never forget it."

68

Motherly Frau Fasold was the first to speak to me, and it was well meant, unlike the questions and consoling remarks still ahead of me. Frau Fasold joined me when I was going to the staff room in the long break. She gave me a friendly nod and walked a couple of steps beside me before saying,

"I hope you won't take that horrible piece in the paper too hard." I knew what she meant at once, but I pretended not to understand her.

I'd read the article in the morning; it leaped to my eye as I was looking through the local paper. At the head of the page, above the article, was a large photograph showing three youths with shaven heads, their mouths wide open, their hands raised to the camera in the Hitler salute. I had put the paper aside after reading it and hoped that Julia wouldn't find the time to look at the article before going to the courthouse.

The author, one of the editorial team who regularly writes as the paper's expert on questions concerning Internal Security, has ranged far and wide. He describes, among other things, the subversive activities of the American businessman Gary Rex Lauck of Lincoln, Nebraska, in feeding propaganda material to German right-wing extremists, for instance in the German-language journal *National Socialist Battlecry* and the video of the film *The Eternal Jew*. I skimmed the life history of Lauck, who according to his own account remains unmarried because as a National Socialist he has "neither the time nor the money for women", and the inflammatory diatribes that he distributes against "those of foreign races who have insidiously made their way into this country", by which he means Germany.

I found the passage that I'd seen coming as soon as I read the sub-title of the article (*A Case Giving the Authorities Cause for Concern*). The author says that not long ago a writer of note from Tbilisi, who was visiting the Federal Republic on a mission from the Georgian government, was beaten up and severely injured early in the evening in a busy street. His attackers, who the doctors say must have used baseball bats, got away unidentified. The Georgian writer, said the paper, was still hovering between life and death.

The author asks: "After the incidents at Mölln and Solingen, do bloodthirsty slogans of the kind disseminated by Gary R. Lauck lead to murder and violence in our city too?" How far and how disturbingly the confusion has progressed, says the article, not least in young minds, can be assessed in relation to the case of this foreign writer. According to reliable information from police circles, those suspected of the crime included some adolescents of – as may be said without reservation here – the most respected local families, among them the son of a highly regarded teacher.

This teacher, the article continues, has only just shown himself uncompromising in opposing an outbreak of right-wing radicalism at his school. He has also been working with great commitment for years to instil liberal principles into his students – "In vain? Does an insidious influence like that of Gary R. Lauck prove stronger?"

I would like to know whether the editorial staff of the paper, led by Herr Heuberger, inspired this article. I wouldn't rule it out, because what is proposed here is only a degeneration of nationalist ideas, and of course our friend with the Nazi sympathies would deny having anything in common with the gang of muggers.

I even suspected that Tassilo Huber, in his pitiless opposition to right-wing radicals, might have cooperated with Internal Security again to win favour with the public. This was indeed my son they were talking about, the son of a friend of Tassilo's student days, but if he went astray then ultimately his father had to assume responsibility, friendship or no friendship. Where would we be if we suppressed the truth?

And after all, what does it matter who inspired this article and why? What counts is the plain fact that I have now been pilloried in black and white.

Frau Fasold said she was sorry that she had made that silly joke at our first argument over Manni Wallmeroth's graffiti, and suggested that perhaps I was in a bad mood because of a little trouble in my marriage. She understood me much better now – "Believe me, Herr Kestner, I have three children myself, after all, and they haven't always brought me joy, God knows. I understand you very well, and I'm so sorry."

She stayed with me all through the break period, talking to me, and protecting me with her dark-toned voice, as if she could hear the vultures calling already and was trying to shield me. I saw the vultures, they were preening their feathers, stalking around me on horny claws, casting yellow glances at me out of the corners of their eyes. Brauckmann, who was in low-voiced conversation with three others, grinning now and then, sensed at some point that I was staring at him. He screwed up his face and raised a hand in greeting.

Elke Lampert took no notice of me. She left the staff room just before the end of break.

69

Small insincerities, little white lies don't have to ruin a marriage. I'd even say they're necessary to keep people living together. Elke Lampert would certainly have been better off if she had believed her husband and hadn't stolen into the car park to find him groaning in the act of love. And what good would it do Julia and me if I confessed to having sex with her friend Erika just because she'd washed the perfume off her plump body?

However, deceptions intended to create a permanent basis for married life are dangerous. They can't be suppressed;

even if you'd like to correct them you can't, not without bringing the whole structure crashing down.

I remember a film in which a man who couldn't bear to go on living in such circumstances escaped them by running away, living in a distant city under a new identity. I forget the title of the film and the actors' names, but anyway it was set in the USA – where else? Given the demographic conditions of Germany, there wouldn't be much chance of a new beginning of that kind here.

The man started a business and a new family under his false name, made a lot of money, lived for many years happy and content with a loving wife and well-brought-up children. But then his past caught up with him.

I don't remember just how it happened, but it was nothing to do with an agent emerging from the shadows to remind him of an obligation from the distant past. Nor had the man in the film done anything in his first life so serious that it could have branded him a criminal. But his loving wife couldn't get over the deception on which he had built their life together, and the children were too well brought-up to forgive him either. They all turned away from their husband and father, and only the youngest child showed any sign of sympathy, saying, "Daddy, I'm sorry. I'm terribly sorry!" or something like that.

The film didn't have a happy ending, and I remember that it affected me deeply at the time. I had to suppress a sob when, at the close, the man boarded a train to take him away again to yet another city far away. He pressed his forehead to the window pane and looked out into the dark as the train rushed through the night.

This evening, when Ralf had gone out "for a breath of air" after supper, I helped Julia clear away the dishes. I waited until, with a sigh, she had sat down in the living room. Only then did I take the newspaper out of the magazine rack. I found the article and handed it to her, opened a bottle of wine and poured two glasses. She read the article in silence, put the paper down and looked at me.

I sat down beside her and sipped the wine. "What do you think of it?"

"It's absolutely scandalous. Very likely we wouldn't be able to pin anything on the journalist, but I'm going to raise all hell with Hochgeschurz's boss. And Steguweit's. I shall ask them how the press came by such information." She picked up her glass and drank.

I shrugged my shoulders.

"Or do you think it's better to ignore something like this?" she asked.

"No, of course not." I drank some wine. "I'm just not sure if we'd get anywhere."

She put her glass down and sat in silence for a while. Then she said, "If you have any reason for keeping quiet about this thing, you'd better tell me."

I looked at her. "What do you mean?"

She smoothed her skirt down before returning my glance. "Was Ralf really at home until nine?"

I refrained from wriggling out of it. No, I said, Ralf had been to the cinema, but couldn't give me the name of anyone who could prove that, and I hadn't wanted to let the police put any more pressure on our son, so I had given him a false alibi.

After a moment's silence she said, "And you'd have done the same even if he'd been at the scene of the attack, wouldn't you?"

I said I had no reason to suppose that he had anything to do with the incident. But yes, she was right, even if he had I would have tried to shield him. Nothing was going to keep me from defending our family, and I still hoped she would understand that.

She looked at me in silence. I wondered if she really knew what difficulties Ninoshvili had brought down on our son. She did not react.

I said Ralf believed that she had slept with Ninoshvili. And he had been dreadfully upset when he found out that Ninoshvili was obviously planning in all seriousness to make himself permanently at home here. At least, that was the conclusion Ralf had drawn from finding an application form for political asylum that Ninoshvili had brought home. I wasn't suggesting that she had been helping our guest there, but very likely he had taken her into his confidence.

"No. I didn't know about that." She passed a hand over her forehead and looked at me. "Did Ralf search David's case, then?"

I said I didn't know, but even if he did I could understand him. Our son had realized, I said, that Ninoshvili was someone to beware of, a very dangerous person, and there I was afraid I couldn't contradict him.

She said, "Christian, what you're saying is very close to persecution mania. The poor man's in hospital, badly injured. A very dangerous person? David is an unfortunate trying to make his way and meeting with failure after failure. Can't you see that? Are you really so blind?"

I asked if she knew that our guest was suspected of being a KGB agent. Not just by me, no, Internal Security suspected the same. And did she know that Hochgeschurz was interested in the question of whether Ninoshvili had known the woman who was murdered recently in a hotel in the city centre? Not a normal tourist, oh no, and it hadn't been a case of sexual murder. The woman had been in the Stasi, with the rank of captain.

She was staring at me wide-eyed.

I drank some wine. "I'm sorry if I've given you a shock. But it was possible you might have known all this already."

"No, I didn't." She rubbed her forehead. "And I didn't know, either, that you are obviously in close contact with Herr Hochgeschurz. Is there anything else you're keeping from me, Christian?"

I said I probably had more reason to ask that question than she did.

"I'm not keeping anything from you, Christian. Nothing that you need to know."

I was silent for a while. Then I asked whether, in her opinion, I didn't need to know that the man we had gone out with on our first visit to Halle together had not been Erika's boyfriend, he hadn't lived in Halle, he had come from Leipzig on purpose to see her, Julia. And I asked whether she was surprised if I wondered why she had staged that pretence.

She asked, "Did Erika tell you this?" I said it made no difference who told me, I knew it anyway. And was it her opinion that I didn't need to know?

She said, "He was a man I once had a relationship with in Halle. I was eighteen at the time. I wanted to see him again, it was just an idea, rather a childish idea. It wasn't worth it, it was a disappointment. But I didn't want to make you jealous. There was no reason for jealousy anyway." After a pause she asked, "And what have you been imagining now?"

I said imagining wasn't quite the right word, but very well: I had imagined that the man was a member of the Stasi. And he had reminded her of a commitment she had made so that she could leave Halle and settle in the west. So he had tried putting her under pressure, just as Ninoshvili was putting her under pressure now. And I also wanted her to know that I had decided to prevent any attempt to make her atone today for a mistake she had made in her youth.

"Christian… this is sheer lunacy!" She stared into space for a moment, then took off her shoes, lay down on the sofa and closed her eyes.

I asked, "Do you call it lunacy for me to defend you? For me to defend our family?"

She replied, without opening her eyes, "I don't think you're bothered about defending me." After a moment she said, "You've been intriguing behind my back. Spying on me. You have not been honest with me, Christian. And I'm afraid you still aren't being honest."

"Have you been honest with me? Are you at least being honest now?"

She did not reply. After some time, we heard Ralf's moped. Julia stood up, put her shoes on, and went to open the front door to Ralf. I heard a few murmured words, and then they both went upstairs and the door of Ralf's room was closed.

I wondered what Ralf might be telling her. I had reminded him again not to burden his mother with what he had done to get rid of Ninoshvili, whatever nonsense it had been.

Fifteen minutes later Julia came back and stood in the living-room doorway. I looked at her with a question in my eyes.

"He sticks to his story of going to the cinema."

I nodded. She said, "Perhaps it will be difficult for you to understand this, but I'd like to be alone tonight. I shall sleep in the spare room."

I did not reply. She said, "Good night," and turned away. I stood up. "No, don't do that. I'll sleep in the spare room." She did not protest.

The sheets looked as if they hadn't been slept in, but I wanted to make sure. I took them off the bed and made it up with clean sheets. I glanced into the wardrobe and tried the clasps of the suitcase; they were locked. Then I opened the drawer of the bedside table. I found Matassi's photograph under the street map of the city. I looked at the photo, and then went to bed.

70

Perhaps Mr Perelman is right. *School's Out*, as the title of his book runs: we ought to tear down our school here, the classrooms where we try to confront our students, the school hall and that ridiculous platform, and replace it all with a building like a honeycomb full of cells all connected to the Internet, where the kids sit at their computers easily learning what old fogies like me can never drum into their heads. Information at your fingertips, get clever at the touch of a key, as another educational expert, the boss of Microsoft, has put it – and he ought to know, since after all he is selling the programs for it.

Teachers like me and the classrooms of the old style of school, says Lewis J. Perelman, that progressive educationalist, have about as much place in the learning process of tomorrow as the horse-drawn carriage in the modern transport system. We're *out*. I'm out, along with my school class. That's right, interactive learning is the name of the game, hyper-learning, not head-on teaching of the kind I practise. Head-on teaching, says Mr Perelman, is the outcome of the typical philosophy of indoctrination in the industrial age of the past; the teacher speaks his words of wisdom and the students have to listen and keep their mouths shut. All that's out, mega-out.

What, perhaps I say, staking my own claim, if I never try to drill knowledge into my students, if I have always tried to

266

keep a dialogue going with them; what if I have done all I can to teach them not just knowledge but social competence as well? That's a mistake, says Mr Perelman; by comparison with my outmoded old school there's far more social interaction in playgrounds, in swimming pools, in cafés. Not to mention computer studios.

And the educational success of those machines is very impressive. A professor from Oldenburg found out by means of a questionnaire that between seventy-five and ninety per cent of the students she asked had enjoyed learning English more through working with electronic sources of information. No wonder. As I have learned from an article in a progressive magazine praising it, there is a computer program that can tell you within a fraction of a second the meaning in one language of a word in another. Fundamentalists like me, used to looking such things up in a dictionary, can only envy it.

And that's not all: more complicated subjects, such as violence, can be made interesting and accessible in the classroom with the help of computers. For instance, students at Bad Essen Grammar School discussed that very subject for weeks on end – think of it, weeks on end without getting tired of it! – in electronic data exchanges with students of their own age at Northeast High School in Oklahoma City. The American kids contributed brand-new material. In the school next to theirs, a ninth-grade student had just been shot dead by another boy. I can hardly compete with that by reprimanding Christian Berkhan in front of my class for hitting little Rudi Ballensiefen over the head with a lath from the fence.

I ought to remember what Professor Seymour Papert of MIT prophesies, to the effect that in future school will be much more natural, and learning, living and loving will no longer be artificially divided. I'm not sure whether, among the forms of social interaction to which schools of the future will devote themselves, Papert includes the practice of sexual intercourse, but why not? When I was in the sixth grade myself, I'd have liked that better than anything else as an educational aim.

And then again, if we were all working through the Internet, Manni Wallmeroth could have committed his graffiti to the computer instead of messing up our stage set. Using a graphics program, he could even have painted his swastika onscreen. The computer might have answered back – *Arsehole* or some such comment – and that would have been the end of it. Or perhaps the computer would have rejected it as unauthorized data. Manni would have turned pale and to mollify the computer would have made haste to ask it a question about the translation of a given word into another language.

And if I were not an old fogey but an interactive presenter, the teacher of the future, then I would not have had to concern myself with the question of whether Manni Wallmeroth deserved to be punished by exclusion. I wouldn't have had to do battle with half the school, Dr Lawrenz, and the editorial team of the local paper.

And I'd long ago have forgotten the educational aims I have been pursuing. I'd have understood the point of what Pink Floyd said in the charts as early as 1980. *We don't need no education.* Education is out, edutainment is in. Kids can get what they need to know interactively, from the computer, and have fun at the same time.

If my school were already open to progress, I wouldn't have had to deal with the moment when, in my class, no one opens his mouth when Helmut Freese puts his hand up and asks why we are studying the Georgian civil war – after all, the Russian guns had put an end to it, and didn't

I now think that Shevardnadze had betrayed his people and handed them over to Moscow? And I'd have been spared hypocritical questions at break, such as hadn't the police stopped investigating my son yet, it was absolutely scandalous, of all people *your* son, Herr Kestner! No one would have avoided me. No one would have made me feel that it was embarrassing to meet me.

Brauckmann had the nerve to ask me, looking grave, how that Georgian writer was doing, or wasn't I in touch with the man? I said yes, I was, Herr Ninoshvili was well on the road to recovery, my whole family was concerned for him. After all, he had been staying with us.

"Really?" Brauckmann raised his eyebrows. "I never knew that! Oh well, then he's in the best of hands."

I said he could be sure of that.

Brauckmann nodded. Then he asked, "What are his plans? Is he going to stay here?"

I said it was perfectly possible, but in Georgia it was considered extremely uncivil to ask a guest how long he was going to stay, and I thought that a very good custom. I too would find such questions extremely uncivil.

"And I'd have expected no less of you," he replied. "Well, good luck!"

Of course people made consoling remarks too. Obviously not all the kids thought I ought to be declared obsolete as soon as possible.

At midday today, when I was on my way to the car park, Günsel Özcan suddenly appeared beside me. She said, "Hello."

"Hello, Günsel. Is there a problem?"

"Oh, nothing special. I just wanted to ask if it would be all right for me to come to the rehearsal a quarter of an hour late tomorrow."

269

"Yes, of course. I'll switch something around."

She didn't turn away, but kept step with me. When we reached the car park she said, "I thought what Helmut asked you was plain silly."

"Then why didn't you say so?"

"I don't know. Maybe I hoped you wouldn't take something like that seriously." She looked at me. "You don't take it seriously, do you? I mean, you'll go on the same as before?"

I unlocked my car. "I'll tell you something, Günsel, but you mustn't pass it on to anyone else."

Her dark eyes widened. "Of course not, Herr Kestner! You can rely on me."

I said, "Günsel, I don't know how things will go on. I wish I did, but I really don't know how things will go on."

71

Ninoshvili wants to go home. He wants to get back to Tbilisi as soon as possible. He's told Julia he didn't want to wait until he was completely better. The contacts he's made in the Federal Republic would have to be enough to open Georgian literature up to German readers. Perhaps he might come back some time.

He's suffering badly from homesickness, Julia has told me. He knows that medical care in Tbilisi probably isn't up to the standards of the Marienhospital, but he's not letting that deter him. He has kept talking to Julia about Tbilisi these last few days, he's described his apartment to her, the balcony he steps out on in the morning, the early sunlight, the busy streets. Perhaps snow will already have fallen in Tbilisi, covering the city, the mountains of the Kura Valley and Narikala Fortress like a glittering wedding dress.

Ninoshvili shed tears describing this picture to Julia. They streamed down his discoloured skin and seeped into his bandages. He shook his head and said, "It is my home, Julia. Never mind what happens, it's my home!"

Julia, she tells me, has reached Matassi in Tbilisi. Matassi answered the phone in Ninoshvili's apartment. She is looking forward very much to David's return. She is going to take time off work to look after him.

However, the doctors at the Marienhospital are making things difficult. They say Ninoshvili is far from fit to travel yet. If he insists on discharging himself from hospital, they must disclaim any responsibility. They're trying to convince him that he ought to stay in their care for a little longer.

72

Who was the hawk, who was the woodgrouse? If Ninoshvili really said these plaintive goodbyes, in a hurry to go, dissolving into tears, nothing on his mind except getting home, whatever awaits him there – well, in that case then I was seeing our roles the wrong way round. I wasn't the one who plunged to the depths of the sulphurous waters below, caught in his talons; he fell held in mine.

Perhaps that's why confessions of guilt and declarations of remorse are so seldom made, because they almost inevitably shrink to embarrassing banality. Self-righteousness can cloak itself in many fine words; like malice, it can be elegantly phrased. But someone who really wants to admit to guilt and remorse can't avoid hackneyed phrases. *Pater, peccavi!* I am sorry. I will improve. I ask for mercy. Over and out.

I'm not asking for mercy. But I can't help realizing that I have brought my misery on myself, and David Ninoshvili's on him too.

It all began because I was afraid. I was afraid in Tbilisi when Matassi sank on my hotel bed beside me and Karl-Heinz Dautzenbacher knocked on the door. I was afraid of David's revenge, as if I had done something far worse than commit a peccadillo. Because it was no more. It was improper, but it wasn't a crime.

And to suppress the thought of that impropriety, I made up a story for which there was no evidence at all, the story of a couple of secret agents, and it frightened me even more. I got myself into a state of such confusion that I couldn't decide which of my fears was to be taken seriously. Was Ninoshvili bent on revenge because I had put my hand under his wife's skirt? Or had he sent Matassi in the first place so that I would put my hand under her skirt and lay myself open to blackmail? They couldn't both be true. But together they made my fear even worse.

And my fear led to hatred when Ninoshvili obviously won the liking of not just my son but my wife, and both suddenly changed sides. It wasn't just his nationalism and a hint of racism that influenced my own opinion. I could have discussed that with him, I could have come to terms with it; I didn't feel called upon to educate a grown man, however foolishly he might express himself. But I was afraid this man might take my wife from me and estrange my son even further.

It's easy to condemn xenophobia as long as you are seeing foreigners only from a distance. But it's obviously very difficult to live with a foreigner under the same roof in practice.

I would never have thought that someone who thinks himself enlightened could react with such irrational lack of inhibition as I did. I didn't take up a clear position, I didn't draw an unmistakable line between what I didn't like and what I was ready to accept. No, my fear was too great for that, not least the fear of having to admit that I wasn't as tolerant as I had always made out. I hid, I began snooping around, I indulged in intrigue and denunciation.

The clues, yes. Ninoshvili's lies. The gloves, the flick knife, the photographs in his case. To this day not even Herr Hochgeschurz has found any evidence that my guest killed the woman in the hotel. Perhaps he never seriously suspected him, and I was the one who tried to send Hochgeschurz down that trail.

Perhaps if I had taken the agent to my house and got him to open Ninoshvili's case, it would have turned out that the blonde in the photograph wasn't the murdered Stasi captain, but a Georgian writer, a blonde Georgian woman, why not? Herr Hochgeschurz could have photographed the notes in the Georgian alphabet on the back of the photograph with his mini-camera, and had them checked out by the languages department of Internal Security.

Fantasies born of sheer fear, no more.

Of course, if David Ninoshvili had really come to us to avenge himself on me, for whatever reason, he had achieved his aim. He could leave with his mission accomplished, a Georgian hero whose greatest courage is not in killing a defeated enemy but in showing mercy at the right moment. He defeated me, but he didn't stab me with his flick knife, he let me live.

The mercy he showed me would then indeed resemble a terrible revenge. I must go on living in the ruins of the life I have built up over the years. I have wrecked it myself, for fear the Georgian might dispute it with me.

I don't know whether my wife will ever really come back to me; I doubt it. Conversations between Julia and me are confined to the insignificant subjects essential to keep the household running. I am still sleeping in the spare room. So far Julia has not shown any sign of wanting to end our separation. I don't get to feel her closeness any more, not even the "perfume of her countenance" that a merciful wind blew towards Shah Moabad's brother Ramin when he despairingly followed his beloved Princess Vis in her litter. What the deserted man suffered I could read in the tale told in the *Visramiani*, and I felt it daily for myself. "When man and woman do not bring each other joy, what is there left in life?"

I have lost sight of my son. He is talking to me again, not so long ago he even challenged me to a game of chess (and beat me), but he leads his own dubious life as before, going in and out of Herr Schumann's summer house. If I were to take him to task, he could ask, "What are you after? You don't take what you preach seriously yourself. You covered up for me, didn't you?" And he would be right to say so. I have stopped asking him questions to see if I can find out after all whether he is in league with Herr Schumann's skinheads. I'd only be inviting the question, "Why don't you stop going on at me like that?"

I haven't just cheated on my wife with her best friend; I deceived her with Herr Hochgeschurz, going behind her back to spin a web with an agent to catch my rival, and in the end I was entangled in it myself.

I tried to deliver David Ninoshvili up to the knife just because I was afraid of him. I realized that danger threatened him as soon as Ralf told me to leave him to sort out the problem. But I delayed, instead of doing what I ought to have done about that at once. I stood by and saw a man, who had suffered humiliation after humiliation, and needed my help, a poor fellow who perhaps really does have friendly feelings for me, beaten to within an inch of his life.

So much for the indictment. *Pater, peccavi?* Over and out?

Yes. I won't make excuses for myself. If I wanted to do that I'd begin going round in circles again. I'd replace one suspicion full of holes with another, coming up with more and more explanations for my fear, more and more self-justifications for my hatred.

For example I would, or could, ask whether it's really just homesickness making Ninoshvili want to turn his back as soon as possible on the Federal Republic, that fine country where even in times of need you find out that life is worth living. I could give free rein again to my unloving suspicions of Julia. I have told her in confidence that Herr Hochgeschurz suspects the Georgian of being a KGB agent. But perhaps she has passed the information on to Ninoshvili.

I could suspect that our guest decided to go back not because he was homesick but on account of this information. No one told him to go; the doctors even warned him against travelling too soon. But perhaps it's getting too hot for him in the Federal Republic.

And if, as Julia insinuates, I was not really concerned to protect her, then I could entertain an even uglier suspicion of my wife. Has she really spoken to Matassi on the phone, did Matassi really pick up the receiver in Ninoshvili's apartment? If I were still going to distrust my wife, I could for good or ill try reviving my terrifying theory that Matassi was kept alive only so that there'd be a means of blackmail available, the accusation that I had tried to rape Ninoshvili's wife.

Perhaps even I wouldn't really believe that Julia's understanding with the Georgian went so far as to deceive me in such a malicious way. But I could construct another and sounder reason why Julia told me about a telephone conversation that she never had.

In that case Matassi – so I would tell myself – is still only a phantom; perhaps she has separated from Ninoshvili, or perhaps she is dead. But Ninoshvili needs her to cover up his tracks. With Julia's help, he lets everyone in this country who might be interested in his whereabouts know that he is going back to his loving wife in Tbilisi. But really he has a very different destination in mind. Julia books him a flight to Tbilisi by way of Vienna. In Vienna, however, he gets off the plane and goes underground, hoping that the Federal German Office for the Protection of the Constitution will not pursue him there.

Of course in that case I would have to suspect my wife of being in league with Ninoshvili. But if I wanted to lay myself open to my fears and suspicions again, then I would find my reasons for that too.

I am sure I'm not doing Julia an injustice by assuming that she also likes Ninoshvili as a man. Whether Ralf is right in thinking that she has slept with him of her own free will I don't know. But if I still wanted to give my fantasies free rein, I could imagine Ninoshvili using gentle persuasion to get her into bed.

I would call to mind her remarkable reactions to my question about the man in Halle. And I would persuade myself that Ninoshvili knew the same as the Stasi officer did, thus having a strong means of blackmailing Julia to hand, and she succumbed to it.

I could get carried away into drawing the conclusion that my wife, once that had happened, was willing to help Ninoshvili escape and lay the false trail to Matassi, so as to deceive me yet again. I could even, if I were unable to quell my fear and my distrust, make an assumption with even farther-reaching consequences.

Ninoshvili doesn't intend to leave the country at all. Julia has told him that I know he is planning to apply for political asylum. They have worked out together how they can get a breathing space. For the moment they can rely on the doctors who so urgently advised him against travelling. And later they will manage to find more and more reasons to postpone his departure indefinitely.

73

Ninoshvili left the Federal Republic of Germany this morning. An ambulance took him to the airport. Julia went in the ambulance with him, I followed in my car.

He isn't flying by way of Vienna. Julia has booked him an Aeroflot flight to Moscow. He can stay on the plane in Moscow, and then it flies on to Tbilisi by way of Rostov on the Don.

Yesterday evening Matassi called us at home. Julia took the call. She told Matassi what the hospital doctors have prescribed and how to give the medical drugs that Ninoshvili is taking back with him. Then she handed me the receiver.

I heard a distant rushing sound, but I recognized Matassi's deep-toned voice. She said, speaking English, "Hello, Christian. I want to thank you for everything which you have done for David. You have done so much for him. I'm very grateful, Christian. I send you my love. I hope we shall meet again. I send you my big love. And I send you a very big kiss."

I was able to park my car just outside the airfield and followed the ambulance on foot as it slowly drove on. It stopped by the movable steps set up to the door of the plane. The paramedics lifted out the stretcher on which Ninoshvili had been lying during the drive, he sat up, they helped him to his feet and gave him two crutches.

Julia took one of the crutches from him and put his arm around her shoulders. With small, careful footsteps she guided him to the foot of the steps, where a sturdy man in civilian clothes and a handsome blonde stewardess were waiting.

They stopped there. Julia hugged Ninoshvili and kissed him. He held her close and buried his still-bandaged head in her shoulder. When he straightened up tears were pouring down his face.

I came up, he gave me his hand, clasped me to his chest and kissed me on both cheeks. He said, in a muffled voice, "My friend! Thank you. I ask you to forgive me. I will always be your friend!"

The sturdy man picked up the leather suitcase that one of the stretcher-bearers had taken out of the ambulance. The stewardess took the crutch from Julia, placed her hand on Ninoshvili's back and helped him up the steps.

He swung himself up from step to step, leaning on the other crutch and using his free hand to clutch the rail of the steps. Halfway up he stopped, with the leg in plaster stuck on one step, and began to sway dangerously, as if he might fall backwards any moment now. Julia's hand flew to her mouth. The stewardess took his arm and steadied him.

In the doorway of the plane he turned back, smiled, and was going to wave, but the stewardess made him go on. A steward appeared in the doorway. The steps were wheeled away, the ambulance engine started. The steward pulled the door back and shut it. Julia was craning her neck, but you couldn't see anyone through the windows of the plane.

While the plane engines were turning over, we walked together to the airfield gate. Halfway there we met Herr Hochgeschurz. He nodded a greeting. Julia said, "I'll wait at the car," nodded back at the agent, and walked past him.

Herr Hochgeschurz offered me his hand, and I took it, but I went on walking. Hochgeschurz followed me. "Well, there we are," he said.

I didn't reply. The agent said, "He has courage, one can't deny that."

I looked askance at him. Hochgeschurz went on, "I imagine there'll be certain people waiting for him in Tbilisi. People who have a bone to pick with him. Well, you know these Georgians better than I do. Revenge to the bitter end. He'll hardly get off scot-free."

I asked, "How do you know that?"

Hochgeschurz laughed. "Yes, you're right. What do any of us know about it?"

BACK TO THE COAST

Saskia Noort

Maria is a young singer with money problems, two children from failed relationships and a depressive ex-boyfriend. Faced with another pregnancy, she decides not to keep the baby, but after the abortion, threatening letters start to arrive. She flees from Amsterdam to her sister's house by the coast, a place redolent with memories of a childhood she does not want to revisit. But when the death threats follow her to her hiding place, Maria begins to fear not only for her life, but also for her sanity.

Saskia Noort is a bestselling author of literary thrillers. She has sold over a million copies of her first three novels.

PRAISE FOR SASKIA NOORT
AND *THE DINNER CLUB*

"A mystery writer of the heart as much as of the mind, a balance that marks her work with a flesh-and-blood humanity."
Andrew Pyper, author of *The Wildfire Season*

"Affairs, deceit, manipulation, tax dodges and murder – there's nothing Noort shies away from stirring into the mix, nicely showing off the sinister side of the suburbs." *Time Out*

"While there are echoes of Desperate Housewives here, this is closer to Mary Higgins Clark and is a good bet for her fans."
Library Journal Review

£8.99/$14.95/C$16.50
CRIME PAPERBACK ORIGINAL
ISBN 978-1-904738-37-4
www.bitterlemonpress.com

THE VAMPIRE OF ROPRAZ

Jacques Chessex

Jacques Chessex, winner of the prestigious Prix Goncourt, takes this true story and weaves it into a lyrical tale of fear and cruelty.

1903, Ropraz, a small village in the Jura Mountains of Switzerland. On a howling December day, a lone walker discovers a recently opened tomb, the body of a young woman violated, her left hand cut off, genitals mutilated and heart carved out. There is horror in the nearby villages: the return of atavistic superstitions and mutual suspicions. Then two more bodies are violated. A suspect must be found. Favez, a stable-boy with blood-shot eyes, is arrested, convicted, placed into psychiatric care. In 1915, he vanishes.

PRAISE FOR JACQUES CHESSEX
AND *THE VAMPIRE OF ROPRAZ*

£6.99/$12.95/C$14.50
CRIME PAPERBACK ORIGINAL
ISBN 978-1-904738-33-6
www.bitterlemonpress.com

A NOT SO PERFECT CRIME

Teresa Solana

MURDER AND MAYHEM IN BARCELONA

Another day in Barcelona, another politician's wife is suspected of infidelity. A portrait of his wife in an exhibition leads Lluís Font to conclude he is being cuckolded by the artist. Concerned only about the potential political fallout, he hires twins Eduard and Borja, private detectives with a knack for helping the wealthy with their "dirty laundry". Their office is adorned with false doors leading to non-existent private rooms and a mysterious secretary who is always away. The case turns ugly when Font's wife is found poisoned by a marron glacé from a box of sweets delivered anonymously.

PRAISE FOR *A NOT SO PERFECT CRIME*

"The Catalan novelist Teresa Solana has come up with a delightful mystery set in Barcelona... Clever, funny and utterly unpretentious." *Sunday Times*

"Teresa Solana's book may be full of murder and mayhem, but it's also packed full of humour, acute observation, a complicated plot and downright ridiculousness... I cannot recommend it highly enough." *Oxford Times*

"Scathing satire of Spanish society, hilarious dialogue, all beautifully dressed up as a crime novel." *Krimi-Couch*

This deftly plotted, bitingly funny mystery novel and satire of Catalan politics won the 2007 Brigada 21 Prize.

£8.99/$14.95/C$16.50
CRIME PAPERBACK ORIGINAL
ISBN 978-1-904738-34-3
www.bitterlemonpress.com

DOG EATS DOG

Iain Levison

Philip Dixon is down on his luck. A hair-raising escape from a lucrative but botched bank robbery lands him gushing blood and on the verge of collapse in a quaint college town in New Hampshire. How can he find a place to hide out in this innocent setting? Peering into the window of the nearest house, he sees a glimmer of hope: a man in his mid-thirties, obviously some kind of academic, is rolling around on the living-room floor with an attractive high-school student... And so Professor Elias White is blackmailed into harbouring a dangerous fugitive, as Dixon – with a cool quarter-million in his bag and dreams of Canada in his head – gets ready for the last phase of his escape.

But the last phase is always the hardest... FBI agent Denise Lupo is on his trail, and she's better at her job than her superiors think. As for Elias White, his surprising transition from respected academic to willing accomplice poses a ruthless threat that Dixon would be foolish to underestimate...

PRAISE FOR IAIN LEVISON
author of *A Working Stiff's Manifesto* and *Since the Layoffs*

"The real deal... bracing, hilarious and dead on."
New York Times Book Review

"Witty, deft, well-conceived writing that combines sharp satire with real suspense." *Kirkus Reviews*

"There is naked, pitiless power in his work" *USA Today*

£8.99/$14.95/C$18.00
CRIME PAPERBACK ORIGINAL
ISBN 978-1-904738-31-2
www.bitterlemonpress.com